'In some families ... love is a paltry emotion compared with the ties of blood.'

Storm Jameson

For David

Ties of Blood

By the same author

Angel's War
Mirror on the Wall
Mirror Images
To Reason Why

Ties of Blood

C.W. REED

ROBERT HALE · LONDON

© C.W. Reed 2000
First published in Great Britain 2000

ISBN 0 7090 6654 6

Robert Hale Limited
Clerkenwell House
Clerkenwell Green
London EC1R 0HT

2 4 6 8 10 9 7 5 3 1

Typeset by
Derek Doyle & Associates, Liverpool.
Printed in Great Britain by
St Edmundsbury Press Ltd, Bury St Edmunds, Suffolk.
Bound by WBC Book Manufacturers Limited, Bridgend.

PART I

'Peace in our time'

Neville Chamberlain, British Prime Minister, on his return from Munich, 1938.

Chapter One

John Wright forced himself to glance away as Jenny Alsop half turned from him in a token gesture of modesty and adjusted her dark grey stocking, lifting her polka-dotted dress and showing a generous lacy froth of petticoat as she did so. It was a leg well worth looking at. Of course, he had from time to time seen quite a lot of her shapely contours during the six months they had been going together; exquisitely distracting flashes on the tennis court, and more comprehensive, and leisurely, views when she wore her black woollen bathing-costume. But the half-proffered glimpse of a stockinged limb, especially with this half-pretended coyness to go with it, was altogether more intimate and disturbing.

He was smitten with remorse at once for his ignoble thoughts concerning the girl he loved, and for his own physical excitement, which he could feel detumescing while he continued to stare out of the narrow, leaded window, down at the figures scuffing about on the gravel tennis-court below. It was a sultry June afternoon, the sun beating down heavily, but with bruised, swollen thunderclouds gathering behind the solid, dark grey mass of the cathedral opposite, which dwarfed the college buildings. As though to remind them of its pre-eminence, the chimes of the quarter-hour rang out over the drifting voices and laughter.

The room was dark, he blinked when he turned back from the

brightness of the window-arch. Jenny was smoothing out his crumpled counterpane, fluffing up the single pillow.

'Just checking. Don't want to give poor old Irene another heart attack.'

'Gosh no!'

Irene was the 'gyp' who cleaned the room he shared with Colin Turnbull. She had made a great play of carefully laying out the hairpins she had found on the bedside locker. 'Found these in your bed this mornin',' she declared accusingly. 'Not yours, are they?' Apart from a scarlet-faced denial, he had offered nothing further, and Irene had not pressed. He was rather rakish about it when he told Colin, who had chortled pruriently, and spread the word among their fellow students. John's protests were half-hearted; he felt he had gained a lot of kudos.

But it was a frustrating business, courtship, he had to admit, if only to himself. It was doubtless a valuable part of the privileged education he was receiving. Having the freedom to bring a female up to your room – a room where the twin single beds shrieked their unspoken message – even if she did have to be gone, like an early Cinderella, by five p.m., was a heady experience, one he was entirely unused to.

He had had little to do with girls until he had come to Durham. At eighteen, he was a five-foot eleven schoolboy still; large on talk, low on practical know-how. Then, at the end-of-term hop at Christmas, he had met Jennifer Alsop. She was a first year student also, but not an undergraduate. She was doing the two year teacher-training certificated course at St Hild's, with just the slightest bit of a chip on her pretty shoulder, he thought at first, like so many of her thin-skinned certificate colleagues. But he was astonished, and dazzled, that she appeared to like him well enough to meet him the next day for coffee. And to exchange letters during the Christmas vacation, and begin meeting regularly the following term. His first real girlfriend.

Everything was so transformed. People, places – she was a

part of everything now, and it was all different. At times he was shaken to discover how supremely important she was to him. He wanted to share his feeling with the whole world. That was why it hurt him so much not to mention her at home. His mother, Teddy, the rest of the family – none of them knew she even existed. It worried at him, pricked him like an invisible splinter beneath the skin.

'I can't wait to meet your mum,' Jenny said, her blue eyes shining. 'She will come for Founder's Day, won't she?'

The words were a private torment to him. How could he tell her that he was – what? Ashamed? Afraid to tell his mother of this most wonderful thing? Why? He said he would do anything, go through anything, to prove his love. Why couldn't he even tell his mother of her presence in his life?

His mother would be happy for him, surely, when she understood how much he loved this girl. After all, she herself had known such love. She had proved it, over and over, by remaining faithful to his father's memory all these years. By choosing to remain alone, with her two sons, devoting her life to them. May Wright was a beautiful woman, even now, in her fortieth year. Widowed at twenty-three, without even the comfort of knowing where her husband's remains lay, seeing only his name etched in the marble of a vast column which contained hundreds like his, she had brought up her boys with a single-minded devotion which had allowed no other man to come within the sacred bonds of the family.

And that was the crux of it: that taint of disloyalty which cast its accusing shadow whenever he thought about his mother's reaction to the news. It was there, in the corner of his mind, in all the sunny expansiveness of being in love. When Founder's Day came he was sick, and disgusted with himself for his cowardice. He fumbled red-faced through the introductions, and only he recognized the flinching expression of hurt on his mother's face as she smiled, took the proffered hand.

It had all passed off well enough. Mum was quiet, but he felt he was the only one who saw it. She was polite, even friendly, towards Jenny. Uncle Dan helped a lot with his almost aggressive jollity, exaggerated, John knew, to help along the awkwardness of the situation.

'Well, you're a dark horse, I must say, young John! Where've you been hiding this beauty, for goodness' sake?' He even stood and swayed, stiff-legged, on the dance floor for a few sweating minutes, his large hands heavy on Jenny's thin shoulders while she moved gamely from foot to foot, smiling up at his red, boozy face, until he cried out laughing for his stick and Aunt I, ready as always, hurried forward to give it to him, and he lumbered off with a good-natured bellow. 'First time I've been really mad at those blasted Jerries! I'd've given young John here a run for his money otherwise, you see if I wouldn't!'

It was two in the morning when John and Jenny stood locked in a goodnight embrace outside the digs in Sutton Street where Jenny was to spend the night. The gates of St Hild's had been firmly locked hours ago. He knew as soon as he kissed her that something was wrong. He continued to hold her round the waist, but she leaned back, her head away from him, and said, 'You hadn't told her, had you? About me?'

'I didn't want her to come with any preconceived notions,' he answered, ashamed at how plausible he was sounding. 'We're a funny lot. Very close. Probably with having no dad around,' he ended apologetically. They kissed again, for longer, and he was encouraged enough to say jocularly, 'Anyway, I haven't met your folks yet.'

'They know *all* about you.'

'Oh, God, no!'

In the main, it had gone all right.

'I'm quite jealous,' Jenny told him. 'Your mum's more like your sister. She must have been a child bride.'

'Forty in August. She thinks it's the end of the road. Disaster!'

'Your Uncle Dan's a card, too.'

John nodded. 'My dad's older brother. He joined up right at the beginning, in 'Fourteen. Same regiment as my dad. The Fusiliers. Got right through to the last year. Then he got blown up. He's lucky to be around. At one time they thought he would-n't ever walk again.'

Jenny's face clouded with compassion. 'Does it – it must upset you, when you think about it?'

He shrugged almost guiltily. 'I was only two when my dad was killed. Never knew him. And Teddy was only one. It's Mum it was tough on. It must have been terrible for her, being left on her own. Well, I mean, she had the family, my grandparents and so on, and Aunt I – She was closer to Mum than anyone. She was the one who got Mum started on the café. They built it up together. Aunt I only married Uncle Dan three years ago. She and Mum lived together all the time we were growing up. Our two mums, they used to call themselves.'

The warmth of his love was obvious in his voice. 'She's a real nob, as well. Her father's Sir Nicholas Mayfield, biggest timber business on Tyneside.'

'She seems good fun,' Jenny offered, recalling the smart, bulky figure who complemented her husband's *bonhomie* so admirably, with a no-nonsense modicum of common sense to counterbal-ance his exuberance.

John chuckled. 'You should hear them telling the tale of how Mum and her first met up. Aunt I was a suffragette; she chucked a brick through the local Labour Exchange window, and Mum came along and saved her from an angry mob. Not to mention a bobby who was just about to arrest her. She took her back to my grandad's.' He swiftly dismissed the notion of telling Jenny the highlight of the story, though he could hear Iris's rich laughter as she recounted it. 'Your ma had to take me back home to change. I'd peed my knickers with fright!'

He went on, 'You can imagine how Aunt I's folks reacted when they found she'd chummed up with the daughter of a joiner from the shipyards.' He lapsed into a broad Geordie twang. 'So ye see, hinny, aah's not much of a catch like, me bonny lass. Me granda still works ower the river at Swan's, ye knaa.'

'Don't come on with those foreign tongues, you devil!' she laughed. 'Remember, I'm just a simple country lass meself.'

The revels of Founder's Day in May led straight into the ordeal of first year examinations. But by the time John and Jenny were recovering from their sweetly frustrating display of passion on but not in his bed in college on this humid June day and Jenny was straightening twisted seams, John knew that he had done well enough to return in three months to begin the second year of his Honours English degree. No September resits for him to worry about. Though there was enough to disturb his equanimity, apart from his sternly repressed sexual desire. In spite of his staunchly concealed disquiet, he wondered if he had perhaps unconsciously transmitted something of his feelings to Jenny, for she was now showing a suspiciously similar unease.

Tomorrow was the end of term, and she was to accompany John back to his home in Hexham for a week's visit before returning to her own home across the country in Cumberland, where, later, in this long vacation, roles would be reversed and John would be the visitor,

'Are you sure your mother doesn't mind my turning up right away? Wouldn't she rather have had you to herself for a while first?'

'Of course not!' John assured her, with far more assurance than he felt. ' "Let's get it over with!" that's what she said when I told her, honestly!'

'Pig!' She punched him above the elbow hard enough to leave a bruise.

'There! That'll have to do. Think this will be all right?' May glanced round the neat bedroom, where she had just laid out a

14

crisp, new, striped bath-towel and matching face-cloth over the wooden rail at the foot of the bed. 'I thought I'd put her in here. The guest wing!' she intoned, with mock grandeur, and Iris joined in her laughter.

'And suitably distant from young Lochinvar's room,' Iris murmured, twitching her eyebrows.

'Pack it in, Iris,' May scolded, with suitable shock. But underneath the light-heartedness, she acknowledged the edge of seriousness in her thoughts.

'There've been a few changes in the old place since we moved in here,' Iris observed, as she followed May down the narrow staircase which led into the long passage. 'How long is it now? Must, be all of fifteen years.'

She knew, to the day. She would never forget any of those mostly happy, hard-working days they had spent together here. For a start the guest room they had just left had not even existed until four years ago. May had had it built on in 1930, not long after Dan and Jack's father, Ted, had died, in the hope that his widow, the formidable Sophia, would move in from the family home in Low Fell. Hope, or dreaded expectation? Iris wondered wryly. Either way, it had not materialized, probably to her daughter-in-law's secret relief, Iris suspected, though May would loyally deny it.

'We get on fine – as long as I don't argue with her!' May would always declare good-humouredly, whenever Iris enquired. Those were the days during the war, when May and Jack and the baby, John, had moved in with her in-laws, just before the birth of the second baby, Teddy. But this place, ramshackle as it had undoubtedly been when the two girls took it over, had been a godsend, a lifeline for the grief-stricken May after Jack's death. If I never do another decent thing, I made a right move there, Iris thought, with justifiable self-pride, for it was her idea, and her money. Well, all right, her family's money, but it was the same thing; she hadn't had to go, cap in hand, and ask daddy to put his hand in his pocket for it, and it had got the Tea Cosy Café started. And what a treasure it had turned out to be. Partly because of her; she was ready to take the credit that was due. But largely, and particularly over the past four years almost solely, through the acumen of the still trim figure moving ahead of her into the comfortable, sun-filled drawing-room.

This elegantly homely room, with its deep armchairs and sofa, with bright chintz that matched the flowered curtains at the two wide bow-windows, had been the café in their days together. Then they had purchased the lock-up premises in town, close to the high street, only a matter of months before Iris had moved out after their ten years of sharing the cottage. And now May had taken over most of the building in town, moved the café up to the first floor and opened up the shop underneath: the bread and cake shop which was doing so well. A far cry from the few fruit cakes and scones they used to bake out the back here and offer on a side-shelf to augment the takings from the café.

That first kitchen was now May's 'office' – a jumble of cardboard boxes, bills and files, with a cluttered table and an old captain's chair. She was always threatening to 'sort it out', but had never managed to get round to it yet.

May glanced fussily round the sunny room, fiddled with the vase of freshly cut flowers on the window alcove. She opened the door on to the garden. A stone-flagged path led between the neat flower-beds to the long lawn where, at its furthest end, a figure could be seen finishing off the cutting of the grass with a hand mower.

'I love the smell of cut grass!' Iris exclaimed, breathing in appreciatively. 'Have you got the kettle on? We've got loads of time before the train gets in.'

Iris had offered to pick John and Jenny up from the station in her motor car. John would have his luggage, including his cabin trunk, which he had sent on ahead from Durham.

'You won't forget the front lawn, will you?' May called out to the gardener, who nodded.

'Aye. Ah'll do it now. Just givin' the dew a chance to dry out a bit.'

'Don't get yourself in a state,' Iris said, as they turned back and moved through the drawing-room and across the narrow passageway which led to the original three-bedroomed cottage and the much smaller parlour. Iris poked her head round the door of the long kitchen at the rear of the house. 'Hello, Ruby. How's the family? Good. Pot of tea, eh?'

'I'm not getting in a state,' May countered querulously, as they settled in their chairs. 'I just want things to be right. The little madam's eyes will be everywhere, I bet.'

'Oh, come on,' Iris said. 'She seemed a perfectly sweet girl.'

'Yes, she did. Butter wouldn't melt. She's obviously made a big impression on John, at any rate.'

Iris gazed across at her with tender concern. 'He's a good-looking boy. It was bound to happen.'

'Good God, Iris, he's only just got to college. He's got another two years to do, at least. Nineteen! He shouldn't be thinking of lasses!'

'For goodness' sake!' Iris burst out, laughing. 'He'd be in a bad way if he wasn't.'

May had the grace to laugh. She blushed a little, then went on, 'No. But you know what I mean. He sounds so serious about her. And I mean, it's the first girl he's ever had. Practically the first girl he's been out with. Properly.'

'Don't worry. John's a good lad. And she seemed quite sensible. Not as flighty as some I could name!' All at once, Iris felt the love for this woman well up so strongly it seemed to fill her breast, tighten her throat. As so often, over the more than twenty years of their friendship, she was almost taken aback by the strength of the ties between them. There was no one, not even among her own family, to whom she felt closer. It was stronger in its unique way than her feelings for Dan.

She recalled how difficult it had been for her to accept his proposal at last. He always claimed, grinning, that he had worn her down eventually, and it was true. She had wept, suffered acute pangs of guilt, when she told May that she had accepted him. It was almost as if she wanted May to beg her not to leave her, to stay with her in the comforting insulation of the closeness they had built up between them. Of course, May had expressed her delight at the news: 'I couldn't be happier – for both of you.' And she meant it, Iris was certain.

But still, glancing round at the old place now, which would always seem like home to her, and seeing the worry on May's face which she could not disguise – she had never been good at keeping things from her – she felt the longing, and the tinge of sadness that things could not be the way they were. For any of them. The ghosts of the two noisy, laughing children, insepara-ble in their boyhood, still seemed to fill these rooms.

'Will Teddy get home while Jenny's here?' Iris asked. And even this was a painful nudge to remind them that time, and life, could not stand still. May had been upset when her second son had announced his determination to quit the grammar school early, without even waiting to take his school certificate. 'It won't do me any good, Mam!' he had argued strongly. 'Swan's will take me on in the drawing office now. I can start my appren-ticeship. Grandad was talking to Mr Webster.'

May had felt resentful towards her father, still working at the Neptune Yard, believing he had unduly influenced his grandson in his choice of a career as a marine draughtsman. There had been a lot of tension, until, reluctantly persuaded by Dan and Iris, as well as Teddy's mutinous obstinacy, she had agreed to his being articled with Swan Hunter's at the same Tyneside yard where her father still worked as joiner and carpenter.

He had started work only weeks after Iris and Dan's wedding. Then had come further strains when Teddy objected to the

18

wearyingly long time he spent travelling to and from work, by train into Newcastle, and then by tram out to the Walker yard. 'It's ridiculous, Mam!' he argued practically. 'I'd be better off in lodgings, and coming home on a weekend.'

'Why, that's a daft idea if ever I heard one!' his Grandfather Rayner announced, in his usual forthright manner. 'There's me and your nana rattlin' aboot like two peas in a pod. You can get yesel' in with us, lad. You can have your mam and your Aunt Julia's old room.' Of all May's siblings, there was not one still at home. They were all married, except for Bernard, and he was in the Royal Navy and came home rarely and briefly on leave.

The Rayners still lived in the terraced house in Gateshead that they had occupied since May could remember. She often felt guilty at the long periods which passed by without seeing her parents, or indeed any other members of her family. When she and Iris were just getting the Tea Cosy on its feet in 1920, she had tried to help her younger sister, Julia, who, as she approached her twenty-first birthday, was drifting discontentedly through a series of uninspiring jobs, from domestic service to shop-girl at a greengrocer's in the Bigg Market. 'You can help with the boys,' May told her. 'And help out in the café when we get really busy.'

The arrangement had not lasted long. Unlike her sister, Julia found the life in the quiet little market town extremely dull, particularly in the almost hysterical fervour of released gaiety that had come in the wake of the Great War. 'You just want a skivvy!' she had snapped accusingly at May. She then went on at bitter length about how 'posh' May had become, with her 'fancy ideas, above her station'. 'And ah'm not gonna be bossed about by your lah-di-dah friend, neither!' she declared fiercely, referring to Iris.

She left after only a month or two, to their mutual relief. Two years later she had married a pitman from one of the local mines, and now she had three surviving children, all girls. In 1927 she had given birth to twins, a boy and a girl. The girl had died after less than two weeks, the boy at three months. She had never been easy to get on with, even in adolescence; after this loss she was practically impossible. Closed up, embittered, she snapped at everyone, fought with many, and her husband took refuge by burying his head in a pint pot whenever he wasn't working. She had had a further child, a girl, again, who was now three. May scarcely saw her, they had not met since little Rose was one year old.

The accusation that she was getting ideas above her station in life was not a new one from her family. But it hurt just as deeply each time it was flung at her, as it was on the occasion when Teddy told her of his wish to move nearer to his place of work in the city. She made a point of making the trip over to Gateshead to see her parents, still half hoping she might somehow persuade Teddy to change his mind. During her visit her dad rounded on her aggressively, 'What's wrong? Havin' him lodging in this place not good enough for ye? Not grand enough for you now, is it, Lady Muck?'

She had found herself trembling inside, tears dangerously close as she swallowed back wounding words to lash out with. They could even find fault with the way she spoke nowadays. 'Like ye've a moothful of alleys in yor gob!' her youngest brother, Jimmy, had sneered, deliberately coarsening his own accent.

Anyway, Teddy had got his own way and stayed with his grandparents, to their doting delight. He was supposed to come out home every weekend, but gradually that had slipped, too. It would be, 'I've been asked to go into the office on Sunday morning.' Or, 'a few of the lads are going to a dance at the Oxford on Saturday night.' Over the past two years he had gradually let his home visits lapse, especially after John went away to Durham, until May sometimes never saw him for two months.

It was difficult to get used to being on her own after so many years of close-knit fulfilment with Iris and the boys. It was just as well that the business, particularly the shop side, had needed so much of her time. And, of course, Iris and Dan had bought a small house in neighbouring Corbridge. 'You don't get rid of me that easily!' Iris joked, but she made a point of dropping round whenever she could, which was most days.

May brought her mind back to Iris's question about Teddy. She nodded determinedly. 'I told him he'd better get his backside home this weekend. I think he will. He'll be curious to get a look at her, like a good many more.'

As they climbed into the Morris Oxford parked in the front drive, Iris said, 'You should have got a licence, you know. Too late now. You'll have to take one of these driving tests if you want one now.' May had steadfastly refused all Iris's urgings that she should learn to drive. The unpopular practical-skill tests had been made law just three months ago.

May was surprised to find how nervous she was as they stood on the platform some minutes later and watched the three-carriage train steam into the station. Doors rattled, and there was John, hauling out suitcases, then turning to help the dainty, slim girl stepping down from the high doorway and the narrow, wooden step. She was wearing a dark blue summer dress, with tiny white dots all over it. The silky material clung to her figure, the skirts flared at mid-calf round her stockinged legs. She wore a small beige beret perched on the side of her head, and her dark blonde hair hung in loose curls just above her shoulders.

May's gloved hands felt damp, clutched tightly in front of her. She smiled brightly, moved forward towards them. John's sensitive features looked tense, uncertain. She knew how he was feeling.

'Hi, Mam. Hello, Aunt I. Here we are then.'

'Hello, Mrs Wright.'

'Which one do you mean?' Iris quipped, and Jenny looked startled. 'We're both Mrs Wright,' Iris explained, gesturing at herself and May. 'I still haven't got used to it.'

Jenny laughed politely. Her blue eyes carried the same vulnerable expression of unsureness as she shook hands with May. Then she turned and cast a swift glance at John, as though somehow appealing for help, and May was caught by the naked look of love, of closeness. She felt the sweetly remembered pain of it like a sharp pang about her heart.

Chapter Two

'What do you reckon then?' John's glance betrayed the apparent casualness of his tone. It was important in this new world of love that everything should be as harmonized as possible. He needed the approval of his brother; he wondered if Teddy felt as keenly as he did the element of separation which had crept into their relationship over the past two years, particularly since he had gone away to college. Not just the geographical distance, which meant they had seen each other infrequently over the past twelve months. The differences were beginning to emerge before that.

Teddy showed little interest in the academic pursuits which were important to John. He couldn't wait to get away from the grammar school. He was aggressively proud of the fact that he was in the 'general and practical' stream; showed scorn for John's more intellectual cronies. 'You can keep your iambic pentameters and your Petrarchan sonnets!' he sneered. 'What good's that going to do you?'

John felt the same way about Teddy's slide-rule and other TD instruments, though he professed rather more tolerance. In fact, there were times when he felt uncomfortably on the defensive, as though there was something slightly shameful about his leaning towards the arts, particularly when he was in Grandad Rayner's company, or any of his mother's family with their challenging pride in their working-class traditions. Not that there was anything wrong about that, he would always assure himself hastily.

23

But he would never forget a remark of Aunt Julia's, tossed out at one of the Christmas gatherings in the little house in Sidney Terrace, bulging with visitors. It was only two days after his fourteenth birthday – he was already growing out of that sense of being vaguely cheated at having been born on Christmas Day, of all days – and his nana had been making him blush with her proud boasts of how well he had been doing at school. Aunt Julia had called out, cruelly he thought, 'Eeh, our May! I wonder where he gets his brains from? I reckon he'll end up bein' a schoolmaster. He doesn't look as though there's a day's work in him!' He smarted under the roar of laughter which erupted all round him.

Later, travelling back to Hexham in the freezing dark, on the last train, he had muttered of his hurt, and his mother had said, 'Don't take any notice, pet. She's got a tongue like a razor, our Julia. Always did have too much to say for herself. And don't forget, she's a lot on her plate with your Uncle Alf, and losing both her babies last year. That was terrible for her.' It made John more ashamed of his resentment, but it still rankled.

Teddy seemed to be inclining more and more towards his mother's side of the family. As the boys grew into their teens John could not help the sneaking suspicion that, somehow, his Grandad Rayner secretly favoured Teddy; identified more closely with his younger brother. And it was reciprocated, for Teddy liked nothing better than to spend Saturday nights at Sidney Terrace; to accompany his grandad down on to the Quayside to the Sunday morning Paddy's Market held there; to wander through the stalls that sold all kinds of things, or to watch the street entertainers, like the man who festooned himself in chains and padlocks, and writhed around in the dirt in a frenzy, crying out as he fought to set himself free. John remembered as an infant being scared almost to tears by the madman's antics, and being doubly glad of the comfort of his grandad's work-hardened hand clasping his.

The two brothers had been inseparable as youngsters. John had rarely felt the responsibility of being the older of the pair. The sixteen months between them sat very lightly on their shoulders. Indeed, it was often the more outgoing Teddy who was the leader in their escapades, with John happy to follow, though often sounding a note of caution which was sometimes heeded, sometimes not. John realized more and more as he grew older that not having a father, or any male figure to take his place, had had a great effect on their unity, as it had on their relationship with their mother. 'We're all right as long as we've got each other!' he could remember Mam declaring, her hands round their shoulders, gathering them into her sides. 'We'll always stick together, eh, lads? Like the three musketeers.'

An apt comparison, he reflected now, watching for Teddy's reaction to his question. Was poor Jenny to be a latter day d'Artagnan striving to break into their exclusive solidarity?

'Do you approve?' He kept up the light-hearted note, and waited anxiously for the answer.

'Oh, aye, she's a reet bobby-dazzler!' Teddy grinned.

For an instant John was irked by his facetious thickening of the accent. 'I'm glad you agree.' He paused, said awkwardly, 'I'm really keen – it's the real thing. I want to get engaged.'

'Bit early for that, isn't it? You've hardly known her—'

'Six months now. I know her better than anybody. We're really close.'

'Oh, aye?' Teddy looked at him quizzically.

John flushed, deciding to ignore the innuendo. 'You'll see. When you and Mam get to know her—'

'Nowt to do with me, is it? Up to you.' John was disappointed at the swiftness of his brother's disclaimer. Of course it's something to do with you! he wanted to answer passionately. Such an important thing, it's everything to do with you and Mam. But Teddy was already continuing. 'What about college? What you going to do? You've another two years, haven't you?'

'I know that. Of course, I know – we've got to wait before we can get things started. But – I just – we know what we want. We're both certain.' He felt that sinking feeling, lodged heavily within him. And the sudden uncertainty, the disruption of his life. Even as he answered Teddy with such brave maturity, he was groaning silently inside at the notion of having to wait in this limbo. Two years was an eternity, beyond imagining. That was why he wanted so much to become engaged. It was a step, a positive one, a public recognition of their love.

His mind turned back to Jenny again, with the now all too familiar sensation of uneasiness. He knew his mam had got Teddy and him out of the way with the excuse of sending them down to the café to shift some of the stuff from the store in the back, to give her the chance to get Jenny on her own.

It disturbed him to find how deeply his loyalty was torn. The visit so far had gone off perfectly well. His mother had got on well with Jenny; how could she fail? He wanted so much for the bond between them to be strong and right from the start. And yet he knew, too, without a trace of anything being said, or even implied, that somehow his mother did not approve. It mattered so much, it was so vital, that he tried to dismiss his misgiving, to reassure himself that all would, indeed, be well. A little more time, and his mother would love Jenny, would open up and admit her to their exclusive union. Nothing to be lost, and all to be gained.

Jenny waited apprehensively. She wished that John were here at her side, but she knew full well that his mother had engineered this opportunity to get her alone.

'I love Sunday,' May said, turning to Jenny with a friendly smile. 'It really is my day of rest. The one day the Tea Cosy isn't open.' She reached down, carefully cutting the stems of the long bluebell hyacinths, which she passed across to Jenny who stood on the grass at the edge of the flower-bed. 'Ruby moans like heck about me cutting so many flowers,' she confided. Ruby was the local woman who came in to help in the house, with the cooking and the cleaning – 'chief cook and bottle-washer' was the way she herself described her duties.

' "Flowers are meant to be growin', not stuck in a pot!" ' May mimicked accurately. 'But I like to see fresh blooms in the house. Maybe it's with being brought up in town, with nowt but a back-yard with a tin bath hanging on the wall.'

Jenny noted the colloquial turn of phrase. Several times over the past five days May had slipped such expressions into her speech, as though to draw the girl's attention to her humble origins. She wondered, uncharitably, if the idea was to highlight what she considered to be the social differences between the two young people. As though that could matter a jot. In any case, it was many years since John's mother had left that tin bath back-ground behind. She had built up a very successful business. This house and garden, on the edge of the pretty market town, in the unspoilt countryside, was proof enough of her achievement. Not to mention the formidable fact that her bosom companion was the daughter of a knight – one of the big barons of industrial Tyneside.

May's voice cut in on her thoughts.

'I'm sorry, Jenny. You probably think we're a right set of heathens not going to church on a Sunday. It's my fault; I've been a bit lax with the boys, maybe, although they never missed when they were younger, of course. And Sunday school. What about you? Are you a regular church-goer? Or are you chapel? We're Wesleyans, our lot.'

Jenny nodded. 'I go most Sundays at home. Daddy's a sides-man at St Mark's. We're C. of E.' No doubt that was another black mark, she thought despondently. In spite of Mrs Wright's perfect friendliness, and her sometimes beautiful smile, Jenny could sense with absolute certainty her disapproval of the young couple's friendship. That was the trouble: John's mother knew very well that there was far more than friendship involved, even though nothing had been said. In fact, their behaviour towards each other had been guarded, to say the least, so that, despite her unease, Jenny partly welcomed this move towards some acknowledgement of the truth which she felt his mother was initiating.

The interrogation into Jenny's background had been conducted, with reasonable subtlety, throughout her stay. 'What does your father do? Have you any brothers or sisters? Your folks must be proud of you going to college.'

Jenny felt she could pass muster. Her father was the area manager for the Allied Assurance Company, and one of the numerous pillars of respectability at his local church. Mother was an active member of the WI, involved in her good works and jam making. Older sister, Rosemary, employed as lady typist with a Keswick law firm and engaged to Gerald Simmons, bank clerk at National Provincial with 'Prospects'. Younger brother, Paul, approaching fifteen, at the grammar school, and 12-year-old Joan, the baby, enrolled as a day pupil at a private girls' school.

In fact, if she were being honest, and she usually was with herself, it was her own parents who might well baulk at John's background. Not at these immediate circumstances, she was quick to acknowledge. The solid trade prosperity, this lovely house and garden, could not fail to meet with approbation. But just go back one remove – a grandfather who was a shipyard carpenter!

Jenny found it intriguing; she could almost feel a smile tugging at the corners of her mouth as she pictured Mummy and Daddy's reaction, their striving not to be shocked or dismayed. And then, to counterbalance all that, John's Aunt I. Not a relative at all by blood, but married to his uncle, and, it would seem, closer in friendship to May Wright than any of her family could ever be. And daughter of a knight of the realm! No wonder Jenny found John so fascinating, with such a romantic provenance surrounding him. Not that she cared a jot for any of that, she corrected herself. *He* was the one she loved, and would do wherever and whatever he came from. She hoped devoutly that he felt the same way about her.

The sun came out in spite of the drifting clouds. It picked up the brilliant, early-summer green of the grass, the freshness of the shivering leaves, the bold colours of the flower-beds in the first surge of their plumage. Jenny savoured its caressing warmth through the thin cardigan she had slung over her shoulders and through the lightness of her summer clothing, and on her bare arms.

'When's your birthday?' May asked, as they moved back down the lawn towards the weathered stone of the cottage, Jenny still holding the long, freshly cut blooms across the crook of her arm.

'First of September. I'll be eighteen in a couple of months,' she added, forestalling May's next question.

'Your folks must be worried for you, being away from home and everything. So young!' She shook her head, laughing softly. 'Gosh! When I think of myself at your age! I don't think I'd spent a night away in my entire life. I'd've been petrified.'

Jenny stood in the kitchen, leaning against the dresser, watching the older woman efficiently trimming stalks, arranging the flowers and greenery in two blue and white vases. She knew what May was leading up to. She prepared to resist.

'You don't look much older than me now,' she said. 'No one would believe you're John's mother. You must have been very young.' She felt the beginnings of her blush and rushed on, 'When you met John's father – when you married.'

There was an instant's pause. May's hands moved lightly, competently, rearranging.

'I was nineteen. I suppose I *was* young. Girls seem to wait a bit longer these days. They want more out of life, maybe.' She picked up one of the vases. 'Could you bring the other one, love?' They moved along the passage to the large drawing-room and stood the vases one in each window. 'There! That's fine.' Her neat, slim figure was outlined against the wide expanse of light behind her. Jenny felt she was being scrutinized. 'We were engaged a year. We had to wait, of course, till Jack had finished his training.'

'Yes, of course.'

'It's not always easy – when you're young.' Now it was May who suddenly seemed awkward, hesitant. 'You're obviously a clever girl, Jenny. You've got a good head on your shoulders, otherwise you wouldn't be doing what you're doing. A good career ahead of you. You're just starting out—'

'Mrs Wright!' Jenny's eyes were full of naked appeal. 'John and I – we – I'm very fond of him. I feel . . . he's very dear to me!' Her breath caught in a hiccuping sigh, almost a sob. There! It was out. The words she had wanted to proclaim from the rooftops. And now the air in the sun-filled room crackled with tension.

May looked strained. Shocked even, though she had surely known what was coming.

'You're both very young. You don't know – you're too young to know your minds, the pair of you. You mustn't be so hasty. There's plenty of time.'

'I know how I feel!'

'You've got a long way to go, both of you. There's college to get through. Two more years, at least. Maybe more. And then jobs. John hasn't known many girls. None, really. Bits of bairns, aren't you?' She tried to smile, not very successfully, and struggled on. 'It's nice that you've made friends so quickly. But, like I said – you're both so young. Give yourselves a chance. Don't get too keen. Not yet.'

Jenny felt her throat close. Her eyes filled with tears. She couldn't trust herself to speak. She tried to fight the fierce resentment welling up. And the sense of failure. She had wanted so much for this woman to like her. Had hoped to establish the closeness which would mean so much, was vital to complete her

30

happiness. Perhaps May sensed her desolation and sought to alleviate it, or perhaps she simply drew the scene to a conclusion in the immediacy of her triumph.

'Where have the lads got to?' she said briskly, and, somehow, consciously or no, her words brought a final, stabbing sense of Jenny's exclusion from this precious world. 'Dan and Iris will be here any minute. Can you give me a hand to start bringing the food through?'

John and Jenny walked Teddy to the station after tea.

'It's all right for you college toffs,' Teddy mocked, 'us peasants have to be up grafting in the morning.'

'Take no notice of him,' John told her. 'To hear him talk you'd think he was spitting hot rivets all day. He's the one who's the toff. A collar and tie man. Drawing office, my God! It's a wonder poor old Grandad doesn't die of shame down at the yard.'

'Get away, man! I'll probably call in at the club and have a pint with him on my way back home.'

Jenny knew that 'home' referred to his grandparents' house in Gateshead. She held out her hand, held him with her clear gaze. 'Well, Teddy, it's been lovely getting to know you. And thanks for coming back to meet me. I hope we'll be great friends.'

'Mam would've personally slaughtered me if I hadn't got myself back this weekend.' He took her hand, held on to it firmly. 'Not that it hasn't been worth it!' he added, with a laugh. 'It almost makes me wish I'd been a swot, if they all look like you at college.' He was still holding her hand, and now he darted his face forward and gave her a bussing kiss on her cheek. 'You get off now, and say one for me, don't forget.'

They were going to the abbey for evensong and left Teddy outside the station entrance. John slapped at his shoulder, received a swat in return.

'Take care, wor lad! I'll probably see you at Sidney Terrace soon.'

'Right you are. Gan canny! Bye, Jenny.'

The sun was still shining brightly, the faded blue and white of the evening filled with the stirring carillons as they made their way along the path through the weathered and blackened tombstones towards the dark solidity of the church. For a few seconds, their vision faltered in the contrasting dimness of the interior. The coolness settled over them, and Jenny shivered, her arms goose-bumping under the thin, linen, oatmeal jacket she wore over the spotted dress. Her fingers toyed with the edges of the light-coloured cloche hat which fitted closely to her skull, and round which her soft curls clustered.

Every cough and footfall echoed in the lofty, timbered nave, the pew cracked and creaked as they knelt on the dusty hassocks when they had taken their places. The central body of the church was nowhere near filled, and though Jenny found some comfort in the familiarity of the prayers and the responses, and the well-known words and music of the hymns, her mind was too distracted to pay proper attention to the sermon.

They were both relieved to get out again into the now long shadows and the final mellowness of the fading sunlight. They took comfort from the reassuring clasp of hand on arm and their proximity as they turned off and strolled slowly through the trees and meadowland beside the river. There was a sudden, damp chill along the river path, in spite of the late sun sparkling across the ripples. Jenny sought his hand, hooked her fingers in his, drew them up to rub briefly over her cheek.

'Your family don't really care for me, Johnny.'

'That's nonsense!' he declared hotly, feeling the sickening inner clutch, even as he spoke so vehemently, that she was probably right. 'They don't know you. It's the first time they've met you. They're dazzled by you, that's all. Like I was. Still am.'

'Oh, John!' She stopped, pulled him round to her, and their bodies pressed together, his arm round her waist held her excitingly against him. Their mouths stayed together, searching, tender and hungry for the love coursing through them. 'I *do* love you!' she whispered unsteadily, fighting against the threat of tears. They moved on, awkwardly, arms still about each other. 'I wish they could see – know – how I feel,' she continued sadly. 'Before lunch, while you and Teddy were out, your mum sort of – warned me off. In a nice way.'

'I'm sure she didn't mean it to sound like that,' he said quickly.

She could see the hurt in his troubled gaze and sensed the conflict that caused him pain. 'She told me we were both too young. How impossible it was to think of a permanent relationship.' She paused fractionally, plunged on. 'I told her how I truly felt. About you.'

She knew, in that even briefer hesitation before he answered, that his immediate reaction was one of trepidation, that his first thought was of how his mother had taken such a bold and challenging assertion, and for a while Jenny was filled with a pure, elemental jealousy. Even more upsetting, just for an instant she saw herself as standing all alone with John ranged opposite her, squarely at his mother and his brother's side in solid antagonism.

He was the one who now stopped their slow forward motion. He held her once again close to him. 'And I feel just the same way about you. You know I do, don't you?' His kiss and his hands on her body were powerful advocates, and she was comforted, and deeply ashamed of her view of his mother as her enemy.

The sun had gone by the time they got back. Through the greyness of the last of the chilly daylight the cottage windows were lit like small stages. The curtains had not been drawn and they portrayed the clear, lamplit warmth and brightness within; sharp-edged, the reflection spread in a dim carpet on the darkness of the grass. Dan and Iris and May were sitting playing cards in the small parlour. The oil lamp spread its magic little pool of light on to the rich green nap of the cloth, which hung in tasselled, heavy profusion over the table's edges and cloaked the sitters' knees.

'Well, well. Back among the sinners, eh? You've caught us at it. Cards and strong drink, and on the sabbath, too! Have we shocked you, Jenny?' Dan Wright's heavy face, overfleshed like his body, was florid, the whisky bottle set on the table was well down.

Jenny slipped off her jacket and John took it from her. Careful not to disarrange her hair, she removed the close-fitting hat, shook out her loose curls.

'I'm a modern young woman, Mr Wright, we're unshockable, didn't you know?'

'That sounds like a bit of a challenge to me. But if that's the case, surely we can dispense with the formality, for goodness' sake? Mr Wright indeed! If you're going to get mixed up with our young reprobate there, can't I at least be Uncle Dan?'

Jenny moved forward into the circle of lamplight, and with a quick smoothing motion of the back of her dress against her thighs, slipped into the empty chair on Dan's right. Her eyes locked briefly with May's as she took her place.

'Be careful,' she said, with a fetchingly roguish smile, 'you'll be making me one of the family next – Uncle Dan.'

'Uncle Dan indeed!' Iris grunted sarcastically. She squinted into the headlight beams through the insect-spotted windscreen. Dan's war disability ensured that Iris did all the driving, but, given her husband's propensity for alcohol, she would usually have insisted on doing so anyway for the few miles back from Hexham to their small house in Corbridge. 'Tactful as ever, that was. After all May had been telling us about the pair of them, and in you jump with both feet, encouraging them in their silliness.'

Dan's hand fell heavily on Iris's leg, his fingers dug in, feeling the soft rasp of her Sunday skirt against the silk stocking beneath. 'You know me, old girl!' he grinned provocatively, 'never did know how to conduct myself like a gentleman.' She gave an irritated snort, jerked her knee up, and he lifted his hand away. In the same tone he continued, 'But their young fancies are lightly turning, et cetera. They are mightily smitten. Just 'cos it took you and me years and years to spark off the glowing embers – and just because May let her fire go out altogether, after Jack went—'

'Oh, shut up, Dan! I've had more than enough of your maudlin whisky prattle, thank you. May is genuinely concerned, and quite right, too. They're both far too young. They're still children. First time away from home and they're falling into each other's arms like that. It's absolute nonsense! I don't blame May for being worried.'

He had heard the real anger, the edge of contempt in her voice, and it stung him, as always. The vision of that sordid room at Amiens came back to him as it so often did. The little table, the poor meal, the wine. And the tense, frightened features of the tall young woman who undressed so quickly, slipped into that shabby bed still wearing her petticoat, and would not look at him. The pain of her unwilling surrender, his own brute insensitivity. It still startled him, to be sitting side by side with her, man and wife, in a marriage that took thirteen years to come about.

Then, as quickly as it had surged up, his wounded anger died again. He leaned back against his door, let his temple rest against the bumping coldness of the glass.

'You and May can worry all you want, old girl, but it won't make a scrap of difference. I'm afraid our John has fallen, and that is definitely that.'

Chapter Three

'We'd like to announce our engagement on the first of September. That's Jenny's eighteenth birthday. Just like you and Dad,' John added, watching for his mother's reaction. He felt that was hitting below the belt somewhat, but he was nervously steeled up for battle. He saw by the closing down of her expression that he had struck a telling blow, but he knew that by doing so he had not furthered his cause. He waited tensely for her answer. 'I hope to be through at Jenny's then.'

'Don't you think it's all a bit premature?' She found it hard to look at him, was glad of the distraction of reaching for the cosied teapot, pouring them both another cup. It was nice, she thought, now that John was home again, that they could enjoy a proper, leisurely breakfast set out on the dining-table in the large room whose double windows looked out on to the garden. They had never been certain what to call it, ever since it had ceased to be the café. Dining-room wasn't right, she felt, even though it was where she served the meals when she was entertaining or when she and the boys were not sitting down in the kitchen, as they so often had in the past and as she did now when the lads were away and she chatted in companionable ease with Ruby, or bolted down a hasty bite before heading for the café and shop in town.

Perhaps she should start calling it the morning-room, she thought self-mockingly, and almost smiled as she imagined her parents' scathing opinion of such delusions of grandeur. But she really had little to smile about this morning. She tried to choose her words carefully, to deliver them in tones of calm reason. To hide the very real and sickening weight of disappointment she felt at her eldest son for his foolishness and his startling lack of concern for her.

'Don't you think you might be jumping the gun just a little? You haven't known one another *that* long, have you? And what about Jenny's folks? You haven't even met them yet. And in waltzes this stranger who announces he's getting engaged to their daughter. Not a good start, is it?'

'Jenny's told them – they know all about me.'

'Oh, well, that's something, I suppose.' Her tone was one of martyred reproach. 'At least they'll have had a bit of warning. Not like your Aunty I and me, turning up at Founder's Day without the slightest idea of her existence.'

I didn't tell you – couldn't – because I knew exactly what it would be like! he retorted angrily inside his head. But he kept the words to himself, felt the sickening hopelessness of this breakdown in communication, or understanding, with the person who mattered most to him.

'Surely you can wait a bit longer?' May resumed, in that voice of maddening reason. 'If you're that certain of how you feel for each other, then it won't make any difference, will it? Why not wait a few more months? Give yourself a little more time. Just to be absolutely sure.' She went on over the beginnings of his protest, her tone growing more urgently pleading, belying her earlier calmness. 'Let's be honest, you've not had much to do with girls. You haven't mixed much with them, socially. How do you know you won't—'

His face reddened. 'I know how I feel about Jenny, Mam! It's – we're both serious.'

'But announcing your engagement! It's a commitment. Don't you see? It—'

'We *want* that. We want to make a commitment. Look,' he went on, speaking in a rush, as though he were trying to convince himself as well as May, 'I know we've both got college to get through, careers to think about. I know we can't marry for another two or three years, at least.'

He tried not to feel the enormity of those words, the groaning desolation they unleashed inside him. As for May, she flinched at the word 'marry'; it was an instinctive reaction, like that to a sharp physical pain.

'It won't be easy, you know!' she said, more harshly than she had intended.

He caught her look, understood the meaning behind her words, and he flushed again. 'I know,' he answered stiffly. 'We'll just have to put up with it. We'll manage.'

She could feel her own cheeks growing warm. She remembered the day she and Jack had travelled out to the coast on the electric train. The sand-dunes, the warm summer day. It was one of the first times they had been truly alone together. She remembered their embraces, their bodies touching, straining together, in that shocking intimacy. The power of that sexual yearning she could not properly understand coursing frighteningly and thrillingly through her young body.

Now, still, after all this time, overwhelming her with its force, catching her in breathless surprise, came that physical ache and appalling sense of loss which had so stunned her. In the years following Jack's death, she had somehow learned to seal it off, to keep it within some secret, sealed compartment in herself, so that, as now, its rare and sudden eruption forth was all the more devastating.

She could scarcely speak, her throat felt closed up, her chest restricted, labouring for breath. She was appalled herself at the hissing fury, the vehemence of the reply she spat at him. Yet she was helpless to stop it. 'Manage? You know nothing. Nothing! The first little chit that comes along, flashing her great cow eyes at you! You're nothing but a bairn still. She'll manage all right. Manage to get you into trouble you can't get out of, and that'll be it, me lad. Finished before you've even begun to live your life! Well, don't expect me to give my blessing to your foolishness!'

They stared at each other in mutual, shocked dismay before May turned and hurried away from the bright room, with a bang of the door that set the teaspoons chinking.

Jenny was standing waiting for him, next to the iron gate leading from the platform. Buffeted by the streams of holiday-makers pouring past them from the train, they clung together, expressing in the fierceness of their embrace the pain of the four-week separation and their delight at being reunited after such a desert of loneliness. They had written every day. There had even been a kind of sweetness in the pangs of their mutual deprivation. And certainly their love had been penned with a freedom of eloquence made possible only by physical absence. But, breathless and dizzy as they still clung together and let themselves be propelled down the hot, glass-covered walkway leading from the railway station to the square at the town centre, they were both united in their conviction that words, however moving, were a poor substitute for the taste and feel and sweet, sweet smells of their hugs and kisses.

'Gosh! I've missed you, Jen!' John told her dizzily, proving the point about the inadequacy of words.

'Me too!' She dragged his hand up to her moist red lips, which moved over his fingers in worshipful nibbles. 'Shall we leave your case at the Left Luggage? I thought we'd spend a little time on our own before I took you home. I'll show you the lake, if that's all right?'

'Perfect!' The word 'home' had already stirred that anxious cloud so ready to build up to a stormy sky which threatened their private Eden, so that he was more than willing to postpone such a possibility as long as he could.

They walked along the narrow margin of Derwent Water, past the busy landing stage, where picnicking family groups covered almost every yard of available ground and there was a long queue for the rowing boats.

'We'll come down early one morning,' Jenny promised. 'There's the ruin of the old monks' cells,' she said, nodding towards the thickly wooded island which seemed close by. 'We can row over. Fight our way through the jungle!'

They kept on, moving off the narrow road and passing through the woody slope of Friar's Crag. In spite of the holiday crowds, they managed to find a relatively peaceful patch of cropped, green sward close to the water. He tried not to stare too closely at Jenny's bare brown legs as they sat, and she gathered the skirt of her light summer dress round the backs of her raised thighs. She was wearing brown, open-toed sandals, and he decided it was not too wicked to gaze at her exquisite toes.

He took off his sports jacket and rolled the sleeves of his open-necked white shirt above the elbows. His forearms were pleasingly tanned and stood out darkly against the whiteness of the cloth.

So, did you enjoy meeting His Majesty?' he teased fondly. She had written him a full account of her trip to Liverpool with her sister and her fiancé to see the king open the Mersey Road Tunnel.

But soon the tension that hovered close about them made its presence felt in spite of their bliss at being together again. John was anxious about meeting Jenny's family, doubly so in view of his mother's attitude towards the proposed engagement. He was also weighed down with guilt and resentment at the atmosphere his relationship with Jenny had caused at home. However much he rationalized, he could not shake off the feeling of having let his mother down somehow. Through the weeks they had spent with each other after Jenny's departure, the situation had lain constantly between them, colouring everything, making both mother and son miserable, for neither could forget it, or discuss it.

As it was July, moving into the full swing of the holiday season, May spent long hours of the day down at the café and the shop beneath it, though Ann Swainsby, the go-ahead manageress who had taken over three years ago from Laura Davies, had already proved herself capable of running the whole show on her own, even at the busiest of times. John, left alone in the peacefulness of the cottage to get on with his vacation studies, wondered if his mother was not glad of the excuse which work gave her to avoid his company until the mellow evenings.

He was glad of the solitude himself at first. He did not put it to much use as far as his studies went. His emotional state was far too disturbed to find solace in the intricacies and distinctions of Anglo-Saxon and Old English. But it gave him a chance to think – and to pour his heart out on paper, for Jenny's eyes only, an exercise he found well worthy of his time and skill.

Although May's hurt and displeasure hovered like an obstinately unpleasant smell about them, she made no further reference to the topic that lay between them. John, motivated by a desire not to hurt her further, and a less noble inclination for keeping the peace, kept quiet too about the subject dearest to his heart. But he felt a double sense of betrayal when he found that Aunt I was so resolutely allying herself with his mother. He had hoped that he would be able to enlist her invaluable support. After all, in the past she had often proved a liberal champion on the boys' behalf.

He still recalled her vigorous defence of him when he was sixteen, and had stayed out until dawn after a tennis-club dance. Mam had really torn into him next day, as he knew she would, ordering him back up to his room. 'Good God, May!' Iris had exclaimed, 'it's *nineteen* thirty-one, not eighteen! He's practically a young man.' It was one of the rare times he had heard them really quarrel. Which had made him feel even worse, until he had heard them weeping on each other's shoulders and making up afterwards.

But now, Iris was as bluntly disapproving as his mother. 'I think you're just being pigheaded about this. There's absolutely no need for a formal engagement at this stage. Your mother's quite right.'

He had bitten his tongue, managing not to be rude, but he was desolate, and suffered a painful sense of isolation. He wished that Teddy were around, though, uncomfortably, he suspected that even his brother might fail to understand how important it was to him.

It wasn't long before Jenny detected his unease. His hesitant answers to her probing questions were merely confirmation of what she had rightly feared all along.

'Your mother doesn't approve, does she? Of our getting engaged?'

John's brown eyes reflected his pain at the situation. 'What about your folks? How do they feel?'

Jenny replied, with more confidence than she felt, 'They'd prefer us to wait. They think I'm a bit young. They don't understand how we feel for each other.' John had wondered if she were having doubts herself. Ashamedly, he wondered also what his own reaction would have been if she had expressed them. But her look as she answered and the tightness with which she gripped him and offered up her mouth to be kissed made him ashamed anew.

Her family made him very welcome. Alexander Alsop, Sandy, though short in stature, was an impressively solid figure, with brown hair, thinning at his brow but compensated by longer than average flowing locks in two wavy wings at the back, which gave his dignity a slightly theatrical air. There were even faint hints, John thought, of the romantic poets with which the region was famously associated, but the abundant, neatly trimmed moustache countered such fancy. Inevitably waistcoated and watch-chained under a dark jacket and pin-striped trousers, replaced at weekends by striped blazer, panama and cream flannels, he was warily polite with John, encouraging him to give his opinions, to which he listened with grave attention.

'I think the disarmament conference was a wonderful idea,' John ventured, referring to the meeting the League of Nations had at last organized two years earlier at Geneva. 'But you can see already it won't work. Japan's already left the League. And look at Italy and Germany—'

'You can't blame them,' Sandy Alsop cut in. His dark eyes carried a hint of challenge. 'A right mess Germany's in, and no mistake. Adolph Hitler may be a rough diamond, but they need someone to sort them out. And Benito's the same. They need somebody to take charge and no nonsense! We're going to end up in the same mess ourselves if we don't sort these trade unions out. I know a lot of people get hot under the collar with Mosley, but some of these socialists are nothing short of Bolshies.'

'I don't think the Fascists would ever get popular support here,' John said, 'but I certainly think it's crazy to talk about disarmament with Europe in its present state.'

John was relieved that their views on world affairs were far from diametrically opposed. He had more grounds for concern closer to home, though. It was Jenny's mother, Moira, who made the first direct approach. At forty-four she still showed the lines of face and figure whose attractiveness Jenny had inherited, though overlaid with a matronly, bustling solidity that went with her busy social life of good works. He was not surprised that she should be the one to bring up the subject of John and Jenny first. The females in the Alsop household, outnumbering the males two to one, were independent-minded in their views and quite used to taking the initiative.

'Jenny tells me you want to announce your engagement next month. On her birthday, in fact. Do you think that's a good idea?'

Hopelessly, John felt the colour rising to his face, heard the quiver of unsteadiness in his voice. 'I haven't mentioned it to Mr Alsop yet. But it's right.' He flashed an appealing look at Jenny, who had also pinked. 'I'm very fond – we both feel the same way about each other. We're quite sure of our feelings.' He continued hastily, 'I realize we're both – we've a long way to go – before we can do anything. I mean, we have to finish college. Find a job—'

'I think you should wait. Finish your studies first. Then you can start planning for the future.' Rosemary, Jenny's older sister, spoke even before her mother. She was sitting at the breakfast table in a flowered silk housecoat, her fair hair, shades lighter than Jenny's thick, dark-honey colour, and far more fluffily abundant, was clamped in tight, jag-toothed metal crimps, and hidden by a thin cotton scarf bound turban fashion about her head. The eyes, too, were lighter than Jenny's clear blue. They were a pale grey, and when carefully made up with mascara fluttered with confident drama. Now they fixed him with a steady hint of contempt, a coolness that bordered on disdain.

He felt himself blaze with helpless anger inside. The flat tones of her pronouncement indicated her superiority. He had already met Gerald Simmons, her fiancé, considered him rather stuffy, well suited to his bank clerk position. Like Jenny's sister, he looked down with the condescension of his four years' seniority on what he considered John's callow youth. They deserve each other, he thought uncharitably.

'We're quite prepared to wait,' he returned, striving to keep the tremor from his voice, and the smile steady on his face. 'But we want to make the commitment – to each other – now. We've known each other eight months. Like I said – we're sure of our feelings.'

Jenny reached over pointedly, took his hand, held on to it. 'We love each other,' she declared with brave simplicity. 'We'll wait till we can get married. But it's a case of when. Not if.'

Mrs Alsop's lips drew in, her face severe, as if Jenny had

committed a breach of taste. 'Young folk often think they know best. Feelings change.' Her tone lightened, grew more affectionate. She smiled. 'You might think you know all there is to know about each other, but it takes a long time to get to know somebody really well.'

'That's true,' Rosemary chipped in with a chuckle, 'I'm still learning things about Gerry. It's—'

'And you've been engaged for a year now.' Jenny smiled at her with malicious innocence. 'Has it put you off?'

'Of course not! That's not the point—'

'Isn't it?' asked Jenny sweetly, and Rosemary frowned in annoyance.

In the event, tears won the day. Jenny insisted on being present when John made his tense formal approach to her father, and, in the face of Sandy's initial stiff disapproval, and his urging that they should wait at least another year until Jenny had finished her course at St Hild's, she wept passionately and insisted it would make no difference what her family said – or did.

'If John will buy me a ring, I'll be proud to wear it on my birthday – and forever after! And as far as I'm concerned I'll be engaged to him until we can be married . . . and that can't come soon enough for me!'

Sandy loved his children. He was no match for such fervour and gave in with outstretched arms. Faced with a *fait accompli*, his wife accepted with surprising ease. Rosemary shrugged dismissively. The younger siblings, Paul, fifteen, and Joan, twelve, were only vaguely interested, and Gerald Simmons gave John a manly, welcome aboard, hand-clasp. Plans were made to incorporate the announcement into the celebrations to mark Jenny's eighteenth birthday.

'You'll have to learn patience,' Moira Alsop told them again, and the warning hint in her gaze reminded John uncomfortably of his mother's words to him.

Their real significance came home to him just a few days before the party. After several days of chilly mist and frequent showers, the 27 August swiftly transformed into a day of bright sunlight and high, white fluffs of cloud. They packed a rucksack and set out past the pencil factory, over the bridge, and followed the path to Portinscale. They strolled through the woodland, then crossed a marshy area which brought them back to the lake shore. They stuck to its margins round the bay, met up with the Borrowdale road, along which they tramped at a steady pace until they struck off, climbing up through the wooded slopes leading towards Lodore.

They rested and ate their packed meal on a jutting rock near the cataract, which was gushing plentifully after the recent rains.

'That noise,' Jenny giggled. 'I'll have to go. Stand guard for me.' They had come across a number of walkers, but there was no one in their vicinity, and Jenny found the required privacy to relieve herself behind a bush, 'You're used to this, aren't you?' she grinned. When she visited him at Hatfield, he was required to station himself outside the lavatory at the end of the corridor to avoid any embarrassing encounters while she made use of it.

They climbed on, up the steep slope, the trees thinning, until the roar of the falls grew muted. They found the solitude they were seeking, and settled themselves in the grass, with a slight bank and a thick growth of bushes to screen them from any prying eyes.

'Are you happy?' she asked him, her eyes holding him as she moved into his arms.

They moved rapturously, limbs and bodies touching, pressing, their mouths searching ever more urgently. They could both feel the control slipping away, dizzily, dangerously, yet they were unable to stop, aware of their desperate hunger for each other. John's hands moved wondrously over her body, his fingers slipped inside her unbuttoned shirt, felt the warm, yielding softness of her breast under its thin cotton cover, felt the thrust of the little nipple against his touch, She squirmed, did not deny him, even offered herself more blatantly, and his fingers fumbled with the underclothing, found their way through to the silken, blossoming warmth of the skin itself, and she shook with passion.

Now it was her fingers, digging into him frenziedly, pulling him on to her, lying back, taking his weight on her, and their bellies thrust together. He felt his throbbing hardness trapped in his shorts, pressed against her. His left hand dropped, cupped her bare thigh, savoured its proffered curve, slid up to the gap of her shorts, and beneath, encountered tight elastic, moved on, beyond redemption, felt the warm moistness, the forbidden, cushioned flesh, the feel of springy curls beneath the cotton of her knickers, the seep of wetness.

She was sobbing harshly, tore her mouth from his, rolled and kicked under him, and he dragged his hand free, rolled off her, sobbing himself, blood roaring, his aching erection withering wetly away.

'Oh God! I'm sorry!' She sat up, swivelled right away from him, presenting the hunch of her back, the shaking shoulders. She cried noisily, accusingly. 'I didn't mean . . .' he muttered, appalled, completely unknowing what to say or do.

After a long while, he reached out with his handkerchief, touched her upper arm, held the cloth over her shoulder, and she took it, kept it to her face, wiping, sobbing. She snuffled, at last calming, blowing her nose, gasping, until she had exerted control over herself. He was kneeling on the crushed grass, keeping a yard of distance between them. Her hair was hanging in untidy wisps over her brow. Her face was red, blotched, the tip of her nose shining redly. Their glance when it met was painful with guilt, and shock.

'I couldn't go on. I had to stop. I was so frightened.' Her voice was small, almost the whisper of a scared child.

'I love you,' he said, with desperate pleading.

Her eyes widened, she stared at him, fear pinching her face, reinforcing his notion of her as a child. 'I love you,' she murmured, seeking comfort from the trite phrase. 'You do understand, don't you?'

His eyes stung with tears, his throat closed. He nodded. He wanted to crush her to him, let her feel the love which beat through him. Instead, he reached out gingerly, took her hand, swung the rucksack on to one shoulder. They moved slowly, with great care, making their way back down the slope, towards the roaring tumbles of foam below them.

Chapter Four

Dan Wright lay with his head pressing uncomfortably against the wooden headboard of the bed. The tangled sheets clung about his middle, revealing the nakedness of his upper torso, its pink fleshiness, with the thin line of fine, dark curls between the swells of his breast. He could see the outline of Madge Wheeler's spine; the long, knobbed curve of it under the pink silk of her slip as she bent to adjust her stocking. Her, tight, neatly curled dark hair stood out above the slender shape of her neck. As always, he felt the tenderness which came to him only now, in the splendid peace after the hectic lovemaking.

He thought of her wild thrashing, her thin body writhing, shaking above him as she straddled him, rode him furiously; the wonderful, groaning abandon of her as she brought him, too, to the same mad pitch of bodily fulfilment. Affection stirred even stronger in him now at her simple, glorious shamelessness, her accommodation of him, of his equally fierce need of her.

She had been his mistress for six years and more. He had thought that, soon after the consummation of their 'affair', he had lost her for good when she announced that she could no longer work for the firm, now that they had become lovers. 'I don't think I can cope with seeing you every day at work,' she said, gazing at him in that direct way of hers that so attracted him. 'Not that I'm being silly or anything. Not going soppy on

49

you. But it would be too awkward, seeing you in the office. Now that we're – like this.'

She was married. He. had met her husband, Peter, several times, at the work functions and the odd time when he had called in at the works to collect Madge. A nice fellow: quiet, self-effacing. Dull as ditch-water, Dan's inner voice mocked, much to his discomfort. And totally unaware of those secret, sensual fires which could blaze through Madge, in spite of the two children he had fathered with her.

Not that Dan had ever discussed such things with her. 'I'm a wicked woman,' Madge declared unsparingly. 'Peter's a good man. Far too good for me. He's given me a good home, children. What I always wanted. I ought to be perfectly happy with him. I'd never want to do anything to hurt him. I love him.' Dan had felt that inner flare of real anger, a desire to lash out scathingly at her for her falsity, until she had added, with that simplicity of hers, 'I couldn't bear it if he ever found out about you and me. But I can't help myself. That wickedness in me. I need you so bad, Dan. It's the way I am. Same as you need me. Or someone like me.'

She knew about his peculiar relationship with Iris. Even when he told her he and Iris were getting engaged, marrying the following year, she showed no trace of jealousy or even hurt. 'Does that mean it's over between us?' she asked, quietly, unfussily.

He had blushed for shame. 'I think it's got to be, don't you?' She had nodded.

Less than a year after his marriage, and shortly after his father's death, he had called her at the place she was working. When he asked if she would meet him for a drink, she had agreed at once. At their next meeting, he said, taking a leaf from her simple book, 'I still need you, Madge.' Without question, she had resumed her former role with him, making no demands, and bringing all the fire of their passion to the various clandestine beds where they came together.

He tried to explain something of his marital relationship to her. He owed her that, at least. 'Iris and me – it's never been a sexual attraction. At least, not on her part,' he added, with commendably foolish honesty, and Madge smiled. He told her about the strange night during the war, at Amiens, when Iris had given herself to him like some reluctant virgin sacrifice. 'I never slept with her again. Not until we were married last year. And even now,' he glanced at her with a diffident little smile of confession, 'she allows me my conjugal rights. Not that I demand them often. But it's not ...' he shook his head hopelessly. 'I still feel she's suffering nobly. In fact, I damn well know she is!'

In some ways, it was his relationship with Madge that had helped to push him towards marriage with Iris. The secret meetings for illicit sex, the furtiveness, the careful planning, their infrequency – all seemed to combine to emphasize his loneliness. In spite of their passionate intimacy, he felt more and more cut off from Madge the fonder he became of her. He felt part of the secret little compartment she had created within herself, isolated from the reality of her home world of husband and children, friends, family. He began to resent this divorce within herself, until he harboured wicked and disturbing thoughts of disrupting, destroying it.

When he sought a more healthy avenue of escape and took himself off to Hexham, the insulated domesticity of the household there, the two women and the boys, grated on him. How apt the name was, he thought ironically: The Tea Cosy. May and Iris, tucked up under the warm, protective cover of the snug little world they they had created for themselves.

He often wondered about his brother's widow. May was a beautiful woman. It was a tragic waste that she should have lost her love so young, and found no other; diverted all of herself into such a small compass. The café. The boys. Iris.

It was their mutual love for May which was the strongest bond between Iris and him. It brought them closer and closer as the years passed, until, after the watershed of his father's death, and his bleak assessment of his inner emptiness, the idea began to grow on him that he and Iris could bring each other a companionship which, uncomplicated by the flares of passion, could prove strong enough for them to make the rest of their lives together.

The truism about the willing spirit and the weak flesh had never been truer than in his case. His marriage was not as serene as he had at times anticipated. Iris had taken some persuading. It was several months before she finally, with uncertain reluctance, agreed. He knew she had had many long, intense discussions with May. He also knew that it was largely due to May's urging that she had at last said yes.

'It won't be love's young dream, you know,' Iris declared forthrightly, slapping her ample hip. 'I'm fair, fat and forty. Well, thirty-eight to be precise. And very set in my ways. May and I have been together ten years now.'

'I know, I know,' he replied good-humouredly. 'If we were Muslims I'd marry the pair of you.'

'Ha! May wouldn't have you if you went down on your bended—' she stopped, reddening as she perceived her insensitivity, but he chuckled, unfazed by her gaffe.

'And that'd take a bit of doing, eh, old girl? But what about you?' He looked at her seriously. 'It's you I'm asking. Will *you* marry me? Let me make an honest woman of you after all these years,' he dared to add.

For once she met his gaze without that flinch of embarrassment, and reached out briefly to touch his face. 'There's never been any other man since. As you well know. I thought I'd die an old maid. But yes, I'll be happy to accept your proposal – old friend!'

Dan was all too aware of the tensions surrounding their first night of marriage. They had both anticipated them. 'There's no need to rush things,' he said, striving for easiness. 'We've got the rest of our lives together.'

Deliberately, he turned his back on Iris, letting her see the cruelly scarred tissue which covered his back, and the deep furrow gouged from his right buttock and the top of his thigh which had so damaged his lower spine that he could walk only with a stiff, open-legged, lumbering gait, and the aid of his specially adapted metal walking-stick. It was not the first time she had seen his injuries, but it was the first time she had been able to study them in such leisured detail.

She had witnessed some terrible sights during her war service in the ambulance corps, and though her eyes moistened with compassion for him, there was no trace of reluctance or repugnance in her glance or her touch as she moved to him and put her arms round him. It was her own condition which preoccupied and alarmed her. There was no physical sign of *her* scars, if that indeed was what afflicted her. She scarcely knew. All she knew was that she had been dreading this moment, that inside, her body and spirit clenched with a revulsion she could not dispel, no matter how hard she tried.

This pitifully marked figure, revealed so nakedly to her, was the only man she had ever lain with. The memory of it, though it happened thirteen years ago, remained vividly and terrifyingly with her. She had not properly understood why she had done it. She was little wiser now. Though she despised herself for a coward, she nevertheless gratefully seized on his generosity of spirit and took his proffered avenue of escape.

She came back from the bathroom clad in her beautiful bride's nightgown, by which time he was pyjama-ed and decently covered beneath the sheet. She got into bed beside him and took his hand, with a shy, sad smile. 'You're a good man, Dan Wright,' she murmured unsteadily. 'I don't deserve you.'

'That you don't, old girl,' he chuckled, and slipped a companionable arm round her shoulders. She settled down with her head trustingly on his chest.

Mechanically, the problem of their sex life was solved,

awkwardly, with attendant humour, but not without trauma. 'Crippled but unbowed!' Dan quipped, at the physical evidence of his potency when they prepared to make love. 'I'm afraid you'll have to do most of the work, old girl. Just imagine you're off on a good gallop!'

He lay on his back, a pillow under his spine, and propped on one elbow. He had tried to rouse her with gentle touches and embraces, to ready her, and she lay tremblingly still until she could endure it no longer. She squirmed free of his arms, managed to prevent herself from saying, 'Let's get it over with!' and awkwardly spread herself over him; forced the union of their flesh. She could not altogether stifle the whimpers and grunts of pain. Even though he was in her, he could sense her clenched disgust, and all at once he let himself go, hurting himself as he tried to thrust savagely into her, gasping with pain and relief when he felt himself discharge.

He knew she took precautions to ensure that she should not get pregnant, and sadly agreed with the common sense view, backed up by her doctor, that she was too old to have a baby. In your mind if not your body, he mused, but kept his thoughts to himself.

Dan felt disappointed and disillusioned. True, he had never fooled himself that passion would rule in their relationship. But he had, perhaps foolishly, hoped they would find the physical expression of their union mutually satisfying. Sex rapidly became infrequent, its indulgence something which Iris clearly endured, with tight-lipped martyrdom. They quarrelled, and Iris wept, was forced to a tortured admission that she did not 'like it'.

She could never express the horror and shame she felt each time, as she straddled herself over him, opened herself to that priapic, thick manhood ready to stab itself into her, or her enveloping shame at the enforced activeness of the role she had to assume. She could not help the painful feeling that he should not demand such a sacrifice from her. Soon, he did so less and less. As the end of the first year of the new decade approached, with its festive, nostalgic atmosphere, he found himself seeking Madge Wheeler's whereabouts, speaking to her on the telephone at the city office where she worked, meeting in the discreet, warmly lamplit intimacy of the Turk's Head cocktail lounge.

Her frank sensuality was like cold water down the throat of a desert-parched man. They took up their illicit affair with a mutual eagerness. There were times during the next four years when Dan wished he could adopt Madge's seemingly uncomplicated attitude towards their infidelity. No matter how hard he strove to justify his own conduct, he could not get rid of the guilt he felt at his deception of his wife. Sometimes he wondered if Iris would understand his sexual unfaithfulness, perhaps even condone it. After all, she so clearly found their sexual relationship abhorrent. And he, even though he was now in his mid-forties, could detect no lessening of his carnal appetite. Why should he then live in a miserably enforced celibacy? Surely it was better to break his marriage vows than to force himself on a wife who was repulsed by such congress? But there were other times when he imagined that Iris would be devastated by the discovery of his relationship with Madge. It was not something he would risk finding out.

Now, as Madge finished dressing in the anonymous comfort of the hotel, he said, 'I'm afraid next weekend is out. There's a do on for my nephew. Young John. You remember I told you he's got himself engaged to some girl at college. He's spent almost the entire vacation over at her place. In the Lakes. His ma's giving some sort of do for him before he goes back to Durham. Not that anyone approves of what the idiot's done. What I'm afraid of and so are a few others, I can tell you – is that he's got her into trouble, as they say, and there'll be an even hastier wedding arranged before long.'

A squall of chilly rain rattled against the darkening window. Madge shook down the hem of her dark brown woollen dress and picked up her coat. 'I'll come down with you,' Dan said belatedly. 'See you into the taxi.'

'Don't be daft! You've got hours to go yet. You keep yourself snug and warm. I wish I could join you.' She slipped on the close-fitting brown hat, clipped it into place. 'Aren't I awful? I feel a lot of sympathy for that rapscallion nephew of yours.'

'Hussy!' Dan reached up for her, and she bent, they kissed, slowly. 'I'll phone you next Wednesday. And you drop me a line at work. Let me know when you're free.'

His fleshy shoulders were smooth and warm. She pulled away, straightened up. 'I'm always free for you,' she smiled.

'I love you, Madge!'

She put her hand to her lips, blew him a kiss and went out.

He lay back once more. He felt his penis stir, and lifting the sheet he stared at himself, smiling at his arousal. Love her? He did, too, in a way. How long was it since he had said that to Iris? Guiltily, he pulled his hand away from himself, and stared unseeingly at the neatly impersonal room in which he had found such powerful release.

'Mam! We *are* going to wait, you know. We won't do anything silly. And we haven't, in case you're wondering,' he added, his face crimsoning.

'I'm glad to hear it,' May said drily, disguising her emotion. The house was packed, mostly with friends of the boys, though some of the family had managed to attend. None of her own – John had taken Jenny through to Gateshead soon after they had arrived a few days earlier. She had met May's mother and father in their small terraced house, and May's embittered younger sister, Julia, who had arrived with her three little girls, deeply curious to see what 'John's lass' was like. Jimmy, at twenty-eight the youngest of May's siblings, and working as a rigger in the same yard as his father and Teddy, had also shown up, together with his wife, Kathy, and their three small children.

'Quite a horde, eh? How did you get on?' May asked Jenny when they returned late that night.

'They were all very nice,' the girl replied diplomatically, while May wondered cynically what she really thought of them.

None of them had shown for this second engagement party. Not that she had expected them to, though invitations had been extended. She could almost hear Julia's biting comment. 'Why, no! We're not grand enough for that lot, man!'

Dan and Iris were there, of course. Sometimes May felt more dependent than ever on Iris's support since she had left The Tea Cosy four years ago. Cissy, Dan's younger sister, and only two months younger than May, was also there, dramatically bemoaning the fact that in three weeks she would be forty. 'Isn't it awful?' she declaimed tragically to May, who had faced the same traumatic experience in August, and clutching at her hands. Cissy had been married for almost ten years to David Golding, an enigmatic figure who did very well in some business to do with steel, which involved quite regular trips over to the continent.

They had no children, whether by choice or not, May had no idea, and would not presume to ask. She remembered how Cissy had made her welcome in the Wrights' home, against the cold hostility of Jack's mother, which had lasted up to the time she had presented them with their first grandson. It was Cissy who had come to the munitions works at Armstrong's in 1917, to tell May of Jack's death at Passchendaele. After the war, Cissy had enjoyed an adventurous life as a 'flapper', with lots of young men and lots of intense affairs, until, in 1925, at the comparatively advanced age of thirty, she had met David, and settled down.

Joe, the youngest of the Wright family, still unmarried at

thirty-six, came, too. When he was younger, May would seethe with a bitter, inner fury at his bewailing the fact that he had been too late to serve abroad during the war. He had joined up in the artillery, but the armistice came just before his embarkation for France. Isn't it enough that you've lost one brother and the other is crippled for life? May would cry inside, but she kept her silence. In later years, more tolerantly, she believed that the frustration of Joe's youthful, if foolish, eagerness to embrace danger had somehow quenched his enthusiasm for life in general. Or, if not, he had narrowly channelled all his energies into the family business. 'Just as well,' Dan had quipped, somewhat unfeelingly, May thought, when she discussed Joe's situation with him and Iris.

There was no quenching of liveliness on this occasion. Teddy, and the other local youngsters, had made sure of that. It took a sustained effort to restrain them sufficiently for the brief speech and toast which Dan organized as master of ceremonies, in the crowded front room of the cottage.

'To the happy couple,' he announced, his florid face shining, as he raised his glass high. 'Here's wishing them all the luck for their future and a lifetime of happiness ahead for both of them!'

May raised her glass. She caught John's eye. He looked across at her, smiling brightly, his young features flushed, reminding her so poignantly of his father. Was she being hypersensitive, she wondered, in seeing just the hint of a challenge in his glance?

Chapter Five

'Is she sick of you already?' Teddy's jovial question was like a touch to a raw nerve. John had to force himself not to snarl a reply.

'No. She's got a load of work to do over the holiday. She goes straight into her teaching practice when term starts. I'll go over for the weekend after New Year.' It was true. Jenny's two year course seemed to be crammed with work. There was scarcely time to fit it all in. In comparison, his own existence was indecently slothful. After managing the hurdle of first year examinations, the path to his English degree had eased into the leisurely academic routine traditionally associated with undergrad life. Attendance at lectures was not compulsory, and as long as you turned up for seminars, and for sherry with your moral tutor, no one exerted any pressure on you.

The fitting in of leisure pursuits made most demands. He still turned out at a chilly seven a.m. three times a week to row bow in one of the fours tubs they used for practice, though each time he did so, picking his way gingerly down the slippery steps behind the college to the black chill of the Wear, with the white wreaths of mist hovering like steam over it, he vowed it would be his last. And now it was Michaelmas Term, there was rugger training twice a week, and a game for the college second fifteen most Saturdays, or, if not, vociferously vocal support of the firsts on the touchline.

59

Most days he would meet Jenny outside St Hild's as soon after four-thirty as she could make it, and they would stroll through the stalls in the Market Square, or wander down Silver Street and go down the steps at the side of the bridge to the river-bank. Sometimes, he would treat her to a cup of tea and cakes in the café at the old mill. The autumn nights drew swiftly in, so that it was dusk, the tow-path soggy with mould like wet tea-leaves, as they walked arm in arm, bodies swathed and bundled in sweaters, cardigans, heavy coats and trailing college scarves, Jenny wearing a woollen beret with a pompom, pulled down over one eye, and hiding most of her honey-coloured curls.

They did not spend too much time alone in purely private places. John still shared a room, and Colin still obligingly kept out of the way if requested. But, since that day at the Lodore falls, they both acknowledged the ever constant need for vigilance and restraint. It influenced all their physical contact; the passionate kisses and clinches, which they pulled breathlessly away from, as though they must be severely rationed.

'I want more,' Jenny confessed quietly, her blush showing how difficult it was for her to admit. 'I know how you feel. Honestly I do. And I appreciate – how good you are. Not ... asking. ...'

Does she really know? he wondered, ashamed as always at the heated response of his body. Could she really know that powerful urgency, the animal hunger he felt? It was such a male thing, he was certain, she could not feel that same raw, physical need, it could not be like that for girls. At least, he qualified, not for girls like Jenny. His restraint did not always succeed in making him honourable. But it was there, it became a pattern of their relationship, and only rarely did John feel that secret resentment, an almost despair that made him darkly believe that it could not possibly be this bad for Jenny.

They parted for the Christmas vacation at Durham station, her brief spurt of tears, still shining as she leaned smiling from the

60

carriage window for a snatched kiss, was a great solace to him. Once he was back home he felt guilty at the pleasure he took from its familiarity and the warmth of the approaching festivities, of being back in the familial bosom. His mother was so delighted, so clearly enthusiastic about the holiday, and having her two sons back again. Delighted, John wondered, because he had chosen to be there, instead of with Jenny?

It was not all sentimental warmth and joy to the world, though. Teddy rapidly disabused him. 'Jimmy's on short time again. There's talk of them paying off more men at Christmas.' The world-wide recession was biting deep in the north-east, when other regions were beginning to show signs of recovery. Even the few miles along the river that separated the rich farming land from the industrial mouth was the frontier between two contrasting worlds.

John noticed how Teddy had dropped the 'uncle' in front of Jimmy's name. Mind you, Mam had been twelve when her youngest brother was born, and had been like a second, subordinate mother to him during his early years. He was only nine years older than John himself, but married now, to Kathy, a quietly cheerful girl from the neighbouring Gateshead streets, and with three children, Betty, aged seven, Bill, five, and the baby, Eunice, two.

'There's talk of him coming back home, to Nana and Grandad's if he gets laid off,' Teddy went on. 'It's grim, man. Loads of fellers hanging about the yard every morning. One of the foremen got set on the other night. Somebody put him in hospital.'

'That'll do a lot of good! It's not their fault.'

'There's a lot of bad feeling. Who gets kept on, you know.'

'What about you?' John asked.

Teddy shrugged. 'We've got enough to keep us going well into next year. But things aren't improving. It's just as well Grandad's retiring next year. Things look black.'

The reality of the harsh economic conditions so close to him struck John forcibly as 1934 came to a close. The gathering in the small house in Sidney Terrace on Boxing Day was a tradition which had rarely been broken. John's grandmother, Robina, insisted on as many of the family attending as could make it. She was nearly sixty-one and suffered from angina which, particularly in the winter cold, left her breathless and blue-lipped and sometimes racked with pain in chest and arms that left her helpless. But she played it down and tried to hide the worst of it from her husband, George, who, approaching sixty-five, was gnarled and bowed. His hands were knobbled and twisted, scarred from his lifetime work as a carpenter. John could hardly remember a time when one of his nails had not been deeply discoloured, the black blood beneath it a badge of office.

'Fit as a lop, man!' he insisted when the family came together in the paper-chained, greenery-decked kitchen, large enough for them all to get round the vast old table which filled one wall opposite the black-leaded, gleaming kitchen range. His chest wheezed and his throat rattled and his voice rasped with the Woodbines he had been smoking since he had started at Swan's as a lad of fourteen, in 1884. 'The' built real ships in the old days, mind!' he declared, with a fierce nod in Teddy's direction, and a wink for the rest of the company.

'Aye. Well, the' not building *any* bloody ships now, are the'?' put in Jimmy bitterly from the small bench near the fender, where he was helping Kathy to see to the little ones.

'Language!' said Robina automatically. 'Remember the bairns.'

Julia, May's sister, scowled. Her lips compressed. 'It's not just the yards that's sufferin', ye know. Alf's been out as well. And they've cut back the overtime an' all.' Her hair was tightly crimped in dark waves which clung to her brow. She had had it done by one of her neighbours specially for the holiday. Her bright red jumper, and the string of large beads at her neck, emphasized the pallor of her thin face, as did the glossy cherry

62

of the lipstick she had used liberally. The whole effect was too garish, May thought, sitting opposite her. Her newly festive outfit, her make-up, served only to highlight the pale scrawniness of her frame, and the ugly bitterness which clothed her personality.

Her husband grinned sheepishly at her remark. His big face, roughened and flushed by alcohol, turned even redder. May felt a swift stab of sympathy mingled with irritation for him. Alf Dale was an oaf and a drunkard. He had made good money as a pitman at the coal-face, but, like shipbuilding, the coal industry had been badly hit. It must be hard living with Julia. And as far as May knew, he wasn't abusive to her, didn't knock her about the way plenty of fellows would. But then, what would she know about it? she told herself.

It was as if Julia had been able to read her mind. 'Not that you'd know owt about that, our May. Livin' out there with all them posh folks. And your lads office workers and college students. No wonder you talk so swanky, eh? It's a wonder ye can be bothered with common folk like us!'

The old antagonism rose chokingly within May's breast like hot bile. 'Would you rather I didn't?' she fired back. 'Sounds like a touch of the green eye there! Anything I've got I've got by hard work—'

'Huh! Aye! And friends wi' pots of money to fling around like ah dunno what!'

'You nasty, vicious little bitch!' May's fingers curled, she had an almost overwhelming urge to reach out over the laden table, as she had on more than one occasion when they were both much younger, and hale Julia by the hair.

'Oh! That one got home, did it?' Julia sneered wickedly. 'You've always thought yourself a cut above the rest, ever since you married into that lah-di-dah fam'ly.'

May gasped as though she had been struck. The words stung like a blow. She blinked, the tears stinging in her eyes as she recoiled, unable to think of anything for a second, stunned by the hurt, the cruelty of the attack.

'Howay, lass!' Alf rumbled, his face aglow with his embarrassment. His protest was drowned in the eruption of shock and anger from George and Robina.

'You shut your mouth!' George flashed, his gnarled finger raised, pointing. 'You'll get the back of my hand across your face, in front of your own bairns!'

His wife stood, the laboured breathlessness of her words highlighting her emotion. 'Stoppit, now! I won't have it, ye hear? Not now. Not round this table. For God's sake, there's enough trouble in the world. We'll not have it in the family. Behave yourself, Julia. Let's have no more of it!'

Everyone started talking at once, trying to cover the awful embarrassment of the moment, only partially succeeding. The two principal combatants stared down at their plates. For the rest of the day and evening they were stiff-lipped and markedly polite towards each other.

In accordance with tradition, after tea the menfolk went out for 'a pint', to the Black Bull two streets away. For the first time, both John and Teddy were allowed to accompany them. John had celebrated his twentieth birthday the day before, and Teddy had been legally entitled to drink at a public house since his eighteenth in April. Both the bar and best room were crowded, but the five men stood shoulder to shoulder in the jostling crowd, hugging their straight, foaming glasses to their chests.

'Well, here's to wor Geordie and Bernard,' George Rayner said, raising his glass in honour of the two sons who were far away. The oldest, named after his father, was in the Merchant Navy as an engineer, with wife and four children settled in distant Southampton. The other, four years older than Jimmy, which made him the second youngest in the family, was also at sea, in the Royal Navy, at present serving on a destroyer with the Mediterranean fleet.

Rather self-consciously, they all sipped in unison. Except, John noted with wry humour, that after his Uncle Alf's 'sip', his pint was half gone.

'By, wor Julia's gorra tongue on her, eh?' his Grandad Rayner observed. He nodded at his son-in-law. 'Ye've got my sympathy, lad. But ah did warn ye, didn't I?' Alf gave his customary grin, and accommodating chuckle. George Rayner turned to his two grandsons. 'Tek no notice of her, lads. Ye know we're all dead proud of your ma. And of youse two an' all.' But the clash, and the sour taste of its aftermath, stayed in John's mind long after the event.

It had obviously upset his mother, too. She was unusually quiet during the journey home by taxi cab over to Newcastle followed by the long wait in the gloom of the Central Station for the chilly train ride out to Hexham. Her face was pale with tiredness and the strains of the day. There were shadows smudged under her eyes, yet her set expression and her weariness took nothing from the still young-looking beauty of her features.

'I despair of our Julia sometimes,' she offered at last. 'She doesn't know how near she came to getting her face smacked, the madam!'

John grinned at the incongruity of the remark from such a smartly dressed, ladylike figure. She saw his smile. 'Don't you worry, it wouldn't be the first time, either. We've never got on.'

He kept hearing his aunt's bitter words over and over. The next day, when May had gone after breakfast to the shop and café, opening again after a two-day respite, he took out the heavily bound family album, gazed at the rows of neatly placed portraits. He studied the few photographs of his father, the face of the young man he had never known, the man his mother had loved. The only one in which the family was complete had been taken at a studio. 'Chapman Studios, Gateshead' the caption read on the cardboard mount. There was a larger version of it, framed, on the sideboard in the sitting-room. His father looked oddly vulnerable in the new khaki uniform, which was buttoned ill-fittingly about his neck. The thin moustache added to his pensive expression, and did little to take away this air of youthfulness.

John had been told that in those early studio portraits the sitters had to hold their poses so long that a smile quickly became a fixed idiot grin, which was why so many of them looked so sombre. In any case, he guessed that his parents would have had little to smile about. This was the last picture they'd had taken together, before his father went over to France. May's figure was stiffly corseted, the intricate braiding patterned down the front of her dark gown swelling out over an almost voluptuous bosom. Her pretty face, as set as his father's, gave a hint of the sadness lurking behind that level stare. His own infant body, festooned in what looked like a knee-length, girlish coat beneath which showed black stockings and heavy boots, was jammed between his parents on the narrow, high-backed wooden bench. He was staring, wide-eyed, transfixed. Teddy was a tightly swathed bundle of white lace, with a portion of swarthy face showing indistinctly from under a wide, white bonnet.

John thought of the contrasting freedom of the finely pencilled sketch of his mother upstairs, the erotic beauty of the delicately planed curves, the slenderness of the girl's body. As always, he felt the disturbing mixture of conflicting emotions in himself whenever he did so. He looked again at his father's fine, sensitive features. Why had he done that, for anyone, everyone, to see? In spite of his mother's brave words – 'never be ashamed' – he could remember how she used to blush if she saw himself or Teddy looking at it. And later on, when he was growing up, she had confessed to him that she used to take it down and hide it in a drawer when any visitors were coming, in the early days.

Aunt Julia's words came again: 'that lah-di-dah family'. He had long ago realized there was a social division between the Wrights and the Rayners. Though both were careful not to make disparaging comments about the other, even as a young child John had understood that this was so. Indeed, the careful neutrality observed by both sides reinforced his feeling. And there was very little mingling, even at Christmas and at birthdays. There were visits to one, then to the other. Christmas Day with the Wrights, Boxing Day with the Rayners.

From a practical standpoint, John supposed he had been closer to his father's family, with Uncle Dan and Grandpa and Grandma Wright on hand to advise, as far as schooling went. He knew that it was money from the printing works which paid for his secondary education, and that a considerable sum had been put aside in trust for him on his Granpa Wright's death. Now a grown man and with a love of his own, he looked with a new appreciation on the difficulties his mother must have faced. Difficulties which were reflected after all these years in Julia's bitter words and attitude. He guessed that his mother must have felt more and more alienated from her own family – her roots – and how upsetting it must have been.

He felt a new irritation with Teddy. In his cocky, often belligerent way he was reviving this old division, with his parade of affiliation with Mam's side of the family. And yet, John admitted to himself, it was inherent even within himself. Why did he feel such confused emotions? Why did it disturb him so much that he felt he could never quite categorize his own roots to his satisfaction? Why did he sometimes feel a kind of shame that he was so divorced from the Rayners' background of physical skill and labour, that he was, for want of a better word, so 'intellectual'?

In his late teens he had been both moved and excited to discover the writer D.H. Lawrence, and to find the divisions which so interested him explored and expressed powerfully in his poems and then in the two novels 'Sons and Lovers' and 'Women in Love'. But then had come the rumours about Lawrence's life-style, and, just before the writer's death in Italy, the outrage about a novel too obscene to be published. A version had come out abroad which one of John's worldly wise sixth-form colleagues claimed to have read: 'filthy as you like, man!' the erstwhile critic had declared enthusiastically. Subsequently, at Hatfield, John had been shown an extract which, sadly, appeared to confirm the opinion his school-fellow had some-what childishly expressed. Shocked at the graphic crudity, and deeply disappointed, John had failed to bring himself to discuss or even mention it to Jenny.

His convoluted thoughts brought him by a roundabout route back to the sketch of his mother, hanging in her bedroom. Some people would surely claim it to be obscene also, even though it was beautiful. He had, with great misgiving, taken Jenny into his mother's bedroom one morning when they were alone in the cottage together. 'Ma doesn't like anyone to see it,' he told her. 'Don't say anything. She'd be mad with embarrassment. She usually hides it away when we've got visitors,' he lied, hating himself, watching her face anxiously. He saw the pink creep up under her skin.

'It's lovely,' she said, a little stiffly. 'Your father – he was very talented.' There was plenty of other evidence of his artistic skill. The water-colours were hung downstairs for all to admire. Jenny had said no more about the portrait, never mentioned it again.

How would he feel about seeing Jenny's picture like that? he asked himself yet again. If he had the skill – his father's skill – would he have done something like that? He could not come up with a convincing answer, but he did not like putting himself into the position of having to defend Jack Wright.

His reflections had a considerable influence on him. When he returned to college in the new year, he noticed a poster advertis-ing a Socialist League project, designed to further the educational opportunities of the working man. He went along to a meeting in the union building on Palace Green, where a suitably regionally accented speaker urged the necessity of developing and stimu-lating the intellectual capacity of the working class.

'You lads, the intellectual cream of our society, have a duty to help out!' he declared forcefully. 'And make no mistake, there's plenty want to learn. They just need the chance. Why don't you come along and do your bit?'

Stirred by these words, and by his own recent self-examination, John did just that. 'I'm not ready to join the league,' he said honestly, 'but I'd like to help with your study programme.' He found himself helping out twice a week in the evenings, in the upper room of the Miners' Institute building, teaching anything from basic literacy skills to a potted course of English literature, to small but keen groups of manual workers from the city and from the surrounding pit villages.

Jenny was cautious at first. 'The Socialist League?' she queried doubtfully.

'I haven't signed up,' he told her. 'Don't worry. I'm not going to turn into a Bolshevik overnight. I just think that this education programme is quite a worthy cause. After all, I come from the same background myself. At least, half of me does.'

When he went home for the Easter vac he discovered that he was not the only member of his family to take an interest in social or political doctrines. 'Look!' his mother said proudly. She thrust a card under his nose. 'I hope you're going to join, too.'

She had been with Iris to a meeting in the City Hall in Newcastle. The speaker was a Methodist minister, a Donald Soper, the subject, world peace. John had heard his mother's round condemnation of war, her espousal of the pacifist cause. She did not often sound off on the subject. She had no need to. He knew well enough how dear it was to her, how closely her life, like so many others, had been so severely affected by it. In the past he had wisely held back on his own views, which could not embrace the pacifist belief wholeheartedly. Particularly since the upsurge of nationalism in Italy, and now in Germany, too.

He looked at the small card she was holding out to him. 'They've used their common sense. They're getting women to sign up now, as well as the men. Nearly two hundred thousand. What do you think of that then?'

He nodded approvingly, stifling his instinct to argue, and glanced instead at the heading 'Peace Pledge Union Card' and the naïve promise of the words beneath, over May's neat signatureo: 'I renounce war and never again will I support or sanction another.'

Chapter Six

George Rayner retired soon after the New Year, well before his sixty-fifth birthday. 'The's no need for me to be stayin' on when other folks are gettin' paid off,' he told his gaffer. He got his watch, not gold, but inscribed with the details of his faithful service, and he got lots of free pints at the evening ceremony they arranged for him, with a considerable number of the bowler-hatted and suited brigade from management in attendance. But it hit him hard, far harder than he expected, the first morning he watched young Teddy heading off to the tram alone, while he sat on beside the cheerily glowing fire in the kitchen, supping at a second pot of tea.

Robina was doing the washing-up. 'By! Aren't ye glad ye don't have to turn out on a mornin' like this?' his wife said. At the small window above the sink in the back kitchen the late February sleet rattled and clung to the panes.

'I am that, lass!' he answered heartily, but he knew he was lying through his back teeth.

'Why don't ye have a bit of a lie-in?' Robina suggested hopefully, a few days later. Already, his unaccustomed presence weighed on her, disrupting the routine of her own lifetime. She was missing the neighbourly chats with Liz from next door over another pot of tea, half nine, regular as clockwork, day in and day out. But the machinery had been thrown out of joint. It was

71

hard for all of them to break new ground. George could not lie in bed; he was always up, collarless and in braces, to see Teddy gobble his early breakfast and leave.

'Could ye not catch a later tram?' his grandfather asked him. Most of the draughtsmen clocked in half an hour after the workers in the yard. Teddy had always travelled to work with George from choice rather than necessity.

'No,' Teddy assured him, 'it's easier sticking to this time. I have to be in first, anyway.' And it was true, there were a number of chores he was expected to carry out before the more senior staff arrived, though he was no longer the most junior apprentice and did not have to see to such things as filling the large jugs of fresh drinking water, which were set out with glasses beside each of the long, sloping drawing benches, or arranging the newly sharpened pencils and pens laid with military precision at each work space.

The reason he was so keen to stick to the schedule established when his grandfather accompanied him had nothing to do with work. Not long before George's retirement, Teddy had noticed a girl who was sometimes waiting in the queue of early risers standing at the top of the hill to take the tram down and across the river. The bitter gloom of the wintry weather ensured that everyone was bundled up in as many clothes as could be managed. But even with her head bound and hidden in a heavy shawl and her figure concealed in a winter coat that came down to her booted ankles he had formed the impression of a slim form and pretty features. His impression was confirmed by his surreptitious glance when, once aboard the crowded vehicle, she slipped the shawl back off a head of unruly, corn-yellow curls and revealed a pleasing, fresh, young face whose smile was in contrast to the stolid countenances around her.

His grandfather knew most of the people who caught the tram at their stop, and would nod and offer a greeting. Most of them were on their way to work, the vast majority were males.

Teddy was fancifully curious, and attracted to the girl. But in George's presence he was shy about attempting to strike up an acquaintance. Besides, she did not catch the tram every morning, appearing only occasionally. For the first few mornings that Teddy made the journey alone she did not appear. When he saw her, hurrying, head bent, the blustery wind blowing the long black coat against her form, he felt his heartbeat quicken. He took a determined breath, and stepped back so he could join her at the end of the line.

'A bit blowy, eh? Still, at least it's dry.'

She looked at him, a little surprised, and he noted the blueness of her eyes. She was guarded, muttered a scarcely audible reply. He forced the conversation on. 'I've seen you getting on here before. You live round here?'

'Wolfe Street,' the girl answered, still with that hint of reluctance. After a slight pause, she added, 'I'm not from round here, really. I'm stayin' at me gran's for a while. She's not too well.'

He could sense her reluctance easing. He was not given to chatting to strange girls, but he had a certain confidence, and an outgoing personality. Still, he was a little surprised at his temerity when he thought about it later. He sat next to her on the slatted wooden seats of the car, and she did not seem to mind. He continued to take the initiative, but she was answering more readily now, prepared to offer more information.

'I'm not from Gateshead. I'm from Easington. Easington Village, not the colliery.' Teddy was vaguely aware that Easington Village and Easington Colliery were two distinct places in County Durham. 'I go over to a place in Jesmond three days a week. Cleanin' an' that. Housework. It's for a doctor. Me gran used to work for him.'

Her sideways glances were beginning to be tinged with curiosity. His voice was attractive, his accent 'posh'. She could tell by his clothes and his hands that he was not a manual worker. When he told her he worked at Swan's, in the shipyard, he sensed at once by her look that she did not believe him. She looked hurt and offended by what she thought was his dishonesty.

'I'm in the drawing office,' he explained. 'Apprentice draughtsman.' He was not sure whether she was impressed or put off. Hastily trying to change the subject, he nodded through the window behind them. They were crossing the High Level Bridge; the road ran under the railway line. It was like riding through a tunnel, except that between the thick girders they could see glimpses of the leaden river and the graceful curve of the New Tyne Bridge downstream, already a symbol of Tyneside achievement, the largest single-span bridge in the world. 'I was at the opening,' he told her. 'Saw the king himself.'

He was twelve, and his Uncle David, not long married to his Aunt Cissy, his father's sister and a real glamour girl even though she was the same age as their mother, had got them tickets for the stand they had rigged up on the northern bank of the river. David Golding worked for a firm which had something to do with the bridge builders, the Dorman Long Company.

The girl was looking askance at him again. 'How old were you then?' she asked suspiciously.

He confessed, with a grin. 'Still in short pants.' He told her he would be nineteen in April.

'I'm seventeen,' she told him. 'My birthday's November the second.'

'Just before bonfire night. Bet you're a right cracker!' His grin disarmed her. He swung to his feet as the tram rumbled past the solid, crenellated mass of the keep and Black Gate. 'This is where I get off. My name's Teddy, by, the way,' He was almost gabbling now, aware of his dissatisfaction at the nebulous nature of their acquaintance. 'I'm staying with my gran, too. The Rayners. Sidney Terrace. I'll see you again,' he ended hopefully, jostled by the crowd making for the exit at the rear. She smiled, nodded noncommittally.

She hadn't even told him her name, he thought, as he dismounted and waited with the crowd to cross over towards City Road where he would catch the trolley bus along the river to the yards. But her reticence was understandable, he assured himself. Even commendable. It showed she was not one of these bold lasses who loved to have boys running after them. It also made him even more determined to strike up a proper friendship with her.

He had to wait another two days before he met her again, but this time she smiled shyly, with clear recognition, as soon as she saw him. He was not so pushy now that he had succeeded in his purpose of getting her to talk. They introduced themselves formally.

Her name was Marian Graham. Teddy sensed a reluctance in her to talk about her family, and he did not press her for details. She was even quieter when he told her about John being at university, and he cursed himself for his impetuosity. He was sure she was beginning to write him off as a 'toff' because of his speech and his family background, and hastily he concentrated on his Grandad Rayner and his Uncle Jimmy.

'He works at the yard. He's been put on short time. I've an uncle who's a pitman – he's at the Lady Mary pit. You know, just down the road, near Birtley.' Surely, he thought desperately, his pedigree was sufficiently working class for her not to be alarmed?

'I've got a brother and sister,' she told him eventually. 'Half-brother and sister, really. Me mam remarried. Me dad was killed in the war. Before I was even born.'

'Hey! So was mine! I was only one when he died.' He suddenly wanted to hug her, he felt so close and in sympathy with her. But she was blushing, and clearly did not want to talk any further about it. He realized how nervous he was when he said, 'Look, would you go out with me some time? Maybe to the pictures or something?'

She looked doubtful, and for a second he thought she was going to refuse. But at last she nodded, and he grinned with relief.

'When? What about Friday? I'll pay you in,' he added quickly. Perhaps the homely phraseology reassured her, for she agreed. 'Shall I call round for you?' he pursued, and was not surprised when she shook her head.

'No. I'll meet you at the end of your street. What time?' He was too elated to argue.

'What's all this then?' his grandad teased, when, on Friday evening, Teddy came in from the back kitchen after lengthy and elaborate ablutions. 'Ye've got enough grease on your bonce to fill a chip pan! Don't tell me all this is just to gan for a drink wi' the lads!'

Teddy's hesitancy was fractional. He had been bursting to tell someone since Marian had agreed to meet him. 'Well, actually, I *am* meeting a lass. I've seen her a few times. She lives round here. Wolfe Street. You've seen her yourself. She sometimes catches the tram on a morning.'

'Oh, aye.' George grinned with pride. 'Hear that, Bobbie? The lad's gannin' sparkin'! With a lass from Wolfe Street.'

His grandmother's reception of the news was far less enthusiastic than his grandfather's. 'Oh, aye? Ye don't want to start in on that caper, me lad. Spendin' all your money on lasses. The'll be after it soon enough. Ye want to wait till you've served your time before ye start on that lark!'

'What about our John?' he countered indignantly. 'He's got himself engaged, hasn't he?'

'Aye! And look what a fuss that caused. Ye'd better not let your mam know ye're runnin' about after lasses.'

He gave his customary grin, winked at her. 'Well, I won't say owt if you don't.'

'Haddaway with ye,' Robina's mouth twitched in an involuntary smile. 'So she's from round here, is she? Who is she, then, this young madam?'

'Well, she's not really from round here. She's just up staying with her gran for a while. She lives in Easington. Her name's Marian. Marian Graham.'

Robina was busy folding away the clothes which had been airing over the rail of the fire-guard. She stopped, glanced across sharply at him. 'Wolfe Street? Her gran's Peggy Dunn?'

Teddy sensed something in the tone of her questions. He shrugged. 'Yeah. I think that was the name. You know her then?' He felt a little edge of discomfit at his nana's sharpness. 'She's a nice lass,' he added defensively.

'Well, if it's who I think it is, ye'd certainly better not let your mam find out. Her mother's Nelly Dunn. She was a mate of your mam's when they were both bits o' lasses. They worked together on the munitions over at Armstrong's in the war. A right flighty little piece, she was.'

'Like mother like daughter, eh?' George chortled, and was rewarded by a killing look from his wife.

'Don't be late back!' Robina called a little later, as Teddy made to leave. His herring-bone-patterned, thick overcoat had collar turned up, the brim of his dark grey, soft felt trilby pulled rakishly down towards his left eye. He was surprised yet again at Robina's instruction, and a little hurt that she should so obviously consider him not yet mature enough to be dating a girl.

As soon as the front door banged, Robina turned to her husband with a frown. 'I hope to God our May doesn't get to hear about this. The'll be ructions all right.'

George glanced up from the *Chronicle* in puzzlement and dawning irritation. 'What's up now? For God's sake, the lad's eighteen year old. Why shouldn't he be takin' a lass out—'

'Aye, and ye know whose lass it is, don't ye?' She clicked her tongue in impatience at his blank look. 'It's Nelly Dunn's bairn, that's who!'

'So what?'

'So what?' she echoed, with deep scorn. 'Have ye forgotten?

I'm amazed she's let the lass come back anywhere near this place. Do ye not remember the scandal when Nelly left Armstrong's? Just before poor Jack got killed out in France. She was pregnant from a feller at the works. Some married feller. That's why she disappeared so quick. Down to her auntie's or summat. Got herself married some years later. Had two more kids. God knows how she passed the first one off. That must be the lass Teddy's goin' out with. Our May'll go mad if she finds out!'

'For God's sake, woman, the lad's only takin' her to the pictures! He hasn't got hissel' engaged to her yet. Not like that daft brother of his.' He shook his head in baffled incomprehension. 'Anyone'd think ye're terrified of our May, just 'cos she's got on in the world.'

Robina glared at him, her hands folded tightly over her floral apron. 'Don't talk daft, man. But she's lived for those bairns ever since Jack went. She wants the best for them, always has. And that doesn't include the likes of the Dunns. She'll not be best pleased to find out Teddy's knockin' about with Nelly's lass, I can tell ye!'

'I see. So you'll be away four days, will you? How nice for you. I hope you enjoy it.'

John was shocked at the waspishness in Jenny's voice. He was also hurt and puzzled at her attitude. He had been invited to join a group made up of students and young workers to travel down to Oxford for a few days to attend seminars and to visit the Morris motor-car factory at Cowley, to witness the famous new assembly line procedure. There was talk of a revolutionary change, not only in work procedures, but in facilities and support for the factory personnel. 'A happy work force is an efficient work force', proclaimed the leaflets which they had already studied. They emphasized how essential leisure pursuits and educational opportunities were for everyone, from shop-floor to office management.

'Well . . . you'll be right in the middle of finals and everything. And I don't have any exams to worry about this year.' His voice faded at the tense, screwed-up expression she flung at him. Appalled, he realized she was close to tears. 'Look, if you don't want me to go then I won't. It was just—'

'Oh no! You go ahead! Don't let me spoil anything for you. As you so rightly say, I'll be up to my eyes in exams, so why should I worry?'

'You'll be fine, you know you will!' He injected a full measure of vigorous enthusiasm into his remark, which served only to aggravate the situation.

'I don't know at all! How the hell can I know? It's not quite as moronically simple as you seem to think!'

He blushed deeply, even more at a loss. 'I don't. I – look, I'll tell them I can't make it. It doesn't matter—'

'No! You go with your bloody precious workers. It's probably better anyway. Do us good not to see each other.' In spite of her best efforts the tears squeezed out from her eyelids, and she muttered a curse as she strode blindly ahead, fighting not to break out in anguished sobbing. He stood for a second before hurrying after her through the muddy dapple of the late spring on the footpath.

She kept on walking, despite the tug on her arm, the tears splashing down now, while her insides churned and her brain issued a stream of profanities he would be horrified to discover she even knew. Why, oh why, was he so innocently ignorant of her emotional and physical make-up? Why were all men so abysmally out of touch? The heavy pain deep down, and the degrading discomfort of her period seemed to symbolize the despair which clung in its cloud of despond about her.

She longed suddenly to turn and throw herself in his arms, to sob on his shoulder and pour out the truth. Listen, just hold me, I'm having my monthly and it's a bitch, and I'm utterly fed up with work, and studies, and I hate kids, especially seven to eleven year olds. I just want to go somewhere with you, and climb into bed and snuggle in your arms, and last night, when you kissed me in the pictures and you put your hand on my knee in the dark, I wanted you so much – wanted you, properly, making love to me, doing *it* to me, that I was wet for you, I couldn't bear it, the wanting.

The tears came faster. How shocked he would be if he knew the extent of her depravity, how often, and how fiercely, her mind dwelt on what it would be like to have sex properly. And how her body responded to her wayward thoughts. She dug in the pocket of her mackintosh for a handkerchief, held it to her face. Make love? she thought bitterly. Even kissing him she was ashamed of her fetid breath.

'Don't cry,' he said wretchedly, holding on to her arm, and now she *did* allow herself to be stopped, and held in his arms. The wave of sobs which erupted as she pressed her wet face into his chest was a relief.

When the violence of weeping had eased she said wearily, 'I'm sorry. It's not about you going to Oxford. It's just – us.' She shrugged hopelessly. 'I think they were right after all, damn them. Your mum, and my folks. The whole lot of them. We should've waited. Shouldn't have become so involved; so absorbed.'

'You don't mean that!' he declared passionately, holding her a little off him so he could look into her face. 'We love each other, don't we?'

She grimaced, her lips turning clownishly down, with a sheepish nod. 'Yes, but – this – it's nothing, is it? Neither one thing or the other. We could've waited. Like they said. Given ourselves more time. Not tied ourselves like this.' She held up her left hand to show the ring, with its three tiny diamonds. 'I want to be married to you. But another year – like this.' The dark bronze curls shook, her throat closed and the tears welled again.

He nodded, all at once gripped in the same dumb despair. She moved out of his embrace, blew her nose firmly. 'Look, you go to Oxford. Of course I want you to go. Don't let's meet tomorrow. I'll see you next week, when you get back. I'm feeling lousy – a cold coming, I think. And I've got loads to do, you know I have. Walk me back, will you? I'll have an early night.'

All their efforts at chat failed. The evening sky was overcast, and a light shower of rain spattered down to echo their mood. At the gate of the college her brave effort at a smile touched him. 'Just exam nerves, I'll be all right. Enjoy Oxford. You can tell me all about it next Wednesday.' She kissed him quickly on the lips, and he did not try to hold her. She hurried away down the slope of the drive to the already well-lit building.

He walked slowly down towards the river again, his mind racing, his gloom deepening. He knew exactly what she meant about the year that stretched ahead. It seemed an eternity, a torturous period for both of them. Suddenly he felt his body ache, literally, with his love and his need for her. He imagined himself turning, racing back into that feminine bastion, crying out for her. Seizing her hand, fleeing. Finding a room, a bed: they would never be separated again. Dismissing his fantasy he strode out, hurrying as though he would speed up time itself.

The long shed, with its network of girders above, seemed to stretch for ever. The assembly line, on stands about knee high, reached down the length of the enormous room. John counted more than a dozen angular car frames dwindling into the distance. The cloth-capped, white-aproned workers attended constantly to the vehicles. They had no time to glance round at the knot of visitors who stood observing them. Near them, two men were fixing the windowless doors to the boxlike frames. They had less than two minutes to position the doors and to screw on the shining hinges which held them. They worked with automated precision, like part of the machines themselves.

'Our shop-floor staff are the elite,' the manager who was

showing them around, brayed over the hubbub. 'They're all on piece work. They can earn more than a trained clerk. Round here, you'll find everyone treats them with the respect they deserve. They're proud to wear the company badge.'

John tried to imagine working here all day. He wondered what would happen if one of them simply stopped working. Would the whole process break down? The faces looked strained, tense with concentration. They earned every penny they made, John reflected sympathetically. The manager, his white overall dazzlingly clean over his grey suit, his white collar immaculately starched, his company-logoed tie-pin square in the centre of a restrained, dark tie, led them down the wide, cemented central aisle towards the hangarlike doors at one end.

Later in the day, during the lunch hour, they got a chance to chat to some of the workers in the fresh June breeziness.

'Oh, yeah, it's good money, right enough,' a tall, well-set individual told John and two others who formed the small group. 'But it's bloomin' hard work, see? I mean, there's no let up. Apart from the breaks, you don't have time for nothing. You can't stop for a smoke or a chat, like.' He glanced over to where some of the foremen stood. 'You're just stuck there. And they're always workin' out ways of speedin' up the line. More cars we turn out, bigger the bonus, see?'

John remembered some of the tales, perhaps exaggerated, which his Uncle Alf Dale told about the conditions at the coalface. Everything was relative, he supposed. Men like Alf, and like Jimmy, his mam's youngest brother, would jump at the chance to work at a place like this, and to earn even half these fellows' money.

A little over a month ago, Neville Chamberlain had bragged that the country was 'eighty per cent recovered' from the Depression. 'Aye, and we know where the other twenty per cent of the poor buggers are!' the ship-builders and the mine-workers of the north-east muttered with justified bitterness. The general feeling of unrest and division was reflected in the election caused by Ramsay MacDonald's resignation because of ill health. His successor was Stanley Baldwin; the national government led by Conservatives.

John was staying with six others of the party in St John's college. Their host was an expansive character in his third year, from somewhere in Surrey, not far from London. He made jovial reference to the 'ecclesiastical slum', as Durham was known in academic circles, but otherwise he was free from condescension and friendly enough. His name was Martin Cox, and he was reading history. John's recently acquired interest in social affairs seemed to strike a chord and they got on well together.

'There's another group over here you ought to meet,' Martin told John eagerly. 'You can come along tomorrow night, if you like. Have you heard of *Kraft durch Freude*? Strength through Joy,' he translated. 'There's a bunch over from Germany. Very interesting chaps. Not so different from our ideas, either.'

John's curiosity was indeed aroused, though he went along with a certain measure of reserve; he would not describe himself as left wing; he had read of the clashes between Mosley's Fascists and their opponents, and his sympathies lay largely with the latter. He could not identify with the rabble-rousing extremism of the Communists and their like, but he definitely could not accept the equally wild and dangerous dogma which Mosley espoused.

But the young men and girls he met in the JCR of New College that Sunday evening were a far cry from the screaming fanaticism he had been led to associate with the new German regime. One in particular, a young man called Horst Zettel – a sandy-haired, pink-faced individual who looked nearer sixteen than the twenty-one years he claimed – appealed to him. So much so that they met again, just the two of them, the following day for some private sightseeing and several hours of animated talk.

'You must come over and see for yourself how we do things,'

Horst urged him. 'You can come to one of our summer camps. The Youth League. We welcome visitors. Please. I write to you, yes?'

'I'd like that,' John answered. He thought of the circumstances in which he had left Jenny, five long days ago. 'I'm not exactly a free agent,' he confessed, shyly, but with some pride. 'I am engaged. You know – a fiancée?' He showed the German the photograph of Jenny.

'She is very beautiful, your girl. You must bring her. We welcome the both of you, very much. You must try to come. Please?'

Chapter Seven

'Do you think it's really safe?' Moira Alsop cast a worried glance at her husband. 'One hears such stories—'

'Oh, Mummy!' Jenny exploded in an agony of impatience. 'Look at what's going on in London this minute! Sir Oswald Mosley's thugs cracking heads. What must that sound like to people abroad?' She turned pleadingly to her father. 'Tell her, Daddy. Tell her it'll be all right.'

Sandy winced inwardly, sensing his wife's anger at her daughter's speaking as if she weren't there, or as if she were incapable of reasoned thought. 'Well,' he began propitiatingly, 'it *is* organized by the university. They'll be in a group, with others. . . .'

'Some people will think it very odd, the pair of you going off on holiday together, and abroad, too—'

Once again, Jenny interrupted her. 'For goodness' sake! Like Daddy says, there's at least a dozen others going.' Her eyes flashed towards John, who up to now had been diplomatically and apprehensively silent. 'Tell her!' There was an edge of irritation in her voice, and in her look, and he felt himself colouring slightly.

'There's actually fifteen of us altogether going to the camp. It's all very organized apparently. You know – separate dormitories, and all that.' His voice faded, his blush deepened at the unspoken implications behind his reassurance.

Mrs Alsop surrendered with a show of reluctance. 'I'm just concerned for the pair of you, you know that. It's not that I disapprove of you going off together.' She smiled at John, to show that she trusted him with their daughter's honour, and her innocence.

Jenny hugged her, delighted at her capitulation. 'Oh, thank you, Mummy.' She turned ecstatically to John, seized his hand. 'Come on, let's start a list of what we'll need.'

As he let himself be pulled away, he reflected gratefully on the change which had come about after her successful completion of her final examinations. At least she and her fellow students hadn't been kept waiting for their results. In less than two weeks Jenny knew that she had made the grade and was duly certificated. And, thanks to her father's good name and influence, she had already secured a post as assistant teacher at the Church of England junior school in the town. 'It was entirely on your own merit,' her father affectionately, and half-honestly, assured her. 'If you hadn't come up to scratch at the interview Tom Maitland would never have taken you on. He told me so.'

So, everything in the garden was rosy, and she was transformed from the moody, pale figure who had snapped and grizzled through the fine June days which would be her last as a student at Durham. Disloyal and ashamed though he was, John could not help feeling more than a little piqued at her eager enthusiasm for a future which, for the next year at least, would mean long days and weeks of separation. He had held on to a secret, half-formed and rosy hope that she might apply for a post somewhere in the Durham area, if not in the city itself, and find lodgings, so that they could remain as close together as they had been over the past two years. He had said nothing, and the thought had never entered her head. And why should it, he kept telling himself, when she could be certain of a job in her home town – and could save a great deal by living at home, instead of paying for food and accommodation? Good job one of us has a bit of common sense, he reprimanded himself. But it still hurt.

However, such gloomy thoughts were determinedly pushed aside by the plans for August and their trip, organized through the university and his connection with the Socialist League; a three week stay at Alfeld, a small farming town about twenty miles south of Hanover where there was a summer youth camp. Jenny was overjoyed at the prospect of travelling, for she had never been out of Britain. John himself had only made one trip abroad, as a boy of nine, with his mother and brother and Aunt I. He remembered his keen disappointment when his Uncle Dan had refused to accompany them, though looking back with the wiser hindsight of adulthood he could perfectly understand his uncle's reluctance, for it had been a sombre enough trip, to the former battlefields and their memorials in northern France and Belgium, one of which was etched with his father's name.

He was unsurprised at his mother's opposition to this proposed holiday. He knew of her antipathy towards anything Germanic, but his resentment was sharpened by his belief that equally strong was her objection to anything which involved Jenny. Jenny had only made two visits to Hexham in the year of their engagement, and though his mother had been scrupulously polite, her coolness towards the girl was painfully evident, at least to John – and to Jenny, too, much to his dismay – for once, during the tense period which had just passed, when a miserable quarrel had flared up out of seemingly nothing, she had shed bitter tears and suggested they should end their relationship. 'At least your mother will be pleased!' she had snapped, and hurt him deeply, for which she later apologized.

But May did not force the issue to the point of an outright clash. 'You do what you want,' she said, with dismissive curtness. 'You usually do anyway.'

John knew several of their fellow travellers. There were five other girls besides Jenny in the group, who were noisily jolly and determinedly modern, portraying their feminism with both aggression and, when it suited, flirtatious guile. They endeavoured to enlist Jenny in their company, but when they quickly saw that she and John were a self-contained unit they left them both largely alone and made sniggering remarks about 'the young lovers'. It made John's ears red, but Jenny only smiled with superior and proprietory pride.

Alfeld was in the middle of rich farmland, and the corn stood rustling and golden, waiting to be harvested. The August sun poured down its blessing. The camp itself was spread over two gently sloping meadows, at the bottom of which flowed a narrow stream which fed into a small lake. Their hosts were assembled inside the gate when the bus lurched to a halt. The newcomers were surrounded by sun-tanned, smiling faces. The young men all looked clean and healthy, dressed in pressed khaki shirts, short-sleeved, and khaki shorts. The girls, mostly flaxen-haired, wore similar shirts, with abbreviated skirts above their knees, and white ankle socks which highlighted the brownness of their limbs.

John recognized Horst Zettel. 'Hello there. This is Jenny.'

'Ah, yes.' Jenny felt herself blushing at the steady regard from the almost delicately graceful figure. His white teeth showed dazzlingly against a smooth, fair complexion which would be the envy of any girl, Jenny thought. She was flustered, had to suppress the urge to giggle like a schoolgirl when he held on to her hand, and raised it to his lips. 'You are even more beautiful than your picture.'

With the other girls, she was led away, part of a shrill, laughing crowd, to one of the wooden huts raised on four brick pillars at each corner, with wooden steps leading up to the doorway at its centre. There were three other identical structures for the men.

'We are outnumbered here by three to one. Is good, ja?' Their group leader was a pretty girl, whose blonde hair was thickly woven into a single plait which hung acros her left shoulder. She introduced herself as Heidi Krempel. 'We have over one hundred youngsters here. Schoolgirls and boys, from senior level. You will help us in looking after, yes? They will be very interested to talk to you, I am sure.'

The simple, iron-framed beds were lined against each wooden wall in two rows, with a central aisle. Between the beds were twin wooden lockers, flat-topped, with a shallow drawer, beneath which was a cupboard divided by a shelf.

'There is no locking, but do not worry; there is no stealing here,' Heidi assured them confidently.

Hilary Greenaway, one of Jenny's neighbours, grinned over at her as they unpacked their bags. She winked. 'Bet you didn't expect this, eh? Bet you thought you'd be bedding down with your boyfriend, didn't you?' Jenny felt her colour mount, but as her mouth opened to protest, the girl went on imperturbably. 'Never mind. There'll be plenty of chances for hanky-panky, from what I hear of these places.' She leered as she unfastened her travel-creased skirt and let it fall, then shrugged off her blouse. 'I can't wait to get started! Did you see all those gorgeous German boys? Bet you're beginning to wish you'd come on your own now, eh?'

Though Jenny was shocked at Hilary's outburst, it was soon evident that there was more than a grain of truth in her words, at least for the youth leaders and the more senior members of the camp. Probably for the younger school-pupils, too, Jenny thought, though on a little more discreet level, for they were more regimented, and watched over with a benevolently author-itative eye. Even so, there was a heady and dangerous atmosphere of sexual freedom. The girls' and boys' latrines were adjacent, as were the screened off primitive showers and wash-rooms, and both sexes were afforded generous glimpses of one another passing, towel-clad, from huts to the ablutions area.

'Those devils!' Heidi chuckled one day as she joined Jenny

and John at the long trestle table for lunch. 'You see what those boys do? They cut holes in the canvas at the back of the girls' washhouse. They stand in line to peep-show.' Jenny gasped in comic dismay, and Heidi laughed again, patted her thin wrist. 'Do not worry.' She turned to John. 'They think your fiancée is wonderful!'

In any case, there was ample opportunity to see bare flesh. Most of the time the girls wore shorts as brief in the leg as their male counterparts. They were formed into squads and were allocated to work on neighbouring farms, or in some communal tasks to help the local populace. But after lunch their time was devoted to various sports, or pastimes such as rambles through the countryside – all healthy, outdoor pursuits, supervised by leaders such as Heidi, in their late teens, with only one older supervisor of each sex to oversee the running of the camp.

There were committees for just about everything. Meetings took place every evening before the communal gathering after supper around the camp-fire for the dancing and singing which were a nightly occurrence. Even the visitors were pressed into service, and, after a few hasty and disorganized rehearsals, stood in a self-conscious cluster before the assembly and sang a limited repertoire of well-known folk-songs. *Men of Harlech* was a particular favourite, and their German hosts called for it several times, and joined in heartily when they learned the chorus. Listening to the stirring martial beat of their own songs, John was not surprised at its appeal.

Gradually, he and Jenny became more relaxed towards the attitudes they saw around them. Jenny felt less self-conscious about appearing in her black bathing-costume and joining in the physical exercises which were a prelude to the jog around the large field before the dip in the lake at the bottom of the slope. For John, it was both a sharp pleasure and a private pain to be so close, to observe her slender body so minimally covered. He noted the daily-changing hue of her skin, the marks and bruising on her legs from the vigorous games of rounders and netball, the paler tone of her thighs, and, sweetest wickedness of all, the discreet little swelling pout of the black wool at her crotch, from which he dragged his eyes with tortured guilt.

Romantic attachments flourished in such a free atmosphere. Heidi Krempel was pursued, and pleased to be caught, by a handsome young fellow called Holger. He looked older than his contemporaries. In the glowing embers of the fire, when the ranks of boys and girls had filed off to their beds and the camp settled down, John and Jenny watched the figures fade arm in arm into the quickly deepening dusk.

They themselves followed suit, striking off in another direction, enjoying the enfolding darkness and its ripe warmth, the friendly moon outlining the dark shapes of the trees and hedgerows. They were aware of the dangerous liberality enclosing them. It was an awareness with which they flirted; excitement spiced with a new danger. It showed in the eagerness with which they came together, their mouths seeking, their bodies pressing with urgency against each other. Until suddenly they were shaking, on the very brink of stepping over the bounds of what they thought of as decency, of betraying all that they had been brought up to believe in. It was not easy to step back from those bounds. Especially when, in this magical setting, they were beginning to question those values they had grown up with.

There were other uncomfortable moments, such as those when they stood, at the back of the files of youths as though to disassociate themselves, while the flag, with its new symbol of the new Germany, was raised, and the patriotic oaths uttered; the nationalist songs which were the new hymns sung with such fervour. The new political regime was not thrust at them, but it was evident, its ethos present in every activity.

John tried to talk about it with Horst Zettel, who was eager enough to discuss it. 'If you know Germany, you would know what Hitler has done for us. We are coming from chaos. It is not right yet, but it is coming.' His innocently youthful face frowned. 'There are those who oppose us. There is still a powerful element who wish to suppress the people. The old ones, the Jews – they have the money. They try to control. They tell the lies, the propaganda, to people like you.'

John nodded thoughtfully. 'But there are stories. About the camps—'

'Work camps. And only for the criminals. Those who won't change. They must be caught. Punished. In all countries it is the same. You have your prisons. We try to teach them. To make them contribute. It is good.'

The three weeks passed too quickly. When the time came to leave, many were regretful. Hilary Greenaway cried as she clung to the neck of a German youth. Jenny smiled fondly at Horst, embraced him, kissed his pink cheek. 'I shall like to come and visit you in England,' he said, his blue eyes warm with emotion. 'You will always be my friends. I shall like to come to your wedding.'

John shook his hand, but Horst flung his arms about his shoulders and pulled him close, reaching up so that their cheeks brushed together. 'Ach! You British! You must come back. Please. You write, yes?'

They promised they would, waved vigorously from the windows of the bus as it bumped over the rough ground and through the wide gateway. John felt Jenny's hand grip his tightly. She dipped her head towards his shoulder, and he could see the warmth in her eyes as she leaned in close to him.

'Thanks for bringing me,' she said, like a child. 'It was good, wasn't it? And I *would* like to come back.' She glanced out at the hedgerows, and the waving cornfields where the harvesting was already starting. 'I feel totally different about the place now.'

The bus slowed, came to a halt. They could hear voices ahead, then the shrill sound of women wailing and young children crying. As the bus began to edge slowly forward they saw four or five brightly painted covered gypsy carts drawn up on the grass. The horses had been turned out of the shafts. Clothing and household goods, pots and pans, chairs, were scattered about the hedgerow as though an accident had occurred. A lorry was pulled up in front of the small cavalcade, and military figures in khaki shirts and dark breeches appeared to be ransacking the caravan. The gypsy women were shrieking volubly, their menfolk huddled in sullen silence, observing the police, or soldiers, in their smart uniforms.

'It is nothing,' the guide who was accompanying the visitors to Hanover told them. He gestured angrily at the scene, as they slowly squeezed past. 'Some thievery. They make big problem, these people. No work. Only stealing. At last the government do something.'

John knew there was something seriously wrong as soon as he let himself into the cottage. The atmosphere bristled with tension, while his mother's glinting eyes and the toss of her dark head confirmed his worst fears.

'Ha! And here's the other one! The conquering hero. My two sons. Real men of the world, aren't you? So bright and clever!' She held up one hand. 'I've got more common sense in my little finger than both your brains put together!'

She was quivering with fury, her expression alive with passion. Teddy had risen, and now he gestured his disgust. 'Mebbes you can talk some sense into her. Though I doubt it.' He laughed bitterly, and John realized that his brother was the cause of her wrath.

Her voice was low. John had rarely seen her so incensed. 'Don't you talk to me like that, you cheeky young bugger! I'm still your mother! And you're not too much of a man to feel the back of my hand, you hear?'

'You sound just like me grandad,' Teddy answered witheringly, and for a second John thought she would carry out her threat, though she had not struck them since the slaps on their legs they had earned as little boys.

She stood still, glaring at her younger son. 'Get yourselves something to eat. There's plenty in the pantry.' She went out swiftly, and they heard the door of her bedroom bang shut like a full stop.

'What the hell was all that about?' John said softly. He went over to the cosied teapot, lifted the cover and felt it. It was barely warm. He crossed and filled the kettle at the sink, put it on the stove.

He had been staying at Jenny's for the past week, but, as promised, he had returned home for the weekend, the last one before Jenny started her new job on Monday. He had felt she should spend the final two days with her family, and without the distraction of his presence. Since their return from Germany, apart from the first two days back in England, he had been staying in Keswick. He felt guilty at how little time throughout the long summer vac he had spent at home, Now that they were into September, he must get down to some serious work before his own return to college in five weeks, to what would be his final year.

Teddy's face was almost comically truculent, his lips turned down. Again he gestured his frustration. 'Oh, it's all because of this lass I'm knocking about with. You know, Marian.'

John had heard him mention a girl several times during their infrequent meetings over the past months. 'Why?' he asked in surprise. 'You haven't – it's not serious?'

Teddy pounced on his reply, sensing an unspoken accusation. 'Why?' he echoed belligerently. 'Are you the only one that's allowed to be serious, like?'

John flushed. 'No, of course not. I just didn't know. . . .'

'Look, man, I like the lass, that's all. We've been going out together a while. Since before Eastertime. Not like – real courting, you know. She's been away back home for a while. She lives at Easington.' He gave vent to another movement of irritation. 'But like I said, we get on all right. All I did was ask Mam if I could bring her through for the day. She hit the roof!'

The whistle of the kettle cut in on them. John rinsed out the teapot, made some fresh tea, leaving it to mash. 'It's not fair, is it?' Teddy burst out indignantly. 'You've got your Jenny. You bring her through here.'

John grimaced. 'Not that often,' he said grudgingly, feeling the tug of conflicting loyalties. 'You know Mam wasn't exactly keen. Still isn't,' he conceded, even more reluctantly.

'It's not as if we're too young, is it? And I'm working; earning a reasonable enough wage – or I will be when I've finished my time, in April. I'll be on good money then. I'll be able to please myself,' he muttered darkly.

John felt a vague sense of apprehension, and loss. 'Surely it can't have been just that? There must have been something – what did you say?'

Teddy shook his head. 'Let's face it, it's just Mam, isn't it?' He looked at John as though challenging him to disagree. 'As you said, she's not even keen on a nice lass like your Jenny. There won't ever be a lass good enough in her books for us two. Not her boys!' The last two words rang with ironic grandeur. He went on sullenly, 'I told her who Marian was – I mean her folks. Turns out Mam knew her mother, when they were both young. Used to be mates, right from school.'

John waited, knowing there was more. Teddy continued angrily, 'It's got nowt to do with Marian. Apparently her mam was a bit fast – you know. Got herself into trouble when her and Mam were working over at Armstrong's. In the war.'

'Mam's never said anything.'

'Aye, well, she wouldn't, would she? They were the days before she—' he pulled himself up short, then went on, changing in mid-sentence. 'She wouldn't tell us about something like that. Not fit for our delicate ear holes! Apparently, Marian's mam had to disappear. Got herself pregnant. She went to stay with some aunt, away out in the wilds. Probably Easington Village, I don't know.'

There was another pause, while John poured them out cups of tea. Teddy added milk and two spoonfuls of sugar, stirred moodily. 'Marian told me her dad was a soldier. Killed before she was born. She'll be eighteen in November. Only Mam reckons her ma wasn't married, and the feller that put her up the spout was no soldier, he was a feller from Armstrong's, with a wife and bairns. She reckons that bairn must be Marian, and she was born out of wedlock. It wasn't until a few years after the war that her mam got married.'

He sat staring at his cup. When he looked at John his face was stamped with the remnants of his anger. 'And if she is, so what? It's not her fault, is it?' He frowned. 'And I'm damned if I'll stop seeing her on Mam's say so!'

'Well, you can't blame her, in a way. She's not going to be overjoyed, is she, knowing all the history?'

Teddy looked at him with wounded betrayal. 'Oh, so you're on your high horse and all, eh? Talk about the sins of the fathers!' He pushed the cup and saucer away from him. 'I'm going down the Beehive for a jar. I wish I'd never bothered coming home,' he added feelingly.

He did not invite John to accompany him. John was about to offer to do so, when he thought of his mother upstairs. The rift hung like a pall over the whole house. He had a sudden intuitive feeling of how hurt she must be, of her aggrieved sense of her sons' disloyalty. The unique closeness of their triangle, which had been a seemingly indissoluble bond all through their lives up to now was being shattered. First by him, now by Teddy.

But maybe this girl, this unknown bastard child, was a wonderful person. He thought of Jenny, of his mother's antagonism towards her. Mam was so wrong, and yet he felt for her; could painfully understand why she reacted as she did.

Depression settled on him. 'I won't bother,' he said to Teddy. 'I could do with an early night.'

Teddy was clearing the tea things. 'Suit yourself.' In the hallway Teddy put on his outdoor coat. 'Leave the back door open.' He went out.

John glanced up at the ceiling, wondered whether he should take a cup of tea up. There was no other peace offering he could think of.

'You've got to let go of them, May,' Dan said. 'They're both young men now.' He could feel the hurt in the brown eyes that stared at him. They were the eyes of the girl who had fought so hard to come to terms with the blow which had devastated her life almost twenty years ago. He recalled vividly the dusky November evening when the news of the Armistice had come through, and how she had come up to his room in Belle View Terrace. Both of them caught in the silent intensity of that moment, with the faint sounds of hurrying feet, excited cries in the street below. The feel of her warm body as she had stood over him as he sat twisted awkwardly on his bed. She held his head clamped tightly beneath her breast, while he clung to her slender frame like a drowning man and sobbed his heart out. Her gentler tears had fallen on him like a blessing. They had never spoken of that moment.

He realized again just how dear she was to him, as he saw the injured expression his words had caused. Words that he had wanted to say several times before, but had pulled back from, understanding the strength of her bond with her boys.

As always, his wife leapt fiercely to her defence. 'Oh, for God's sake, Dan! Use some common sense! Can't you see how entirely unsuitable this girl is? It was bad enough John going off half cock the way he did. Goodness knows what effect it'll have on his degree. But this, this . . .' She waved her hands furiously to express her outrage. 'You've heard the girl's history – her family background.'

'You're talking about years back,' Dan argued forcibly. 'It's not the girl's fault she was born out of wedlock. Or what her mother got up to before she was born.'

'It's in the blood,' Iris answered. 'Families like that—'

'What? You mean like mother like daughter, eh?' The scorn in his voice was evident. 'There was a war on. All sorts of things happened.' He paused fractionally, his eyes locked with his wife's. 'Young girls did all kinds of foolish things, made all kinds of mistakes, especially where men were concerned. Surely *you* haven't forgotten that?' he said quietly. He watched the colour mount in Iris's already flushed features, the flinch of her eyes at the telling force of his strike.

Irritation mingled with his compassion for May. 'You and the boys – you've brought them up all on your own. You've done a splendid job, no one could deny that. But there's been just the three of you. . . .'

But already he could see her draw back, and knew that in spite of all his best intentions his words had struck like a blow. He saw her gather herself to repel what in her heart she must be aware was the truth. 'It's the old cry, is it? How could I possibly manage without a man? They needed a father! Is that it? You think I want to keep them tied to my apron-strings for ever?'

Her voice shook with emotion. Don't you? he had an urge to cry out, to fling the words in her face, but he kept silent.

Iris's voice was cold with contempt. 'Look, if you've got nothing constructive to say, why don't you take yourself off? Why don't you go and have a jolly night out – with your *friends*?'

The withering scorn in her final words startled him. Does she know? he wondered, shaken at her vehemence Unconsciously, she had moved closer to May, who was still sitting at the kitchen table. She put her hand on the sloping shoulder, their faces glaring hostilely at him. As it had many times before, the closeness of their relationship, its self-contained solidarity, washed over him like a wave. He felt a thick rage, and a surge of cruel male sexuality, cut off as he was from their exclusive union. He struggled to his feet. Damned right he would get out! He would go to the woman who understood him, who wasn't ashamed to share her body, and find pleasure in his, crippled as he was.

He gripped the handle of his stick, fitted the metal rest into his forearm. 'I'll phone for a taxi,' he said thickly. 'No need for you two to break up your cosy little tête-à-tête!'

Chapter Eight

At times, John was almost glad of the sudden, seemingly interminable piles of work facing him as the new academic year began. Durham was a different, much bleaker place. The familiarity of the scenes around him only served to illustrate that difference. The shining wet cobbles of the Bailey, the vista of the cathedral's splendid rose window. It filled his own narrow panes as he gazed out from the third year luxury of his small but cosy sitting-room, with the even smaller bedroom leading off from it – as a final year student his, and his alone.

Lone was the word. The beauty of the autumnal trees along the steep banks, and the well-loved Houghall Woods, the Saturday morning bustle of the market place and Silver Street, the evocative aroma of coffee in the steaming fug of the union. Jenny's absence from all these places clung to him like a ghost, and he flung himself into his work as a means of distraction. Far too often, in a cruel reversal, it was his missing her which was the distraction, preventing him from concentrating, until he would wind his scarf about him, pull on his coat, and wander about the city hugging his loneliness to him like another garment. You're nothing but a masochist, he told himself, standing one chilly afternoon staring at the gateway of St Hild's. And it was true, there was a poignant sweetness about his mood which was a kind of sombre pleasure.

They had both sensibly agreed that they should not meet up more than two or three times during the term. Jenny was embarking on her new career, and it was essential that he should do as well as possible in his examination. He was sure that a first was out of the question, but a top second would be highly gratifying. Jenny wrote bright, lengthy letters telling him all about school – her colleagues, various children with whom she became deeply and enthusiastically involved.

John poured his heart out. Nothing new happened to him, he told her. There was only his love, and he strove desperately for new and beautiful ways to express it. He wrote poems, working on them for long hours, changing a word, a phrase, refashioning, until he made his final, painstakingly neat copy from the sheets of scratched out, scribbled notes spread out at his desk.

They talked once a week on the telephone, on a Saturday evening. The phone stood in a chilly corner at the foot of the stairs, near the entrance to the hall. At this time it was deserted. Most of the inhabitants were out socializing – John often joined his friends in the Shakespeare, for a late pint after the phone call. Somehow, those calls were never as satisfying as he had hoped. Of course, it was wonderful to hear her voice, even if it did echo a little tinnily in his ear. But he found it impossible to say the things he could so flowingly write. 'I love you,' though it ached with sincerity, was maddeningly repetitive.

She did most of the talking, about her work. She clearly found it fascinating. He was pleased for her, and ashamed of the pique he tried to smother at her cheerfulness. 'Do you miss me?' he would suddenly fling into the conversation, and despise himself for the wheedling, whining tone he detected in his loaded question.

'Of course I do, silly,' she would murmur fondly. And she did, too, he knew that; but sometimes she sounded as though she didn't.

That Christmas was his twenty-first birthday. The vacation

began on 10 December. He travelled straight home. He had arranged a brief visit to Jenny's for the following week, staying two nights with her family, before returning to Hexham. 'You'll have to spend Christmas with your folks,' Jenny said philosophically, and he nodded.

'You can come over after New Year.' He was determined that she should stay. 'We'll be having a proper do then. For the twenty-first. You've got to be there.'

As usual, he felt both guilty and a little uneasy on his return home. He had been back only once since the start of term, and then for a fleeting visit of two nights. He had the excuse of working for finals, and he did make a weekly telephone call. But the tensions which had surfaced at the end of the summer, with the discovery of Teddy's association with Marian Graham, had lingered, like distant but threatening clouds. 'I've seen neither hide nor hair of your brother,' she had told him once, in answer to his cautious, enquiry. 'Not that that surprises me. I'm getting used to living on my own,' she added, with a brittle laugh. 'I can please myself what I do. Don't have to worry about anyone else.' The words hurt, as they were meant to do.

But the morning after his first night back home, there was an air of lively excitement about her which John noticed at once, She even brought him toast and tea up to his bed, when normally she would have allowed him to lie in until noon if he wished.

'It's not a bad day,' she said. 'Come on, get up. Your Aunt I and Uncle Dan are calling in, they said.'

'What? This morning?' he asked, surprised. 'Aren't you off to the caf?'

'Good heavens! It's your first day home. I've seen nothing of you this past ten weeks. Anyway, I'm a lady of leisure nowadays. Ann reckons I'm more of a nuisance when I'm there. They get on better without me. Come on, you lazy lump!' She slapped at the shape of his raised knees. 'Get up. There's bags of hot water.' So he was up, washed and shaved, combed and dressed in slacks and warm pullover, when his mother jumped up from her seat at the table in the kitchen and cried out, 'That sounds like them now!'

The car which drew up on the drive, from which his uncle and aunt waved their greeting, was not their usual vehicle, but a gleaming, smaller, sleeker sports model, in pristine condition, the headlights' polished silver gleaming in the winter dullness from the rakish curve of the mudguards which flanked the long, tapering bonnet. Uncle Dan grunted laughingly as his stiff limbs waved and he fought to extricate himself from the low bucket seat on the passenger's side. The pale canvas hood was fixed in position, in concession to the weather, but John could imagine how magnificent this machine would look with the cover slipped off and folded along the back. The spokes of the wheels shone immaculately silver, too.

'We've tried to keep it as clean as we could,' Dan puffed, at last managing to haul himself upright and lean on his stick. From the other side, Iris came round and hugged John to her bosom, his nose buried in the silky, damp fur around her shoulders.

'Gosh! When did you get this little beauty?' John breathed admiringly. 'Bit racy for you two, isn't it?' he grinned teasingly.

'It certainly would be.' Iris's violet eyes were dancing with merriment. She looked at May, raised her eyebrows questioningly. He saw the same animated expression in his mother's face.

'What . . .' he began, puzzled.

May came forward, caught hold of his hand and held on to it. 'It's a little bit early, but we thought we couldn't keep it secret right up to Christmas. Happy Christmas, and happy twenty-first, and happy results in your finals! It's from all three of us.'

He stared, his heart thumping. He was breathless, astonished by the gift. He felt ridiculously young again, like a little boy who was about to burst into tears. All his emotion showed in his face as they stood surrounding him, smiling. Then they were a huddled scrum, hugging and laughing as he gasped out his thanks.

'I – I don't know what to say.' He didn't. He couldn't find the words to express his surprise, his gratitude and love. He didn't need any, for they could see it plainly.

'Go on! Take it for a spin. It's dying to let rip. Your Aunt's been terrified of getting a splash of mud on it. We were passed by two pedestrians on the way here!'

It marked the start of a truly happy holiday. Even Teddy and his mother called a truce, and the family gathering to celebrate his birthday and Christmas was not marred by the slightest note of discord.

But the new year was only days old when the first of what would be a whole series of turbulent events, both public and personal, occurred. On 20 January the king died, and the Prince of Wales became Edward VIII. And only two weeks later, as John returned from a morning lecture, the bursar's secretary met him at the top of the drive leading down to the college buildings. 'We've had a telephone message, Mr Wright. Would you call home as soon as possible, please?'

It was Ruby who answered. John winced at the hoarsely bellowing voice. His mother's help was convinced that speaking over the telephone required conversation to be conducted at a shout. 'It's your gran. Your mam's over there now. She's been taken to Bensham Hospital. She's very bad.'

'Which one?' He found himself bawling in reply.

'Eh? Oh, aye. It's your mam's mam. Heart attack, the' think.'

'I'll get home as soon as I can. All right? I'll come to the house first.'

John had not brought his car to Durham. He would have difficulty in finding garaged accommodation, and did not want to leave it standing out in the open during the winter. At home, it was securely under cover in the solid brick outhouse which served ideally as a garage. There was no one in at home when he arrived in the icy darkness after a chilly journey. It was odd, and somehow daunting, to find the place cold and deserted. He could not recall ever before returning thus.

Beside the telephone stand in the hall was a carefully printed number. He guessed that Ruby had written it. When the operator put him through, he realized it was the Bensham hospital he was speaking to. He gave details, and waited anxiously. 'There's a message from your mother. You're to come at once.' In response to his question about his grandmother, the female voice said dispassionately, 'She's very poorly, I'm afraid.'

John replaced the receiver on its hook. Poorly? his brain protested. That's a word you use about someone who's got a bad cold, or an upset stomach.

There was a heavy frost whitening the trees and hedgerows. His breath steamed in clouds about him as he adjusted the ignition switch, then swung the starting handle. He was sweating, in spite of the cold, before he persuaded the reluctant cylinders to fire and splutter to life. No doubt the car had been standing for days, although Aunt I had promised faithfully to give it a run regularly. He drove carefully. Under the street lamps when he reached the city, he could see the glint of the frost.

The long ward seemed huge, bed after bed stretching out down its length. John was suddenly reminded of the motor car factory at Cowley. His feet echoed on the polished wooden boards, his shoes squeaked. There was a screened off enclosure near the far door. His mother came out. Her face was etched with the tragedy, and he could feel her shaking as they embraced, knew that she was making a great effort not to break down.

'Your grandad and Teddy have just popped out for a smoke. Jimmy's somewhere about as well.' She nodded, smiled bravely at him. 'You can go and see her. She's awake.'

Robina was propped up in the bed, almost upright, with the pillows piled behind her. She looked old, quite suddenly, for

John had never thought of his grandma as other than a lively, energetic, bustling woman. She seemed diminished, too, as though flesh had fallen from her. The shape of her body under the neatly aligned bedclothes was slight; her face was angular; her mouth so tightly compressed that her lips were all but invisible; her eyes were closed, and the lids were dark, bruised-looking, and sunken in the sockets; deep lines stood out around them, and were chiselled down the sides of her nose to the turned down corners of her mouth. Her skin was parchment pale, and her hair, wispily gathered on the pillow, was thin and fine, and silvery grey.

All at once, the eyes opened, startling him with the intensity of their gaze. They shone, huge and eloquent with suffering, and, John realized after a while, with fear. She was breathing shallowly, the winceyette nightgown scarcely moving at her chest. It was as though she were waiting for something. It dawned on him that she was afraid of moving. It was the flicker of her eyes, the twitch of a gnarled hand, the gold wedding-ring standing out, which indicated her recognition. The clenched mouth moved, she gave a kind of sigh to serve as a greeting. He touched her hand. It felt cold and dry. 'Hello, Nana,' he whispered hoarsely. 'You had us worried for a while.'

She tried to smile, then her pain-filled eyes closed again, and he sat in dumb misery, his fingers resting lightly on her hand. A touch on his shoulder made him turn. His mother was there, standing behind him. 'Have a word with your grandad,' she whispered, and he stood, ashamed of his relief at being able to leave.

There was a bleak corridor outside the ward, which was quiet now that the normal visiting hours were over. Teddy was sitting there, and his Uncle Jimmy. His grandfather stood, came to him and hugged him with brief awkwardness. His eyes were shining with grief, and he had a lost look about him. He, too, seemed older, frailer, crushed by what had happened. 'Thanks for comin', son. She's taken real bad. It's ever since this cold snap started. Plays havoc, man.'

He went in through the swish of the swing doors, and John greeted his brother and uncle, sat beside them. 'It doesn't look good,' Jimmy told him simply. 'The' don't think she'll get over it.'

May was sitting with her again, alone, when it happened. She had no time even to call out for George. Robina suddenly raised her head, those dark, blazing eyes opened wide, and her face wrenched with agony. Her mouth opened, and was drawn into a snarl of pain. She leaned towards May, her anguished gaze bored into her, while the gnarled hand tightened on her own like a vice, crushing its slender softness. There was a gasp, as though she were trying to speak, then she slumped. May cried out shrilly, whimpering in alarm, and pushed her mother back on to the pillows by her shoulders. The eyes were open, staring emptily beyond her daughter into the dimness beyond the bed. May felt rather than saw the life drain from them, and, though the jaw dropped, at last that terrible rictus of agony faded; the muscles relaxed.

A nurse came, other feet scuffed, and someone prised the dead hand away from its grip on May. 'It's over,' someone murmured behind her, and she heard her father give a single, harsh cry; transform it to a cough.

The year rolled on. Not long after Robina's funeral, Germany reoccupied the Rhineland, without any apparent objection. The newsreels showed cheering crowds. 'We should never have taken it off them,' people commented. Closer to home, Palmer's shipyard, at Jarrow, closed, putting hundreds more men on the dole. There was bad feeling made worse when the authorities claimed it was to keep the other, more modern Tyne yards in work. It still didn't help Jimmy Rayner, who was paid off from the riggers' loft at Swan's about the same time as Teddy finished serving his time in April.

'Ye can move in with me, son,' his father offered. 'It'll be smashin' havin' the bairns around. And Kathy to cook for us.'

May had tried to persuade George to come out to Hexham and live with her. 'We've got loads of room. And there's the garden. You could grow some vegetables for us. There's always something needs doing.'

'Why, no, lass. Ah'd be lost out there in the country. And ah'd miss me mates, and the club, ye know. Thanks all the same, pet.'

He was drinking a great deal more than was good for him, she knew. Out every night, and all day on Saturdays. 'It's hardly surprising, love, is it?' Iris reasoned. 'After – what was it? Forty years or more of married life. He must be utterly lost, poor chap.'

'Well, at least he had the forty years,' May answered, and Iris glanced speculatively at her, thinking sadly how changed, and hardened, her darling had become over recent years. 'Well, now that Jimmy and Kathy and the bairns are moving in, Master Teddy will have to get himself home, and lump it!' May declared, with more than a hint of vindictive triumph.

But she was mistaken, and deeply wounded, when she found out what Teddy had done. She learnt of it when she travelled through to Gateshead to visit George after she had called in at the house in Belle View Terrace where her mother-in-law, a sprightly if somewhat stiff-necked sixty-five, still lived, with her unmarried son, Joe.

In the familiar kitchen in Sidney Terrace, where May herself had been brought up, she faced her son across the long table which had seen so many family meals and which recalled Robina's presence more powerfully than any other spot.

He looked at her with that cocky defiance, edged with a nervousness he had every right to feel. 'I've got myself fixed up with lodgings, not far from here. It's too far to travel into work from out at Hexham. Besides, it's cheap enough, and I can afford it now.' He cleared his throat. By the fender, George sat in his

108

favourite chair, and he, too, waited tensely. 'It's in Wolfe Street,' Teddy threw out in challenge.

May stared, poised, anticipating his revelation. 'Oh, aye. And whereabouts exactly?'

'It's with Mrs Dunn. Marian's grandma. There's a room going spare. And I know her—'

'How very convenient!' May's nostrils were pinched, her anger was like crackling electricity all around her. 'Under the same roof, eh? And in the same bed before long, I dare say!'

'Well, mebbes. Ye never know your luck!'

His brutal unfeelingness was like cold water in her face. She gasped for air. 'Don't bother coming back home as long as you're staying with that trollop,' she said, with venomous quiet.

'Hey, howay youse two!' came his grandfather's rumbling protest, but it lacked both authority and conviction.

'Don't fret yourself, Grandad,' Teddy said, struggling to keep his emotion down, 'you know what Ma's like. Always willing to think the worst of people. Especially if they're lasses. Will you be saying the same thing to our John, I wonder?'

'John at least can recognize a decent girl when he sees one, and knows how to behave—'

'Aye, right! College lads and lasses don't get up to that sort of thing, do they? It's just us peasants that let the side down, eh? Ta-ra, Mam. Grandad.' The door clashed shut on his exit, and May stood, the tears welling up, and a tight pain in her chest as though something was physically constricting her about her heart.

John sat behind the wheel with his left arm stretched almost horizontally, resting on Jenny's shoulders. The collar of her heavy tweed coat was turned up, and the heavy, loose curls of bronze hair spilled over it from beneath the dark blue woollen beret which tilted down over the right side of her head. A sudden slinging patter of hard rain drops beat on the canvas roof of the car, rattled against the celluloid side-window. There was a certain nestlike sense of protection from the encapsulated intimacy of the cramped vehicle, but it could not keep out the April chill. John's feet were cold, in spite of the thick hiking socks he was wearing, and Jenny was hunched down in her seat, her hands thrust deep into her capacious pockets.

They were parked on the narrow grassy verge of a dirt road whose ruts and depressions were already well awash. Falling away steeply, below him on his side, the ground led to the dark surface of Derwent Water. Ahead, through the rain-spotted windscreen, he could see the forested slopes of the private estate of Lingholme, and beyond that, rapidly disappearing in the driving squall, Keswick itself, or at least the beginnings of it.

The weather had been steadily against them during the whole of his three-day visit. He was going home tomorrow, and they had hardly been able to shift out of the house. The only time he had been able to be alone with her had been at night, when her parents rose from the sofa in a flurry of newspaper sheets and cups of cocoa dregs, and departed with an eloquent glance at the clock on the mantelpiece. 'Don't be too late, you two,' Sandy would say, with his usual gruff chuckle.

Now, in this chill privacy high above the lake, John toyed with the stray curls, and clumsily tried to plant a kiss on Jenny's right cheek. 'I don't know if I can hold out much longer,' he moaned, savouring the subtle perfume as his lips grazed her skin and her hair tickled his nose.

'What's that supposed to mean?' she enquired sharply, turning to stare directly into his face.

Hurt at her tone, he grimaced to show his suffering. 'It means I want you so badly it's like a constant pain. It never goes away, not properly. Tomorrow I'll be going, and I won't see you for nearly two months! How can you stand the thought of it?' There was an undertone of genuine enquiry in his voice.

'It's just the same for me, you know.' Her tone was one of

gentle reproach. Again, he heard his mind demanding, is it? It was just too easy for her to say it, he could not believe she felt the weight of frustration, of pain. And it *was* a weight, a constant, dragging burden, like a prisoner's shackles. 'I just keep looking ahead, to the time when we really can belong to each other, in every sense. And all this waiting, this – pain, will have been worthwhile.'

She was right, she was right, he told himself angrily, taking his cramped arm from her shoulders. But being next to her, smelling her perfume, holding her in his arms, the kisses – it was a torment.

His thoughts switched to his brother. From the way his mother had spoken, Teddy was having a sexual affair with Marian Graham, flouting convention, flouting all the moral precepts they had had drummed into them throughout childhood. He had been prepared to believe it was his mother's antipathy towards the girl's family which had caused her to speak like that, but then, the last time he had met Teddy, there was something about him – not bravado, just something different, that made him feel somehow that Teddy was indeed involved physically with this girl; had exceeded, as they say, the bounds of decency.

John was shocked at his own feelings. Trust Teddy to be the first to do it! That was his initial reaction, so childish he squirmed with shame at himself. But, helplessly, he recognized his resentment, and, yes, his jealousy, that his bolder, more adventurous younger brother should be the one to cross that great divide of manhood first.

Chapter Nine

'There's a lady to see you, Mrs Wright.' The girl made a nervous little ducking movement, almost a curtsy, and May's mouth twitched in amusement. The little white lace cap was perched on top of the dark, shingled hairstyle, the short apron a pristine white over the black dress. May found she couldn't remember the young waitress's name. She was one of the extra staff Ann Swainsby had taken on for the summer season. This, and the girl's anxious deference, brought home the fact of May's increasing distance from the day to day running of the café and the shop. Even the ordering and buying was being taken over more and more by Ann. She was beginning to feel an intruder in her own establishment, May thought, as she glanced round the tiny office set to one side of the kitchen. Through the open doorway, she could see the length of the low-ceilinged room, with the windows over-looking the high street. It was pleasingly crowded, with not a table unoccupied.

'Who is it? A customer? Isn't Miss Swainsby—'

'No. It's you she wants, Miss. She says she wants to speak to you. She didn't give her name. She's down in the shop.'

'Well, show her up, then.' May's voice carried an edge of impatience. Iris was coming for her in ten minutes or so. They were going shopping in Newcastle, and then to an auction at Jesmond. Iris was really getting into collecting these days, and her enthusiasm had rubbed off on May. And she had plenty of time to devote to her friend. John, safely through his finals and seeming all too casual about the result, which they would not know for another week, had hardly had time to dump all his stuff and unpack his bags before he was turning round and rushing over to Keswick. He wouldn't be back before Monday, at the earliest.

As for Teddy, she had seen him only once in the last three months and more, and that had been at her father's. He had breezed in, with that cheery, devil-may-care manner which infuriated her – far too much like Dan, at times – and then away off again after ten minutes. The kitchen had been full of Kathy's children, and she hadn't even had a chance to talk to him.

The waitress appeared in the doorway, one thin arm extended to introduce the visitor, then, with another comic little bow, she fled. The woman facing May was a brassy blonde, gaudily dressed in a purple costume, with an ornately frilled blouse beneath. She was heavily built, with broad hips and behind, across which the material of her skirt strained, and her bosom thrust the jacket forward voluptuously.

'Hello,' May smiled, and was lifting her eyebrows in friendly enquiry before she recognized the fleshed-out, made-up face. Her eyes widened, her mouth opened in surprise. 'Nelly! Nelly Dunn!'

'Nelly Graham's the name. Long time no see, eh, May? And you'll not be pleased to see me now, neither, I dare say!' She advanced grimly, filling the space in front of the narrow desk. May's heart was thumping, she could feel the heat rise from her throat.

At that moment, Ann Swainsby came bustling in. She, too, smiled at the visitor, with the same enquiring look. 'Sorry, I didn't know you were busy. It's Farsons'. That order we gave them – can I just check . . .' she paused, aware of the awkward silence, the lack of explanation or introduction. 'Anything I can help with?' she asked, looking from one to the other.

'No!' Nelly replied, with heavy emphasis. 'The's nowt *you* can do about it, hinny.'

May rose, eased herself out from behind the desk. 'Come on,' she said, 'we'd better go outside.'

'Get me away out of here, is it?' Nelly sneered, but she moved, edging past a puzzled Ann Swainsby, out of the confined space.

'Hold the fort,' May murmured, flashing an urgent look at the manageress, who nodded, at a loss.

'Do I not get a cup of tea?' Nelly demanded aggressively, clumping down the staircase in her uncomfortably smart heeled shoes. But she did not pause, and followed May out through the shop on to the busy street. They walked among the passers-by, heading up towards the abbey. By a large department store there was a lane leading to a series of quiet, narrow streets whose old buildings leaned in towards one another. At the end of the lane May stopped.

'Is it to do with Teddy?' she asked abruptly, staring at the features, which looked swollen, the lips thickened, a glossy red. Nelly Dunn had been strikingly pretty as a girl, though with a sharp boldness, and a look which May would later have described as 'common'. Nineteen years on, that look was still there, but the prettiness had fled, leaving the features coarsened.

'You know bloody well it is, kidder! And you'd better be ready to do something about it, quick, because he's got our Marian in a right bundle of trouble, the dirty little sod, and I think you know what I'm talking about!'

May blushed, with anger as well as embarrassment. She was also, she realized, deeply shocked, in spite of everything. It hit her hard that Teddy could behave so irresponsibly, so immorally. 'I've not seen Teddy since he went to stay at your mother's,' she said stiffly. 'I warned him – told him he shouldn't be so foolish.'

'Foolish, is it? She's a good lass, is our Marian.' She pulled up short, as though she had changed her mind about saying something. Her rouged cheeks were glowing too, but with no sign of any shame. The glossy lips curled in an ugly sneer. 'Oh, I know what you're thinking! I can guess what you think of me an' all. You've done well for yourself, haven't you? With your posh caf, and your fancy cake shop, and your big house out in the country.' She glanced round her in scorn. 'Real toff now, aren't you? But it doesn't stop your swanky lad spoiling our Marian.'

'Is he responsible for her condition?' May's voice was cold, her loathing evident.

Nelly's face grew vividly crimson. 'Ye cheeky bitch! I'll knock you on your skinny backside if ye speak like that!'

May instinctively stepped back, her pulse quickening with alarm. Now it was she who glanced round at Nelly's raucous tone. 'Brawling's not going to do any good,' she said quietly. 'Look, there's a little café down here. It'll be quiet. Let's go and sit down. Discuss this thing sensibly. It's all come as a great shock to me—'

'Don't give me that. You must have known what was going on, you're not that much of a fool, are ye? The pair of them living under the same roof. And him with his charm, his fancy talk.'

'It takes two, you know!' May snapped, rallying. 'I warned him not to move in there. We've not spoken since.'

She was trembling, glad to sit at the table, with its stained cloth, and to sip at the weak tea from the cheap, heavy cups. At least this public setting, while it allowed them to talk with privacy, might exert some modicum of restraint on the buxom figure opposite her. The tragedy of what had happened was only just making its full impact on May, She felt a kind of panic, a desperate longing to find it was not after all true. Her neat, safely ordered world was dissolving. It had started with her mother's death – or, more truthfully, before that, with John's engagement, Teddy's moving out. All at once she felt very vulnerable, and lonely.

She took a deep breath, clenched her hands under the table. 'You're sure – I mean, how far on is she?'

'She's missed her second – I just found out yesterday. But they've been sleeping together months. And he's the first!' She looked at May fiercely. 'I know you think – because of what happened to me – but she's a good lass. The's been nobody else.'

'I'll have to talk to both of them,' May said faintly. 'We'll have to see. . . .'

'Talking's not going to cure anything. The's only one thing to be done. And that's the decent thing. He'll have to wed her, quick as you like.'

May suppressed the horrified denial which sprang to mind. Helpless, her thoughts raced. Nelly Dunn was always a schemer. After her trouble with Harry Turnbull she had managed to avoid a real scandal by getting away to an aunt of hers in County Durham. And she'd kept away from Gateshead after her baby was born, even got people believing that the father was a tommy, killed in the war, a hero who had been going to do the right thing. All right, so the bairn had been born out of wedlock, but that was the war for you. It was a common enough tale. She had even married when Marian was still an infant, and had two more children. Mrs Ernest Graham, all above board and respectable.

And now poor Teddy was ensnared. It would be a fine match, a step up in the world indeed, to be allied with the Wrights.

'Does your daughter – Marian – know the truth? About her father?' The question came out before May could stop it, and she saw Nelly's reaction, the bridling as though responding to an insult.

'She does now!' she returned, breathing heavily, her nostrils flaring. 'Thanks to this carry on with your lad! I had to tell her.' Her blue eyes glittered across at May with enmity. 'I'm sure you'd put your Teddy in the picture, hadn't you?'

'He wouldn't say anything,' May said, indignantly, and Nelly shrugged.

'Well, I couldn't have her hearing it from any old Tom, Dick or

Harry. Better coming from me.' She grimaced bitterly. 'It wasn't easy. I'm not proud—' Again she chopped off her words, then glanced at May with that thrusting aggression once more. 'I'm not ashamed, neither. I loved Harry Turnbull. Even if he *was* a bastard!'

'What does your husband think of all this?'

Nelly's eyes narrowed, she shot May a venomous look. But she chose to interpret the 'all this' as referring to the situation of her daughter and Teddy. 'He's as upset as I am. He looks on Marian as his own bairn. He was all set to go round and give your lad a real piece of his mind, and mebbes more. But I stopped him. Our Marian's at home now, with us, and that's where she's staying till we sort this lot out.'

In spite of Nelly's belligerence, May began quietly to assert herself. After all, she was not the ignorant, unformed girl who had been tied to her mother's apron-strings when they had first been firm friends. And perhaps the memory of those distant days calmed Nelly's aggression a little. Such a lot had happened, to both of them, since then. May remembered that Nelly had been her companion that eventful day when she had first met Jack, when she and Nelly had wandered by chance into St Thomas's, to shelter from the June rain.

The other boy, whom Nelly had sparked with, had been Art Mackay. He had been killed, too, not long before Jack, though he had enlisted right at the beginning in 1914. Nelly had written to him regularly, shed tears at the news of his death, though by that time she had been well and truly involved with Turnbull, one of the foremen at Armstrong's. Though it was painful for May, they even found time to reminisce about those far off days.

'You know, there was summat funny there,' Nelly reflected, at mention of Arty. 'His mother got no money, no pension or nothing. Leastways, she hadn't last time I heard. Mind you, it was years ago.'

Gradually, it was May who became more decisive. 'Look. I

117

need to see the pair of them. When can Marian come up? I'll go over to Gateshead. See Teddy. Is he still staying at your mother's?' she asked suddenly.

Nelly actually managed to look nonplussed. She nodded. 'I'm not sure – if he knows, like – about Marian.'

'What?' May's voice rose shrilly. 'All this fuss and you haven't even told him yet? Don't you think he has a right to know what's going on.'

'Listen! He knows what's *been* going on all right. Our Marian's too bloody scared to tell him. That's why she came home. I told you – I only found out meself yesterday. I came straight to you. You're his mam.'

May nodded. 'That's right. And I'm off to have a word with him today. I'll write. Let you know when Marian can come up. Teddy will meet her at Newcastle. Or maybe we can organize a car to come down and pick her up.' She paused, met Nelly's gaze squarely. 'Don't worry. Teddy won't let your girl down, I can promise you that.'

If old Mrs Dunn knew anything of her granddaughter's predicament she made a good job of disguising it, May thought. Or maybe it was just that she was too sick and worn out to care any more, for she spent her days in the chair by the fireside, and even her bed had been made up downstairs, alongside the wall separating the front-room from the kitchen at the back of the small, terraced house. The place looked terribly overcrowded with the shabby old pieces of furniture. Her husband, Nelly's father, had died some years previously.

May remembered vividly the day she had called in here, after Nelly had been off sick from Armstrong's for several days, and the tension she had walked into. That was the day Nelly told her of her pregnancy. They had sat together up in the bedroom, holding hands, while Nelly sobbed out her distress and her fears for the future. Perhaps that was the very room where Teddy and

118

this girl . . . May dragged her mind away from such speculation. She left a message with the neighbour who was seeing to Mrs Dunn that Teddy should come round to his grandfather's as soon as he got in.

'You know what this is all about?' May said, white-faced as she faced him in the familiar kitchen. Kathy had made herself scarce, and her father had used the excuse to get out even earlier to his club. A deeply uncomfortable Iris was with her. She, too, would have been glad to make her escape, having driven May over, but May pleaded with her to stay by her side.

'No,' Teddy answered, but already the brick-red tide which swept up his features showed that he had more than an inkling.

'Nelly Dunn – Graham – came to see me today. She says Marian's going to have your baby.' May was startled at the depth of compassion stabbing at her when she saw the stricken look which fell across him. The 'no' this time was merely a whis-pered reaction, of disbelief, to the bombshell which had landed upon him.

'You stupid young fool! What the hell do you *think* happens when you – sleep with a girl?' She swallowed hard, the tears brimmed dangerously, blurring her vision. She wanted to shake him, to strike at him, to hug him tightly to her breast. 'Is it yours?'

He sat, with that same dumbfounded expression. He looked up at her, his eyes eloquent. He looked helpless, and very young. Finally, he nodded.

'How long has it been going on?'

Teddy was afraid he was going to cry. He shook his head bemusedly. Why hadn't he been prepared for this? He should have known. Should have done something,. They had tried the rubber sheath, and she had been as reluctant as he, had protested tearfully that he should not use such a horrible device again. She had promised to go to one of the new clinics, claimed that she had done so, even showed him the cheap ring she had worn as

119

a subterfuge. There was some cream, and a tube of jellylike substance – an instrument which she said she fitted inside herself. He had never even seen it, didn't want to. It had made no difference to the sex they shared. It was all still wonderful, irresistibly so, after those early, fumbling, clumsy days, or rather nights; now they knew each other's bodies, knew every creaking floorboard, and could lie all night in wonderful naked intimacy in his narrow bed.

'If you were going to be so disgusting, couldn't you at least have taken some precautions?' his mother hissed, while Iris glanced around the kitchen like some trapped animal seeking an avenue of escape. She did not want to hear this, did not want even to think of it, or hear May uttering such words, or his tortured replies.

'I thought we had,' Teddy muttered, and May felt a sudden hysterical urge to burst out laughing, This was displaced by a disgust so thick she could almost taste it.

'My God! Don't you know?' she screeched. 'Were you content to leave it all to her? She was probably as pathetically ignorant as you were!' She stared at him in hard suspicion. 'Was she a virgin?'

'Yes. Yes – I think so.' Teddy had to exert great control to stop himself from leaping up and rushing from this torture. His brain was reeling dizzily. Vaguely he was aware of how foolish and uninformed his answers were. But they were the truth, That first time. He hadn't been able to get it in for ages. She had been so tight, he had put his fingers in, and she had cried, but there had been no blood and his penis, though sore when they had finished, had penetrated her, fully, eventually. He had hated himself for even wondering. Of course she would not lie to him. She had said she'd never done it before, with anyone. She must, surely, have been telling the truth.

'You'll have to bring her through to Hexham. We have to talk. Decide what's to be done.'

120

He gazed at her, sick with despair. He hated himself, yet felt helpless, a victim. Each time he felt the splendid, smooth silkiness of Marian's flesh next to his, saw and felt it spread so yieldingly for him, he whispered, 'I love you!' as they came together and she enfolded him in that rapturous softness. Then there was no need for any words, their bodies spoke for them. Those moments were love; he meant it. But now, suddenly, frighteningly, love was something else, something quite divorced from those magic, private moments of union. Love was worry, and duty, and responsibility. A roof, and children, and providing. A world that seemed to close in on him, terrifying, smothering, burying him alive.

They both travelled to Hexham the following Saturday. John was home, but he made himself scarce during the early part of the visit, so that May could talk to them alone. On her home ground, and without the formidable presence of Nelly, May felt confident enough to dispense with Iris's support, much to the latter's relief. Part of the shock wave had been felt by her, too. Sick with worry on May's behalf, and deeply disappointed with Teddy on her own, Iris had taken out some of her feelings on Dan, as she frequently did. 'You should have talked to him. To both of them! They have no father. You should have taken Jack's place for them.'

Her words stung him. He was feeling privately guilty for that very reason. Not that he would have had a clue what to tell them, beyond that so useless phrase, 'Be careful'. As though care came into such a situation at times like that. Instead he rounded on his. wife, wanting to hit back, and succeeding. 'Oh, it's all just too sordid, isn't it, for such ethereal spirits as yours and May's? The dreaded old Adam! You'd tut-tut with horror at the immaculate conception itself.'

The girl's face was chalk white when they came up the path. They had walked from the station. She clung to his arm as though she might have slumped to the floor without it, and when at last she came face to face with May she hung her blonde head and wept, the tears streaming down her cheeks like a blubbing child. They both looked like children, and again May felt that conflicting emotion of pity and anger.

Marian was pretty, without that bold worldliness which had been stamped on her mother's features. 'Come on, now,' May said briskly, swallowing the lump in her throat. 'Crying's not going to mend anything. Here, get your coat off and come in and sit down. The kettle's boiled.'

Teddy had very little to say. He squirmed at the brutal directness of some of his mother's questions, but he made no protest, just sat dumbly at the weeping Marian's side.

'Is it Teddy's baby?' May asked.

Marian's blue eyes, smeary with her tears, reflected the pain the question caused. But she seemed to have no spirit left for anger. She nodded. 'I've never – been – with anyone else.'

'Teddy was the first? You were a virgin?' She did not even find the question offensive, ignored its challenge to her statement. She nodded again. 'Why didn't you – Teddy said you were taking precautions?'

The crying became more violent, and the girl sniffled to control herself. She did not look at Teddy. 'At first, before I'd done it, I couldn't. I mean – they're not for – at the clinic, the things they give you. They're for married women only. I had to lie. Say I was married. But the cap – it hurt so much. I couldn't fit it, not properly.' Her shoulders shook, and she put her head down, gave a huge, desolate sniff. 'And they told us – the nurse – said it was all right, if it was near your monthly. I left it – didn't wear it.'

She broke down, sobbing bitterly, the tears splashing on to her bare, folded arms as the yellow hair shook. 'I didn't do it on purpose, Mrs Wright. Honest! I never meant . . .' she stopped.

May reached forward awkwardly, put her hand over the thin wrist. Her own eyes were moist with tears, and her throat ached.

It was all such a tragic mess. She was almost angry with herself at the sympathy she felt for this poor creature. 'Do you want this baby?' she asked, and saw the fair head jerk up in alarm, saw the shock in the tear-stained eyes.

'Yes. Of course. I mean – if Teddy wants me,' she ended, in a small, forlorn voice. 'I *do* love him.'

'There are ways,' May said carefully, despising herself as she spoke. 'We could try.' There was a pause. 'Have you tried anything yourself yet?'

Marian glanced up tragically, shook her head. 'Mam said – she would help me. But,' she hesitated, then turned her head to look at Teddy. Tears rolled silently now down her cheeks. 'It's Teddy's baby as well. I didn't want . . . I had to let him know first. If he wants it – me . . .' the weeping took over again.

Teddy's chest swelled. It was like being under water, striving for breath. He could not trust himself to speak. He felt he was on the edge of a precipice, his toes clinging to the very brim of the rock. Then he was over the edge, everything had gone from under him, he was falling headlong into emptiness. 'Yes,' he said tightly. 'We'll keep the baby. It's mine. You're mine.'

John had plenty of his own troubles to reflect on. He had said nothing. His mother was far too distracted to notice his with-drawn manner, his pale moodiness. He hugged it to himself, and was once more disturbingly conscious of a romantic tendency to see himself in this poetic, melancholic light. For a while, he was savagely envious of Teddy, who had forced the issue, done something wildly irretrievable. Done exactly what *he* should have done with Jenny. She's pregnant. We have to get married. How gloriously simple that would be, and how it would shatter this smothering blanket of respectability and decency which was closed all about him.

He guessed from the moment of his arrival at Keswick, Jenny's strained face, her brave smile when she came out to greet him at the car. Her unease was like an aura surrounding her, he could feel it in every tense muscle as they embraced. Typically, it was Moira who braved the subject, that very evening. It had been carefully talked over, of course. Planned, by the three of them, how best to carry out the approach. Jenny and Sandy and Moira, like a council of war discussing tactics. And probably cool, haughty Rosemary tossing in her ha'p'orth.

'Have you thought any more about what you want to do, John?' her mother asked, by way of an opening.

'Well, a lot depends on what I get, of course. But realistically, I think it'll be a two-two, I'm afraid.'

With distaste, he recalled the tutor at the appointments board interview: 'A second-class honours will get you a very decent teaching post, in a good school. You'll be able to pick and choose.'

'I suppose I may well end up teaching,' he announced, with a rueful little laugh.

'There are worse things,' Jenny put in quickly.

Sandy gave his dry chuckle. 'Jenny really loves it, don't you, dear?' She merely nodded, reddening. John waited.

'The thing is,' Moira went on carefully, like someone picking her way over a muddy foreshore, 'we were talking things over. We don't think you should rush into things. I mean both of you,' she added swiftly. 'Jenny's doing so well in her new career. And the authority wouldn't be too pleased at her marrying so soon. And you haven't even settled on a career yet. Take your time. It's very important for both of you. You're certain of each other's feelings now, so there's no worry on that score. Another year won't make that much difference, will it? And it'll give you time to get a bit of your own money behind you. Time to settle into a job before you have to take on the responsibilities of marriage.' She smiled encouragingly. 'Look at Rosemary and Gerald. They know they'll be ready when they tie the knot.'

Rosemary's wedding was planned for November. A big affair,

of course. Sandy had already made numerous jokes about not being presented with the ruinous prospect of Jenny's nuptials as well. John had hoped this would persuade them to allow a much quieter affair, perhaps even a wedding over in Hexham. Now, his own nefarious schemes were being dashed. 'We've talked,' they said.

He glanced despairingly at Jenny, who was pinkly avoiding his eye. She was going along with all this. It was like a stone in his gut. She was actually prepared to put up with this, for another whole year, maybe longer. He faced the daunting prospect that she really preferred to put their marriage off for the sake of another year's teaching at that damned school of hers. He was sure she felt the despondency that settled around him. There was a subtle distance between them. Their kisses were almost chaste, they did not hug and press with that hint of repressed lechery. When he left, their parting was restrained. Almost like a well-settled, already married couple, he thought, and wondered if Jenny felt the same deep irony.

And there was an irony, too, in the situation when he came back home that Saturday evening, to be introduced to the pale, sadly smiling figure of Teddy's girl, who was painfully shy and silent all night. 'Teddy and Marian are going to get married,' his mother told him, with studied neutrality. 'It's what they want. And of course it'll have to be arranged as soon as we can. They're going to see the minister tomorrow.'

'Well done. Congratulations,' John said, the awkwardness of the whole business wrapping them in its stifling folds. He kissed Marian's cool, proffered cheek, he shook his brother's hand. 'Lucky devil!' Teddy's eyes stared back at him, like a prisoner on whom a crushing sentence had just been passed.

Chapter Ten

'Can ye not get yesel' ower to the naval yard?' George Rayner's abrasive voice carried above the buzz of conversation around them.

Teddy shook his head. 'It's different altogether. Be like starting all over again.'

May studied them with an unusual depth of perception. Now that the wedding service was over, Teddy looked more relaxed, He was handsome enough, in his dark suit and stiff white collar, but there was more of the solid, bantam cockiness of her side of the family. John was thinner, had the advantage of height. He was like his dad, May thought, remembering so clearly those sensitive features, the expressive, dark eyes, saw them stamped again on the face of her eldest son, until she felt the familiar, tender ache inside her. Are you watching, Jack? Looking down on us; sad for me? And for Teddy, who doesn't want all this thrust on him – and for the poor girl, scarcely more than a child, sitting there looking so lost and frightened of us all? Is she wishing now she hadn't gone through with it, that she had taken up my wicked, half-offered suggestion to get rid of it? Was that a terrible sin of me, Jack? Did the angels weep?

Emotion choked her, welled up until her eyes stung, and she thought for a horrible second she was going to start crying again. She had done so, in spite of all her resolve, in chapel, and people

126

had smiled understandingly and thought how sweet, not knowing that they were tears of real sadness she was shedding. She knew as surely as she knew anything that Teddy did not want to marry Marian.

That poor chit of a girl knew it, too, but could say or do nothing about it; who herself knew nothing beyond the narrow existence of a working community, and who had been brought up on a lie as blatant as the slick and sugary Hollywood romances she had watched yearningly on the cinema screen since she was an adolescent. She was dumb now, nobody could get a word out of her, other than a husky 'yes' or 'no', and that pasted, anxious smile. A day to remember! It was an ordeal for her, she was praying for it to end, as she sat, looking pretty, the dark costume and the chic little hat with its turned back veil and white blossom proclaiming her wickedness, branding her with her sin as starkly as any scarlet.

But was it a sin? May continued her private communion with her dead husband. Does God really think it a sin? And why does it always seem to be the woman who carries the burden of shame and guilt? Never the man who fertilizes her, only the wicked Eve who consents that he should do so, according to a white-bearded patriarch who sits there on His throne, arm outstretched, letting nations slaughter one another. . . .

She pulled her mind away from her blasphemy, her gaze still resting on Teddy. Yes, he looked like her dad all right. They were arguing about the grimly uncertain future at Swan's. 'The's contracts for three naval vessels comin' up, th' reckon,' George was saying. 'Now that the bloody government's wakin' up at last. We can thank yon Hitler for that at least.'

The anger surged up like bile once more, then the despair. God! Did nobody learn anything from the huge waste of life that had taken place only twenty years and less ago? There was her father talking animatedly about the decision to build more warships, to spend more public money on weapons of destruction, as though, instead of taking lives, it was bringing new life to the region. And ironically, it would, too, for perhaps it would bring work for men like her brother, Jimmy, who had had to leave his family and was working for a builder down near York somewhere. He couldn't even take time off to come up for the wedding. Probably couldn't afford the fare, either, for he was on a pittance of a wage.

Kathy, his wife, was here, with the three bairns. She was turned out smartly, as were the children, but at twenty-six her face was already stamped with the lines of worry that came from trying to make inadequate ends meet. And, May suspected, that did not include a contribution towards the modest rent of her father's house in Sidney Terrace. Mind you, he still had plenty of money for the ale. He was getting the look of a real boozer, she thought, witnessed by the network of broken capillary vessels about his upper cheeks and the sides of his nose which contributed to that permanently ruddy glow. And he was certainly putting enough of it away today. Even now his earnest discussion was punctuated by the waving glass in his hand.

Her general resentment against menfolk surfaced again as she caught sight of Alf Dale's even more florid features, and the empty bray of his laugh, as though he hadn't a care in the world – and he had been laid off from the pit for more than a month now. There was talk of protest all over the region. They were even talking of organizing one of these hunger marches down to parliament itself, like the unemployed had done last year, and the year before. In Jarrow, when the twin towers of the cranes of Palmer's shipyard came down, it was like the fall of the town itself. Three out of four men on the dole.

For once, Julia appeared to be operating on the principle of joining rather than beating, for her cheeks, too, carried twin patches of red which owed at least as much to the number of port wines she had consumed as the rouge she had liberally applied. She was also parading her gaudy best – a thin, floral, summer frock which gave the lie to the chill autumn weather. The hat, too, was an elegantly elaborate affair, with a high back on the crown of her freshly set, dark hair, and tapering down to a long, Robin Hood brim over her right eye. Three cockades of bright plumes, wrapped up in fine net, jutted saucily.

May wondered where she had borrowed it, for she could not remember seeing it before, and she could not surely have afforded such a purchase? On the other hand, she had not seen her since their mother's funeral seven months ago. And they had not met for more than a year before that, so maybe the hat was a buy from better days. If so, it must have been a long while before, for 'better days' had not been in evidence for the pitmen for a good many years.

In fact, not since the general strike of ten years ago. The miners had hung on alone, long after the other workers, carrying on the strike for six bitter months, until the winter forced them to go cap in hand to their bosses and beg for their jobs – at a reduced wage, and not all were successful. May had helped Julia out on several occasions, as discreetly as she could, and with the accepted fiction of 'you can always pay it back when you're on your feet'. May was aware that a bitter sense of obligation had not helped to improve relations between her and her younger sister, for whose situation she could feel sympathy, but whom she could not love.

But, May thought sardonically, she was in her element right now. Nelly, née Dunn, had the same aggressive attitude, as did the rest of her relatives and cronies. Knocking back the booze and the food, and all the while with that challenging air about them: We're as good as you lot, and don't think we're impressed with your motor cars and your posh, countrified ways.

She watched Dan stomp over to the group – another kindred spirit, she thought meanly at his drinker's glow, then felt ashamed. He leaned forward, said something, and Julia's thin face split into a grin, and Nelly's overweight hat shook with her mirth. Good old Dan! Straight over the top and bridging the gap, or trying to, tearing across the no man's land between the Wrights and the rest. For it was so obvious, the divide between May's lot; Iris and Dan; his sister, Cissy, and her quiet, distinguished-looking husband, David; and Joe, still handsome and amazingly youthful looking, though he was nearly a year older than Julia. And, head of the clan, slim and dignified, rigid and stiffly corseted, the matriarchal Sophia, May's mother-in-law, in her mid-sixties and showing no sign of failing physically or mentally.

They had mellowed greatly towards each other over the years. May could still remember with painful clarity how scared of her she had been, when she and Jack were courting. And how hurt when Sophia's freezing politeness had shown her so eloquently how little she rated this chit of a girl from a lower class. But, perhaps reluctantly, she had changed her opinion, and her attitude, when May had presented the Wrights with their first grandchild, and then when she had agreed to go and stay with them, and have the second child in the home where Jack and Dan had grown up.

Their love of Jack had eventually bound them in a unity which May had slowly come to appreciate. In those days when Jack had first left her to join the army, she had relied more and more on Sophia's friendship – and strength. And through the tragedy of Jack's death, the knowledge that her grief was shared had meant much more than May had realized at the time. But it was through her, and, of course, her beloved Iris, that May had found the courage to carry on, to build a new life with her two boys.

Guilt struck again, as May acknowledged how closer now in sentiment she was to Jack's family. She loved her family, her father and her brothers and sister, and their children, of course she did. But she felt her distance from them. Was she nothing but a snob she wondered? But, no, it wasn't just that, she certainly didn't look down on them. But, beginning with her brief happiness with Jack, and then with the precious years she had shared with Iris, her horizons had been so widened, her life had been so enriched. . . .

The laughter burst in another explosion about Dan, Nelly's cackle rising above the rest. Dan was always the rebel, the maverick. It was typical that he should be the one to be crossing the divide, which was spatial also, for the Wrights were gathered in one corner of the room.

Never mind, it would soon be over, She was sure none of them realized what a strain the past weeks had been. The tensions between herself and Teddy remained all the while. 'You don't have to do this!' he had exclaimed one day, when she was trying to get him to take part in the planning. 'We'd be happier with just a registry office. Just you and John – and Marian's mam. We don't want a fuss. It's embarrassing.'

'This is not going to be some hole and corner do!' she fired back. 'You're marrying the girl. You're doing the right thing. Let's start as we mean to go on. You've got nothing to be ashamed of.'

'Hah!' The exclamation rang with his scornful disbelief. 'Come off it, Mam. You of all people don't believe that?'

Well, she was giving them the best start she could. She had offered, then insisted, against Teddy's strong opposition, on giving them a deposit to put down on a house. There were some very nice semis right on the southern edge of Low Fell, off the Durham Road, in an estate called Chow Dene. Red pantile roofs, attractive brickwork, with the upper storeys pebble-dashed. Small gardens front and back, and surrounded by farm fields and unspoilt countryside. They looked across to the green and wooded slopes of Silver Hill, with the turrets of Ravensworth Castle peeping through its screen of trees. Ideal for raising a family.

'You can pay me back some day if it matters that much,' she

snapped irritably at Teddy's protests. 'Anyway, you'll have the mortgage payments to meet every month. I'm not buying the house. Just giving you a start.'

'It's very good of you, Mrs Wright,' his bride-to-be ventured softly, then crimsoned into silence at the look Teddy flashed her.

At twenty years old, May guessed that her son would rather be riding around in a sports car like his brother than thinking of house and furniture. But then, he had made his bed – a bed he had clearly found too tempting to resist, and now he was paying for it.

Her father had fuelled her anger when, only a day ago, she had told him what her present to the couple would be. 'What d'ye want to go buyin' a house for?' he had argued. 'Nowt but trouble. Ye've got to pay for everything yourself. All the repairs. And the's rates and things, isn't there? Rentin's always been good enough for us. Forty year and more we've been in Sidney Terrace. Plenty of good houses to rent round our way. What's he want to live way out at Low Fell for?' His pronunciation of the name carried the wealth of scorn he felt for its pretentiousness.

She could no longer bite her tongue at her father's outbursts. 'What's the matter? You against people getting on, are you? By lad, you must really think the worst of *me* then!'

He had given her a long, hard look with his glittering, rheumy gaze. 'It's what ye think of yeself, lass,' he said, with cutting finality. She could feel herself curling inside with frustration, and cursed her own illogicality at the guilt he could still curdle in her.

Again, she experienced a stirring of compassion when she studied Marian. All the insecurity and fear showed in that shy smile, the blushing cheeks, and uncertainty in those gentle eyes. If only the poor girl had a bit more go about her, a bit of sparkle and life. Teddy would appreciate her far more if she could only show a bit of backbone. Her bitterness rose again at her son. He had found the girl's body fascinating enough, night after night, for clearly their fornication had been going on for months.

She was startled and ashamed at the condemnatory word her brain supplied to describe their action. Grief arose, too, when she thought how complex and full of snares sexuality could be. She remembered how her own had caught her unawares, shamed her deeply at first, when Jack had shown her how powerful sex could be – and how frighteningly pleasurable, too. But they had loved each other. Sex was love for them; they had waited, been sure of one another before they had ever given their bodies.

More guilt, as her gaze transferred to her eldest son. John was doing the honourable thing. He was waiting, denying himself the physical release he surely hungered for. Why then could she not be happy for him? Jenny was a lovely girl, intelligent, clearly as fine a choice as he could hope to make. Unlike his brother – her mind shied away from the odious comparisons, and, with a bright smile, she strode across the floor of the hall towards the group gathered about Dan.

John put down the copy of *New Verse* and stared at the rain blurred gloom from his bedroom window. He could hear Ruby moving around downstairs, and the muted strains of Henry Hall drifting faintly from the wireless in the front sitting-room. 'Won't disturb you, will it?' she had asked, in that pointed tone which dared him to disagree. Not that he wanted to. He couldn't settle himself to any real work, anyway. Reading the poems of Auden and Day Lewis, and now this chap Stephen Spender, only served to make him dissatisfied with his own efforts, which seemed so puny. He was far too subjective, far too inward looking. They were writing about the real issues, in the world around them.

A smile tugged at the corners of his mouth at the sudden image of his maternal grandfather. 'Well now, what are ye goin' to do, son?' 'Well, Grandad, I thought I'd be a poet.' His reaction would be comically extreme. Not that he would ever find the courage to say such a thing to George Rayner. He couldn't say it to anyone. Not even to Jenny.

The frustration and discontent weighed heavily on him when he thought of her. He was supposed to telephone her on Saturday evening. And the first question she would ask would be about Beaconsfield. Beaconsfield was a private preparatory school in an Edwardian country house half-way between Hexham and Corbridge. It was through Aunt I that he had been granted the chance of an interview with the headmaster, James Challoner. Although Beaconsfield was only a prep school, with some eighty boarders and a handful of day boys, between the ages of eight and thirteen, it was already gaining a growing reputation locally and, recently, further afield, due to the advanced ideas and methodology of its head.

Mr Challoner had come from teaching in a traditional back-ground of public school where team spirit and manliness were expected of pupils, and conforming virtues which would enable them to display the qualities of responsible leadership whatever their chosen field, whether at home or in the quarter of the world which comprised the Empire. His own educational aspirations for his charges were rather different. From what he had learnt of them, so far, John was intrigued. Though John was from the humbler setting of a grammar school, his schooling had been privately funded at secondary level, and both methods and aims at the grammar schools were watered down versions of the public school system, in keeping with the more modest ambitions appropriate to the trading and lower middle classes.

At Beaconsfield, individualism was encouraged rather than stifled, and carrots rather than sticks were preferred. Spartanism for its own sake was not encouraged. Cold showers were not considered good for the soul, and, perhaps the greatest heresy of all, prowess on the games field was not the acme of achievement. As a result, the school was attracting the type of boy, or, rather, the type of parent, who was prepared to stray from the norm. In the district, Beaconsfield was acquiring a reputation along the lines of an establishment for problem children. 'Very progressive. Very modern,' Aunt I said encouragingly, in that hearty way of hers.

He knew she was backing up his mother, as always, though Mam had been remarkably restrained in her urgings for him to get out and seek employment. Probably because she was so relieved at the postponement of wedding plans for what looked like another interminable year. Though postponement was hardly the correct term. They had never got as far as setting any kind of date for the wedding.

He ought to telephone the school right now and fix up an appointment. He could hear the disappointment, and unexpressed reproach, in Jenny's voice, if he should fail to do anything positive about it before the weekend. Poetry was not a job, as he damned well knew. Schoolmastering was, and with a bottom second, Eton or Harrow or Winchester were not going to open their hallowed gates to him.

He would be better sticking to the adult education he had gained some experience of over the past two years. After all, he was becoming more involved than ever with the plight of the working, or non-working, man. He had just helped to organize some of the support services and stopping places for the Jarrow lads, who had set off self-consciously yesterday, home-made banners held high. 'We march against starvation', one had proclaimed, flapping in the chilly October breeze, the rough handles quivering in its bearers' hands.

There was a certain irony, he acknowledged, in zipping down the Great North Road as far as Doncaster in his sleek little motor, and there had been one or two quizzical eyebrows raised in various institute halls at his clothes and his accent. But there were plenty like him who were sincere enough in their belief and their efforts. Perhaps more so, he acknowledged, for he was uncomfortably uncertain of what his real sentiments were. Of course he supported them, the thousands who through no fault of their own were denied the right to earn a living, who depended on a hand-out which would scarcely keep their families alive and yet were denounced as 'spongers' by many of their social superiors.

But his leftism was so unsure. He continued to receive friendly letters from Horst Zettel, full of zeal for what the Führer was achieving for Germany. Hitler's party called themselves National Socialists. He was creating work, putting bread in the mouths of the population, working for the common man. Surely that was socialism, even if it needed a strong man at the top and a dose of ultra-patriotism to enforce it? Was it any worse than the decrees of faceless committees in Soviet Russia? And how much of a difference would his own contribution make here at home, if he taught a few kids, privileged enough to have folks who could afford it, to be their own men and enjoy a good piece of literature more than thumping a leather ball about a muddy field?

In two days, Teddy and his new bride would be back from their honeymoon in the south. Blushing was certainly the word to describe poor Marian, he reflected compassionately. She did little else from what he had seen of her. He had already moved his stuff in here, to Uncle Dan's room as they had always called it, so that the larger room could be readied for the newly weds.

It would be a tense time. The atmosphere between Teddy and Marian was far from the rose-tinted romanticism of young love. He had a feeling that his brother was simmering under the surface with frustration, and that was a sickening way to begin married life.

But maybe he would come to an acceptance of his situation. Maybe he already had, now that the strains of the wedding were over, and they had had a chance to relax, to be together as man and wife. Not that the wedding night would contain too many surprises, he thought, and felt warm with shame, a knife-sharp, aching envy. Visions of Jenny's body, its promise, swam before him, mounted hotly within him until he groaned. One day, one day!

Meanwhile, Teddy, you stupid young bugger! Marian's a pretty girl, she idolizes you; you're well set up in a good job you always wanted; you've got your own house, or will have, in a few more weeks. A brand new wife. What right have you not to be happy?

Teddy lay in the darkness, staring upwards into nothing. It felt strange to be lying in such a familiar place with Marian beside him. He still could not get used to sleeping with her in a double bed, even after the week's honeymoon. He had thought he would be glad to be at home. The tensions between them were exacerbated by the strange surroundings of the hotel, their hypersensitive reactions to what seemed like the knowing leers of the staff, and some of the other guests. The two of them had been like careful strangers to each other, painfully considerate and polite, and with nothing to say to each other.

The days had not been too bad. He had filled them as best he could with walks, and sightseeing trips, ignoring the cold and often wet weather of the end of September. He bought the *Daily Mail* each morning, and talked about the latest Loch Ness monster rumours, and the situation in Spain, which, since July, had developed into a full-scale civil war after the failure of the military coup led by a General Franco. As usual, he forced the conversation, all the while knowing that she was feeling as sick and wretched inside as he was.

Nights became dreaded. He sat on in the small cocktail bar, putting off going up to their room, while Marian sat pretty and silent beside him, wrapped in her dumb misery, until he would say, 'Look, why don't you go up? You need your sleep now. I'll be up in a while.' She pretended to be asleep, but he knew full well she was not, that she had been lying weeping. He hated himself, and felt sorry for her, and yet he was helpless to reach out to her, to do anything to ease her pain.

Desire for her had fled. They had made love once, on the wedding night, and he had tried once, and ignominiously failed, his beat of excitement withering as soon as he attempted to enter her. 'It's because of the baby,' he told her. 'I'm frightened I hurt you.' He hoped, but doubted, that she believed him.

Now, back home, it was the same. She had called his mother 'Mrs', then stopped in an agony of embarrassment, and May said almost sharply, 'I suppose you'd better call me Mam now.' She didn't call her anything. Didn't speak, unless she was asked a direct question. And John – he no doubt thought her some kind of imbecile, he talked to her as if she was some backward kid.

He knew she was crying now, in the dark silence. All at once, it was too much, and with a groan he rolled over towards her, lifting himself up to peer at her dim shape. He put his hand on her bare neck and shoulder, felt the thin strap of her nightgown, felt his knuckles brush against the wetness on her cheek. 'For Christ's sake! Say something! Tell me what a rotten bugger I am. Tell me how you hate me.'

It was like breaching a dam. She came at him with a low moan, clutched at him, shaking with the violence of her sobs, trying to muffle them. The only physical changes so far showing were the increased ripeness of her breasts, and the filling out of her buttocks. He felt the soft rounds beneath the lace-trimmed silk. Her nipples thrust erectly against the stretched material across her bosom, and he dug his fingers roughly into her, squeezing the soft roundness, tracing its contours. The lace edging was up, displaced, he felt the warm smoothness of her belly, with its cap of springy hair, and her opening thighs.

Her hand reached down, searched at the flap of his pyjamas and closed round his throbbing penis, yanking at it, jerking him to a painful hardness, pulling him on to her. 'I love you!' she wept, her open mouth against his, her breath hot, rank with her frantic longing. He gave way entirely, thrust into her, stabbing, bucking, in a frenzy, and it was over in a minute, or less, and he lay gasping, wilting out of her, half sobbing too, and lost in a despair that seemed bottomless.

May woke with a dull headache, wondered if it was caused by the tension which had settled like a fog on the house with the return of the honeymoon couple. She hoped the legalities of sorting out the Low Fell house would not take too long. The sooner they were settled in their new home the better. But it would be a while, she acknowledged grimly. At least she could keep busy, maybe even cure the girl of her almost paralysing fright of her, for she must make the effort to help her with all the necessities of starting up a new home.

And as for Teddy. Her jaw set as she thought of his unrelenting grimness. The young fool had to face up to it. Whether he felt life had dealt him a cruel blow or not, he must face his responsibility in what had happened. He must learn to love the girl who was carrying his child. He must be man enough to make a secure and a happy life for them.

She got up, pulled on her thick winter robe and slipped her feet into her woollen slippers. The sky was lowering, it was scarcely light, but she could not face the prospect of lying abed. There was no noise from John's room, or from Teddy and Marian. She would have time to have a leisurely breakfast and have the stove going before Ruby arrived.

She had made the tea, shuffling back and forth to the sink and the cooker, before she saw the folded note lying in the middle of the table. It said simply, 'Mam'.

She read it, her head spinning, unable to take it in, then unable or unwilling to believe its contents. She sat there, drawing in great breaths, giddy enough to wonder if she might be going to faint. Then, trembling all over, she ran for the stairs, clutching the paper in her hand.

She barged into John's room, and he sat up wildly, his striped jacket gaping, showing his thin torso. 'It's Teddy!' she gasped. She held the sheet of paper in front of her. It shook in her grasp. She sat abruptly on the edge of his bed, as though her legs had given way. 'He's gone.' She was whispering, in a hushed tone, suddenly afraid that the girl asleep in the next room would hear. 'He's cleared off. Run away. Oh, John!' The tears came, tumbling fast, she couldn't stop them. 'He's gone to Spain, to fight in their bloody stupid war!'

PART II

'These people are mad.'

Edouard Daladier, French Premier, on his return from
Munich, 1938.

Chapter Eleven

Marian's face looked swollen, her cheeks red, marked with tiny imperfections. She was fleshing out all over, beginning to put on weight in her fifth month of pregnancy, but it was grief which had caused this puffed-up appearance, as May well knew. There were two ruffs of flesh underneath the eyes, whose blue had a faded, washed out paleness from the tears she had wept every day since Teddy's disappearance.

'I don't want to go back home,' she said, in that soft tone of hers, and again the threat of tears lay behind the unsteady croak.

Once again May felt the conflicting twinges of compassion and irritation with the dumbly passive suffering the young figure exuded. The girl had sat crushed and silent during the agony of her mother's visit, listened to the outraged, blustering tirade from Nelly which May had weathered and stood up to. 'Ah've never heard the like!' The silly little hat had quivered with her indignation. 'To go off and leave his wife as soon as they get back from the honeymoon! Not a fortnight wed and he sneaks off like a thief. And who's goin' to be responsible for 'er – and the bairn, eh? That's what ah'd like to know. It's a bloomin' disgrace, that's what it is. If that's how well-to-do folk are taught to go on—'

'He's been very stupid,' May cut in, the pallor of her face betraying her emotion. 'He must have panicked. It just shows how young they both are. And how unready for marriage. Maybe if we hadn't pushed—'

'Oh, aye. And you expect my lass to carry the can? Take the blame for his wickedness while he runs off.'

'I'm sure he'll be back before long. When he realizes how badly he's behaved, how he's let all of us down.'

'Well, he's married to 'er fair and square, he can't get out of that,' Nelly declared vehemently. 'He's responsible for her, and the bairn an' all.'

'Of course he is. There's no question of that. Marian and the baby will be taken care of. He said there's some money coming, from the provident fund he's in at work. And of course, whatever happens, we'll make sure neither Marian nor the baby goes short, or suffers. . . .'

There was no pretence of amicability this time when Nelly, hat still quivering, left the cottage in a cab called and paid for by May. Though her mother had urged Marian to pack her things and 'come home with me' the weeping girl had demurred, and May had managed to get rid of Nelly with vague references to having things to settle first.

Now, in the relative calm of the following day, May and her daughter-in-law were discussing that uncertain future. May was more than a little surprised at Marian's reluctance to go back to her mother's. She seemed the sort of girl who would have returned to the familial nest as soon as possible at this first of life's hard knocks. Especially as she had appeared to be overwhelmed by everything that had happened to her over the past weeks. For the brief period of time she had spent at the cottage, she had scarcely uttered a word except in reply to a question, or to murmur 'thank you' like a polite little girl at everything offered to her. However, May could well understand that Nelly would not make life easy for her daughter after all that had befallen her.

May was disconcerted at first by this unexpected expression of opinion from Marian. Then she was ashamed at the recognition of her own reluctance to be faced with responsibility for the tragic young figure's welfare. She was almost surprised to hear herself saying, 'Well, of course, this is your home now as well. You're welcome to stay as long as you like. Till you can decide what you want to do.' She added quickly, 'Anyway, like I said, I'm sure Teddy will come back soon. He knows how wicked he's been. I'll bet he's already feeling so ashamed – he'll be back, you'll see.' She reached out automatically and patted the cold, plump arm, and felt compassion stab strongly yet again at the pathetic look of gratitude the girl flung at her.

It was a strain, though, even though the girl hardly spoke, and strove painfully hard to make herself useful about the place – efforts which merely served to offend Ruby, who looked on them as some kind of usurpation of her duties and her authority. The atmosphere affected everyone. John felt particularly awkward. His attempts at friendly conversation, even light *badinage*, reduced her to blushful stammerings. He kept out of her way as much as possible. He sometimes heard her being sick in the bathroom on a morning, and was appalled and angry with himself at the disgust he instinctively felt.

Worse still, was the sound of the muffled weeping he heard coming from her room. He had taken to writing after the household had settled for the night. The silence and the solitude enhanced his mood, and he savoured these hours when he sat in the pool cast by his desk lamp, often until 2 or 3 a.m. Padding along the landing towards the stairs for a cup of coffee, he would hear her snuffling quietly, and pause uncertainly, wondering whether he should tap on her door, offer tea and sympathy. Inevitably, he moved away with exaggerated care, feeling guilty and ashamed, on behalf of his brother, and of himself. To add to his discomfort, he could not rid himself of his awareness of her accusingly voluptuous figure, the sensuality he could envision in her open young face, the ripely thick, pale lips, swollen, he felt, with the promise of soft, ardent kisses. All too vividly, he could imagine Teddy's helplessness to resist her appeal.

Innocently tempting, she seemed to John the essence of sex. None of which helped him to feel at ease with her.

It seemed somehow unfair to him that she should have come into their lives just at this time when he was missing Jenny so much, and feeling disgruntled with the shape of things in general. The year was fizzling out, and still he had made no decisive moves concerning his future. He had not made any further approach to James Challoner about taking up a post at Beaconsfield. Jenny was disappointed in him, he knew. He could scarcely understand himself his dilatoriness, his reluctance to commit himself. 'It's just – I need a month or two to take stock – after finals,' he had told her unconvincingly. 'You know, maybe do a bit of writing,' he added apologetically, despising himself for his feebleness.

He was still taking his adult classes, at the Armstrong College in Newcastle, organized through the League. He followed as closely as he could the progress of the hunger marchers. They were down in London now, trying, without success, to gain an audience with the Prime Minister, Mr Baldwin. And no doubt clashing with Mosley and his gang. Only a couple of weeks ago, there had been a demonstration which had turned into a free-for-all, with over eighty people injured. He had been tempted to head for the capital himself, but, as usual, he had done nothing. Besides, he felt he could not truly join forces with any of the opposing factions. Firmly on the fence, as always, he castigated himself.

But he could genuinely ease his conscience now by telling himself that his mother needed his support in this latest crisis, caused by Teddy's act of madness. No sitting on the fence for his younger brother. No sitting anywhere. Up and off, with his typical tempestuousness. John was quite sure Teddy would have thrown his lot in with the Republicans, for his sympathies would lie with the left-wing, anti-Fascist forces. It seemed incredible that Teddy could be in danger, might even lose his life for such a cause. John was also sure that his brother had acted primarily for purely personal reasons, a means of escape from the trap he had fallen into with the girl who wept day and night for him. John was sickened at his brother's unbelievable cruelty. And at the same time secretly angry with himself for his envy at Teddy's dramatic ability to act, however crazily.

Meanwhile, the momentous events at the close of 1936 seemed to mirror rather than outweigh their own personal drama. In the bleak November, a harassed-looking king went to see for himself the plight of the unemployed in south Wales and raised a heartfelt cry. 'Something must be done'. Then, all at once, out of nowhere it seemed to ordinary people, His Majesty was caught up in his own crisis. Three weeks after his visit to Wales, a stunned nation was listening to his emotional speech over the radio-waves announcing his abdication, and his ten month reign was over.

Two days after the reluctant new King George VI had assumed the throne, May received the first communication from Teddy. He had been training in a camp in the Hautes-Pyrénées, close to the border, a remote and wildly beautiful area. Things had been chaotic, with weapons in such short supply that they had had to share the venerable rifles they were using. Hundreds of volunteers were flooding in daily, from Britain and other parts of Europe, until the tented camps were in danger of becoming disorganized health hazards. There were not enough instructors or men with military experience. All they seemed to do was sit around and elect people to sit on committees, then discuss endlessly the intricacies of left wing politics. This was clearly not to Teddy's liking and he sounded delighted at the winds of change which were beginning to stir the mountain encampments.

'The Comintern has at last arrived and started to put things into some sort of order. At least the Ruskies have some idea – they're forming us into international brigades and we're waiting to move off towards the action any day now. The Fascists' attack on Madrid has been halted, so I expect we'll be sent into the line somewhere to the west.'

John glanced up apprehensively from the letter which May had handed over to him. Her mouth was a tight, thin line clamped in emotion, but John could understand something of the turmoil behind the locked expression. He knew his mother's deep feelings on the subject of war, the permanent and deep scar it had left in the centre of her life with the taking of his father. Once more, he was appalled at his brother for the insensitivity he displayed in expressing his apparent eagerness to be caught up in the accelerating violence. As if he hadn't already caused enough hurt to his family – and to the new wife and unborn child he had deserted so brutally. Only in the final paragraph did he refer, briefly, to his own domestic catastrophe: 'It's no use me trying to explain what I've done. Anyway, I don't think I could – even if I did, I wouldn't expect anybody to understand. I'm sorry to land you all with this mess. I hope you got the provident fund money, not that it's anywhere near enough. I'll try to send more when I get some. You won't believe me, but one day I'll make it up to you. Please look after Marian. None of this is her fault. Tell her I'll write to her as soon as I can sort myself out. The way I am just now she's better off without me.'

The paper in John's hand trembled with the anger and hurt he felt coursing through him when he thought of the solid happiness that had made up this home. His mother, Aunt I, Uncle Dan. It had all seemed so secure, rock solid for Teddy and himself. Nothing could ever alter or harm them. And then suddenly it had all seemed so fragile. Things changing every day; other factors; their world widening, involving others. If only he could make his brother listen to that nightly muffled weeping, see the dumb misery stamped on the young features, at a time which should have been the most fulfilling in her life, as her body blossomed with the life it was carrying inside it.

His mother echoed his thoughts as she murmured, 'And he hasn't even the guts to write to her himself. How on earth is she going to feel when I tell her I've had a letter?' She shook her head worriedly. 'I tell you, she'll be lucky to carry this bairn through with all this going on. What a Christmas this is going to be, eh? I can't believe I've brought my sons up to be so wickedly selfish.'

John smarted at his inclusion in May's condemnation, but he knew the great burden of anxiety she carried over Teddy's safety. She was right, however, in her prognosis as far as the festive season was concerned. Teddy's action, and absence, cast an unavoidable shadow, further than John might have envisaged. He had seen Jenny only once – at her sister Rosemary's wedding – since her two day mid-term break in October. She had appeared sympathetically shocked at his brother's behaviour, but when he spoke tentatively on the telephone of the Christmas arrangements he sensed at once the hurt and resentment in her voice. 'I can't really leave Mam now,' he told her. 'With Teddy's clearing off – Marian's still here. And then there's Grandad – you know we always go to Sidney Terrace for Boxing Day. He's insisting we keep it up this year. It'll be the first without Nana. . . .'

He wondered if he was merely being hypersensitive, but he always thought he could detect a slight chill of embarrassment in Jenny whenever he used that word for his grandmother. Hypersensitive or not, there was no mistaking her tone of wounded resentment at her reception of his news that he would not be spending the Christmas holiday with her in Keswick. 'Why don't you come through here?' he offered, striving to disguise his own uncertainty. 'It would be lovely. Give you a chance to meet Marian.'

'Oh, I don't think so. Your mum's got enough intruders as it is.'

'You're not an intruder!' he disputed hotly. 'How—'

'Sorry, but that's how I feel. I can't help it. Oh, well,' her tone of brittle brightness was doubly cutting, 'if you can't make it, I'll just have to put up with it, won't I? I can't make you come.'

'I could try for New Year, maybe,' he said miserably. 'I could come through New Year's Day.'

'We'll probably be going to my Aunt Maud's. Other people have family obligations too, you know. By the way, I don't suppose you've done anything about getting in touch with Beaconsfield, have you?'

'I was going to ring, make an appointment. Things have been a bit difficult here.'

'It's all right. You don't have to explain. Plans for *our* future will just have to stay on the shelf a little longer. I understand.'

He was trembling slightly when he put the phone down. He felt as though they had quarrelled. All at once he wished that they had. A blazing anger swept through him. And a deep, leaden misery, solid in his gut, at her lack of compassion and understanding. There was a frightening hint of despair almost, a shattering recognition that the world of his love, their love, so precious to him, which he struggled each night to establish in all its glory in his head and on the paper, might well be divorced from the harshness of the physical world which surrounded and separated them.

That evening, Marian's eyes were even redder, the puffed-up area beneath the lids even more swollen. When the three of them sat at the dining-table, she said in that husky, almost whisper, 'Do you want me to go back to me mam's for Christmas?'

Her voice was so forlorn that May answered at once, 'Not if you don't want to, love. We'd love to have you stay here. If your mam won't be upset.'

'It's all boozing and that,' Marian answered, with resigned pathos. 'I'd feel right out of it, specially now.' She glanced down at herself eloquently.

John's eyes moved no lower than the splendidly rounded bosom. Suddenly he recalled the warm feel of Jenny's soft, more modestly proportioned flesh, and he blushed, with shame and with longing.

'That's settled then,' May said briskly. 'I've told you. This is your home now, as long as you want. You're one of the family, aren't you? There's three of us Mrs Wrights now! You, me, and Iris.' She gave a snort of laughter and clapped her hand to her mouth. Her brown eyes danced with mischief, like a young girl's. 'What am I saying? Four, for goodness' sake!' She glanced over at John, with a guilty grin. 'Fancy forgetting your grandma. The matriarch of the clan. Wouldn't old Sophie have a fit!'

Beaconsfield was a rambling, red-bricked villa, on the edge of the town of Corbridge, close to the site of the Roman fort at Corstopitum. It had been built just after the turn of the century, so that it had had time to mellow during the thirty plus years of its existence. The gardens were well matured, and the house was well screened from the road by a thickly wooded little copse through which the drive curved up to the entrance steps and the wide lawns and rose-beds which flanked the building on its southern side. John had been invited to visit around teatime. As he drove between the twin brick pillars marking the school's gateway from the roadside, he noticed the grey-jerseyed, scruffy-looking small figures darting about the trees and shrubbery, and gazing with tousle-haired, frank interest at his arrival.

'That's where they make their dens,' James Challoner told him with his engaging grin. 'You have to be careful where you're walking in there. It's full of tunnels and subterranean hide-outs. Bit like the Western Front.'

In some ways, the headmaster looked older than his forty-two years. His tall frame had an academic stoop, and though his long limbs were thin, he had a distinct pot pushing out his tweed jacket and the waistcoat beneath. The top of his head was completely bald, and the fluffy wisps at his temples were already grey. His circular, dark-framed glasses added to the scholarly impression, but then the grey eyes which danced behind them, and the broad smile which, at every excuse, lit up his features, gave him an ingenuously youthful appearance. This, together with his normally enthusiastic, often exuberant manner, in both speech and movement, created an overall concept of liveliness and freshness of outlook associated with a much younger man.

He did not stop talking during the swift tour he conducted of the school and its environs. Since he had taken it over from its former owner, a number of outbuildings had been converted to various uses, including a changing-room and a games-room. A low, long shed, with windows running down both sides which gave it a remarkable resemblance to a greenhouse, was labelled grandly, 'Art Room'. 'I'm afraid it's known universally to staff and boys as "the shed",' the headmaster chuckled. 'Too hot in summer and freezing in winter. Still, blue fingers shouldn't deter the true artist, eh?'

There was a freedom about the place, almost a whiff of anarchy, John thought, which he found oddly exciting. The rest of the small staff were assembled in what was formerly the drawing-room, whose high, wide bay-windows looked out over the level expanse of grass, segmented by the neat rose-beds. Several boys, in a varied assortment of casual clothing, were working on them, and making a considerable noise in the process. 'Supposed to be a punishment,' James Challoner grunted humorously. 'Little beggars are getting far too much enjoyment out of it!'

On the whole, the handful of teachers sitting in the deep chintz-upholstered, solidly comfortable furniture, appeared to be as relaxed and friendly as their leader. John was still waiting for the formal interview to begin. He had met the head once previously, at the end of the summer term, but had not taken up his offer to pursue matters as far as employment went. He was startled therefore when Dr Challoner – 'I only use the "doctor" when absolutely necessary, to impress would-be clients. And in the

152

prospectus, of course' – casually offered him employment over the teacups. Despite his laughter, James Challoner was sincere.

'Well, you've had a look around; met my fellow sufferers; seen something of the rapscallions we nurture here. What do you think? Could you steel yourself to a life of unrewarding toil in our particular neck of the woods?'

'You – you're offering me a post, sir?' John said, taken aback at the head's directness.

'Jumping at the chance, my boy!' the head laughed. 'You said something about being engaged, I believe? Are you still planning to tie the knot? I do hope so. Your fiancée is already teaching, yes? Could we possibly hope to recruit yet another staff member before long?'

He took John's arm as he guided him back to the car parked at the foot of the steps. 'If you don't mind the advice of a crusty old bachelor, don't leave it too long before the nuptials. I was far too reticent myself, and you see the result.' John smiled uncertainly, made a gesture of disagreement, and Challoner shook his arm vigorously. 'Nothing so valuable as a helpmeet on the rocky road. And it's what we need so much here – a woman's touch. It's what our boys need. Such a tender age still. I know Mrs Phillips would be delighted.' Mrs Phillips, the housekeeper-cum-matron who treated pupils and staff with similarly firm kindness, was, John guessed, around his mother's age, or a few years older, and, like herself, a war widow.

The smile faded from the head's face as he stood by the car. It was like the sudden disappearance of sun behind a cloud. 'These are worrisome times,' Mr Challoner said. He patted John's shoulder in an avuncular gesture. 'And possibly worse to come. Don't waste any opportunity, John. You don't mind if I call you John? Seize the day, eh?' His handshake was strong. 'I look forward to having you with us. Enjoy the rest of your holiday. My best to your mother. And to your fiancée. Tell her I'm looking forward to meeting her.'

John was surprised at how much of the head's enthusiasm had rubbed off on him. He was more excited at the prospect of starting work than he had thought possible, and he was eager to tell Jenny as soon as he could. He phoned her straight away, and was disappointed at her guarded reception of his news.

'He'd be delighted to offer you a job as well,' he told her, still swept along on the current of his feeling. 'He's even prepared to offer us accommodation in the school if we want it!'

'That's very good,' Jenny answered. 'I'm so pleased for you. But we mustn't rush things. I mean – there's my job here to consider. I'm settled in now. In any case, I'd have to give notice. There's a lot we need to consider first. We'll have to talk it over . . . When you come through.'

'Of course. Next weekend's still all right, isn't it? I love you, Jen.' When he hung up the phone he was shaken by the note of interrogation he had discovered in his own voice.

Marian glanced shyly at John. With a confiding air, she said softly, 'I'm not lookin' forward to goin' into Leaholm. They seem a bit snooty, you know. And that matron . . .' she gave her characteristic smile of apology. A flush spread over her rounded face. She had lost that bloom which her pregnancy had enhanced, and which John had found so shockingly attractive. Now that her time was near, her features had filled out to a roundness he found almost plump, blurring her beauty. The swollen hugeness of her belly made her clumsy. Its distortion seemed to shriek her condition at John, while the breasts whose fullness had so disturbed him now hung on her lump, sagging overripely. 'I wish I could have it at home – here,' she added wistfully.

Leaholm was the maternity hospital nearby into which May had booked her for the delivery. 'You'll be fine there,' John tried to reassure with false heartiness. 'You won't have time to worry about anything. It's better; safer, with it being the first baby and everything.' He found himself blushing awkwardly, out of his depth. 'You'll only be in nine days or so, won't you? You'll be back home in no time. And we'll be in to see you every day, don't you worry.'

He stood, feeling cowardly at his withdrawal but unable to stop himself. He glanced eloquently at his wrist-watch. 'Well, I'd better be off. I'm supposed to be on house duty tonight. Don't want to be late.'

It was an equal effort for her to chat, but she forced herself, making a brave attempt to sound brightly interested. 'How's it going then? You still like it?'

He nodded. 'Yes. More than I thought I would, really. Not that I'm much good at it yet.'

'I think you'll be brilliant!' Marian declared, with an amount of feeling which surprised and touched him. 'I think it's wonderful, you being a teacher and everything.'

Embarrassment gripped both of them, John nodded, took his chance to escape from the living-room. Though Beaconsfield was only a few miles away, and the head had offered him the chance to live at home if he wished to, John spent most of the time at the school, sharing the cramped room tucked away on the second floor with another member of staff, only spending the occasional night at his home. 'I want to do my bit,' he told Mr Challoner, who was clearly pleased, 'be a proper member of the team.'

He had surprised himself with his enthusiasm for the job. At times, he could stand back and examine his motives dispassionately, though not always comfortably. He was conscious of how enclosed, almost claustrophobic, the school world might become. Various truisms stood out in his mind about the profession: 'Men among boys, boys among men'; 'Those who can do, those who can't teach'. It disturbed him to think how his Grandad Rayner would endorse such opinions. And most of the rest of Mam's family, he acknowledged.

He also acknowledged, painfully, that part of his desire to

immerse himself in his new occupation stemmed from the fact of his secret dissatisfaction with the way things were working out, or rather, failing to work out as he desired, with Jenny. The uneasy atmosphere of their telephone conversation, when he had broken the news of his securing the teaching post, had hovered about them when he had driven over to Keswick for the last weekend of the Christmas holiday. As he had feared, the Alsop family presented a united front, and presented him with what seemed like a *fait accompli*.

Typically, it was Mrs Alsop who made the first assault. 'I think Jenny's being very sensible about this. She was saying she thinks she'd better not give notice just now. Not until the end of the academic year at least. She doesn't want you to have any distractions until you get settled in. You'll find teaching a very demanding profession. As she's already learned.' There was, he sensed, a gentle reproof there, for the term of idleness he had allowed to slip by after he had left college.

His arguments, such as they were, were met with sweet reasonableness, by Sandy and his wife, and the newly married and unctuously superior Rosemary. 'You'll be thankful you waited, believe me,' she told him. 'Start building up a bit of a nest egg. I doubt if Gerald and I could have managed otherwise. We've no regrets about waiting, have we, Gerald?'

Go on, dare to disagree! John thought, but held silence.

The quarrel burst into the open when he was at last alone with Jenny. 'If you'd rather, we can call a halt to the engagement,' she said, twin spots of colour daubing her otherwise white face. 'Suspend it, if that's what you'd prefer.' She tugged at the ring as she spoke, slipped it dramatically from her finger.

'Is that what *you* want?' he asked, his eyes brilliant.

'Of course not. But you're obviously unhappy with things. With what I think. . . .'

It ended with tears, bitter at first, then with kisses as she clung sobbing to him. Then kisses again, building to a passion which had lain like a sword between them for so long, it seemed to him. He left her on the Sunday, feeling both relieved and vanquished. Only when they were separated once more, by an interval of time and distance, did he feel the sweet sadness of their love return with all its force. But he was doubly glad of the challenges and rewards of his job at Beaconsfield, and the absorption with which he was able to fling himself into it.

Chapter Twelve

The whining, angry gnat's buzz of the plane's engine became a demented screaming that filled his head, then his whole shaking body, and transmitted itself to the earth they were clinging to. Teddy felt the thin, hard body of the girl he was covering trembling beneath him. In spite of his terror he looked up, saw the black shapes of the planes transpose from tiny blurs to a distinct silhouette of curiously tilted, angled wings, and short jut of undercarriage still down. They seemed to be screaming vertically in a dive to destruction, but then the siren shriek was drowned in a roar of thunder as they swerved up at the last minute. The farm buildings burst into fragments in front of his eyes, dissolved as though exploding from within. In the centre of the billow of dark smoke was a brilliant flash, to be followed distinct seconds later by the deep thud of bomb burst, and the hot, breathless rush of blast which drove his head down again, his face buried in the coarse dustiness of Rosie's jacket.

The words came rushing, too, into his ringing head. The words that Felipe had shouted mockingly at the red-faced, pop-eyed priest they were about to murder. Words that one of the others had laughingly translated for him: 'Where's your God now, Father? Why doesn't He save you? Send His thunderbolt down to smite us?'

The thunderbolt was on them now, all right. Delivered from out of a blinding sky by these banshee-wailing planes, swooping

158

down to bring death right to them. He couldn't stop thinking about the previous day. Executions, Leonid, the company commander, had called them. Seven frightened young men. Pathetic, boyish faces whey with terror. At least one had a dark stain, spreading, widening over the crumpled expanse of his filthy uniform trousers. His bowels had opened, too, for he stank acridly as they herded him with the others to the long wall of the barn. The wall which had now disappeared in the flash and rumble of smoke.

'You can't just kill them!' Teddy had protested, appalled, and Leonid had rounded on him viciously, in a rare display of emotion.

'That's what we're here to do!' he hissed. 'And these are our orders. You've seen the corpses of the villagers. The women – and the children.'

The priest was a comically rotund figure. They had stripped his soutane from him in a final cruelty, and his paunch stretched the dirty, grey-white vest and the baggy drawers which flopped above his knees. His grey, wispy hair flapped over his sweating forehead. His cheeks were purple, his eyes rolling, starting out from his visage. His lips shone like raw liver, and they moved in a curious chewing movement as he muttered incessant prayers. The young *Fascisti* huddled together piteously. Some were crying, still pleading, their voices soft, like children.

Leonid turned away in disgust, gave the order to fire, swiftly, without ceremony, and the ragged volley rang out, eight lifeless bundles collapsed, flapped on the bare earth. The crop-headed Russian, his dark beard cut close as the hair covering his skull, had threatened to put Teddy under arrest, have him sent back to prison at the coast. But later, in his more usual calm dispassion, he had offered an explanation. 'You have seen the atrocities committed by the Fascists. The raping, the terrorizing of the population. These are the crimes against humanity. They must be punished. And you. You are a soldier now. You must obey orders. That is all you have to do. Obey orders. That is the life for a soldier.'

But Teddy couldn't rid himself of the thought as he lay, deafened and frightened during the air attack, that this was vengeance, the horrifying inhuman screech, the brilliant cascades of the bombs. Everyone had talked of them. The dreaded Condor Legion of the Nazis. This was their first experience of its horror. The minutes of the raid were an eternity. Then they were gone, the blue brilliance of the sky was back, empty, marred to the height of the savaged trees by the orange mist of the dust, the rolling plumes of the black smoke rising way up. The low farmhouse and the barns were flattened rubble.

All at once, Teddy was aware of Rosie's hard, thin, tight little buttocks pressed against his loins. They twitched, thrust up into him, blatant, and he drove himself hard against them, pressing her down, his penis stiffening, his frame charged with the wild arousal. She squirmed around, rolled under him to turn and look at him, her tanned face split by a wide grin. Her small, even teeth showed white against her brown skin. 'My hero,' she lilted. 'Will ye get that cock of yours out of me arse, for God's sake? I might look like a feller, but I'm buggered if I'll be buggered like one!'

He grinned shakily in return, then he reached forward, seized her neck and pulled her to him. He kissed her urgently, hard against her mouth, whose lips accepted him, opened, and returned the rawness of his passion.

'I wondered when you'd get round to it,' she murmured, the caricature of her Irish accent fading to her normal pleasant cadence.

'Do you mind?'

'Not at all. I'd've had to attack you meself if you hadn't made a move soon.'

But then they picked themselves up, and the world of horror engulfed them again in death and pain that made Teddy's gorge rise, until his throat ached, jagged with the vomit of revulsion.

160

Some of the corpses were unrecognizable as his comrades. Some not even whole. Slivers, fragments, and solid chunks of flesh; raw, bloodied meat, smelling of the bits of singed cloth clinging to them.

The living – and dying – were equally horrific. Tomas, with his left arm vanished, mangled strips, flopping obscenely from his shoulder. He wasn't even screaming, just muttering softly, his head constantly rolling, eyelids fluttering, seeing nothing of the carnage around him. Rosie was working furiously, her delicate face screwed in fierce concentration, using the precious, dwindling stock of morphine while one of the others struggled to bind the ghastly stump. The tall, blond French lad, Louis, had had half his face blown off. His chin had disappeared; white jawbone and teeth showed through pale strips of flesh, and he appeared to be choking, his cries of agony drowned in the gurgling of his working throat.

Teddy tried to do what he could. It was more than many, who stood around dazed, or moved away from the nightmare scene around the ruined buildings, glad to be ordered to dig a vast hole to bury the dead. Teddy hung over the still smoking stones of the barn and retched drily, brought up a little bitter bile, his stomach burning. In the distance, the mountains of Cantabria, down which they had swung, full of lively chatter the previous morning, shimmered in the hazy unreality of the late afternoon. Twilight was on them before they had cleared up, buried the corpses in the communal grave, left the wounded in the village waiting for the transport which still had not come to pick them up. Weary as they were, they were glad to move on, through the level fields, putting distance between them and the site of the air raid. It was almost dark when they found another farm, long deserted, the simple dwelling empty, as were the crude barn and the animal stalls, their occupants swept away on the tide of the war.

After they had eaten, round the comforting blaze of a fire lit inside the walls of the farmhouse, Rosie came to him, as he knew she would. She pulled him by the arm. He rose and followed her. No one said anything. No sly comments, crude jokes. There had been none of the usual banter throughout the leisurely meal. People sat staring into the flames, wrapped up in their own thoughts as they would soon be wrapped in their blankets. They were too shaken to talk yet of what had happened to them today. They had lost more men in five minutes than they had lost in two months of the campaign.

'Come. See what I've found.' Rosie led him away from the building, the flickering light which showed dimly through its chinks, and the narrow, windowless openings high in the walls. The April night was overcast, but already warm with promise of more heat on the morrow. She wove her way expertly through the ramshackle fences behind the farm, along a track hedged by the high scrub. The ground dipped suddenly, then he saw the dim gleam of water. There must have been a spring somewhere, for someone had dug out a makeshift little pond, more like a long trough, lined it with wooden boards and old pieces of rusty, corrugated iron.

'Come on. We can take a bath. Get out of these stinking clothes. I want to be clean for you.' She was already sitting, dragging off her heavy boots, tugging at the thick grey socks. She stood, threw off the ragged jacket, the voluminous trousers, the loosely flapping shirt that came to her knees. She peeled the dirty white vest off over her head. Her short black hair stood up in spikes about her face. Her teeth flashed white at her grin. Her dark eyes never left his face as she pushed down the black knickers, and he saw the small dark cap of her pubis.

Her body was thin, elfin, her breasts small, so that he was surprised at the generosity of the nipples and their surrounds, their darkness against the lighter flesh, It was the first time he had seen her naked, though he had often seen her stripped down to her underwear, the childishly baggy knickers and vests she wore and let others see without compunction. 'We're all lads together, aren't we?' she would say, with that cocky, challenging grin. She was always going on about how much like a boy she looked, that they should think of her simply as a comrade. 'Just forget that I haven't got any dangly bits between me legs, will you?'

But he had never thought of her like that. Instead, he found her gamine appearance and manner, as well as her forthright speech, highly sexual. There had been women throughout the training. The sexes had lived and slept together. It had been encouraged, though they were warned that there must be no sexual misbehaviour. Such an offence would be punished by instant banishment. Of course, the regulation was broken, stealthily but often. One or two were even caught. Usually it was the female who disappeared. The male offender remained, chastised by extra drill, guard duties, then forgiven.

Now, though, in the line, things were different. Women were rarer. The comintern frowned on females serving in the battle lines, there were rumours that soon they would be forbidden to do so. There had been many fierce arguments in their own unit, Rosie contesting hotly that women could be just as ruthlessly efficient at killing as men. She was the only female left in the unit, and was fiercely proud of her status.

Teddy was dismayed at his inability to dismiss his sexual attraction to her. He had tried, desperately. She made him uncomfortable, for he sensed that she knew very well how improper his feelings were, and that she mocked him for them, always calling him 'comrade', with that cheeky look, stressing the sexlessness of her relationship with him, and the others in the unit. But one day, after their first spell in the static front line, their first shots fired in anger, he had found himself talking to her truly as a comrade. In real friendship.

She told him her history. Rosemary Connelly, 'bog Irish', she grimacingly labelled herself. One of seven surviving children.

'We worked like slaves for me da, and his measly scrap of land. Every Sunday afternoon he took Mammy off to bed. "Doing his duty", he called it. Putting her up the spout, until at forty she looks like sixty, and I doubt if I'll ever see her alive, again.' She frowned. 'And your man the priest telling him what a good feller he is, pillar of the community and all that shite! And lining me up for more of the same with some fool as ignorant as he is. I tell you, I was away out of it as fast as I could shift meself.' She hawked and spat, in a way that made the corners of his mouth twitch in a smile, despite her seriousness. 'What's done back home in the name of religion, you wouldn't believe!'

She looked at home here, black-haired, dark-eyed, brown as a berry. A regular gypsy. Teddy wondered if one of her ancestors had given comfort to some shipwrecked Spanish sailor boy in days of yore. He had found himself confessing too. He told her of Marian, his helpless feeling of entrapment. The hasty marriage, and his fleeing from it. He had expected condemnation, her rallying behind the banner of femininity at his wickedness. But she had shrugged matter-of-factly. 'The old Adam – and Eve,' she added. Then her face broke into its typical grin. 'Aren't we lucky there's none of that nonsense here, eh?'

When the letter came from his mother he sought Rosie out. 'I'm a father. Of a girl. Edwina Helen. Born on February fourth. That's nearly three weeks ago. And I didn't know. I'll have to write,' he said torturedly.

'I know you're a bright feller, and any seed of your loins must be a feckin' genius, but the poor wee mite's a bit young yet to be reading, isn't she?'

'You know what I mean.' He glared at her wildly, then subsided into a sheepish grin. Her refusal to be judgmental helped to ease a little the pain of his tender conscience. So much so that he was, at last, able to pen some stilted lines of congratulation and, he hoped, of comfort, to his deserted wife.

Distracted memories of Marian, of her beautifully accommo-

164

dating body, came drifting back to him now as he watched the dim shape of the naked girl standing unabashed in front of him. The baby would be more than two months now. Marian had written straight back to him. Telling him of the baby, how lovely she was, how good his mother was, how happy she herself was to hear from him. How much she loved him, and was worried for him. Not a single word of reproach for the awful thing he had done to her.

'Are you not going to join me then?' Rosie turned. He saw the narrow hips, the dimpled buttocks, remembered the tight clenching of them against him. She turned, stumbled, slipped with a little shiver and gasp into the dark stillness of the water, which came just over her knees. She crouched, gave a muted whimper as she lowered herself into the water, splashed it up over her body. Quivering with want, he tore at his clothes, and she laughed joyously, uninhibited, with merry lust, at the sight of his bobbing penis before he sprawled smotheringly into her and they clutched at each other as they sank and flailed in the tiny iciness and the oozing mud.

Their flesh felt frozen, dead, and they were out in seconds, lying on a sloping bank, and she was under him, pulling him on to her, lifting her thin legs, wrapping them about his hips, taking his hard penis and guiding it to her. No kisses, just urgent fumbling, thrusting, rutting, until he was lodged within her, then she clamped her mouth avidly to his.

She felt tight and small and virginal. He was sore when the brief frenzy was over and he had spent himself inside her. Appalled and helpless to stop himself, he recalled the vastly different feel of Marian's body. Its round softness, his slow and leisurely explorations of it, its proffered abandon to him through hours of loving.

After a while he slipped in cold detumescence out of Rosie, rolled off her, but held her in his arms. Guiltily he let his hand fall between her thighs, probe at the sticky wetness, the furled flesh, until she gave a sharp cry as though of pain, and thrust his wrist away from her. 'Jesus! Dont do that! Are ye trying to kill me or what? I cant bear it.'

'Was it all right?' he asked humbly. Her hard, skinny arms twisted round his neck, pulled him tightly against her breast.

'What do you want? A flaming citation? It was wonderful, wasn't it? Just what the doctor ordered.' She scrambled up from his embrace, turned to the chill water again. 'Now let me get cleaned up and get some clothes on again, before Leonid finds us and has us shot at dawn.'

When they were dressed, they crept back towards the farm-house. The huddled sentry saw them, said nothing, lifted his arm in tired salute. Teddy grabbed at her, pressed his lips to hers. 'Rosie! You know how I feel about you—'

She pushed her hand up against his mouth, to stop any further words. gave a little shake of her spiky head, a flashing grin. 'Good-night, bucko. Sleep well.'

'Here, get yourself a pint. And stick a whisky in there. Save my old gammy legs, there's a good lad.' Dan pushed across his empty glass. 'Not with your pal this evening?'

John shook his head. 'I just fancied nipping out for a quick one. Had an idea I might find you in here.' He turned to the bar, ordered the drinks with the money Dan had given him. The Angel was quiet on this weekday evening. It was less than a mile from the school, a handy watering hole for those on the small staff who liked a drink. James Challoner occasionally accompanied them, at end of term and so on, but he claimed he was 'no pub man' himself. John was sure that the head was sensitive enough to obviate any awkwardness which might occur if he made more frequent trips to the Angel Inn.

Not like his Uncle Dan. If anyone deserved the epithet of 'regular', it was him. Not many evenings passed when he didn't call in for a 'swift one', both words far from accurate to describe his visits. Now, John could tell from his uncle's brick-red countenance that he had taken more than a few shots of the Bell's that was his favourite tipple. 'How's Aunt I?' he asked, as usual, when he brought the drinks back to the narrow table. Though he sometimes popped in to their house in Corbridge, he had found that, despite its proximity to Beaconsfield, his duties at school precluded his dropping in more than two or three times throughout the term.

'Oh, she'll be out at one of her good works, no doubt,' Dan answered. 'Or else she and your ma will be gloating over their latest purchase at some sale or other.' He paused, then added sympathetically, 'I hear May's not too pleased with you chumming up with that Jerry friend of yours.'

John grimaced, took a pull at his beer, wiped the foam from his lips. 'Horst. She thinks I'm some kind of traitor having anything to do with a German. She seems to hold the whole nation forever responsible for my dad's death.' He glanced up in quick half apology, remembering his uncle's permanent disablement. But he knew Dan was far more tolerant of his former enemy. John had often heard him condemning the harsh peace terms exacted by the Allies, which had led to the present upsurge of German nationalism and the spectacular rise of Adolf Hitler.

'You cant really blame her,' Dan put in gently. 'You can imagine what it must have done to her, can't you? Think about you and Jenny. All your plans. Your whole life in front of you. How you feel about her. And to have all that snatched away from you . . .' He let his voice die away, staring into his glass, and John felt a sudden surge of affection, of love for the battered, rugged figure slumped next to him, and for his understanding. He felt a close sense of bonding, an alliance against the often bitter criticisms of his uncle he heard from his mother, and from Aunt I.

'He's coming over on a visit next month. He gave Jenny and I such a good time when we were over there. I thought we might offer him some hospitality in return. He's expecting to stay with us, but Mam says she won't even meet him. Makes things very tricky.'

'I'd offer to put him up at ours, but . . .' Dan shrugged, gave a resigned chuckle. 'You know how it is. The auld alliance. It'd be more than my life's worth.' John knew exactly what he meant, in turn understood Dan's not wishing to upset May by appearing to side with her son against her. Besides, Aunt I would never tolerate such an idea for a second. As always, she was solidly on Mam's side. No logic or shades of grey could influence her unwavering loyalty.

'It's all right. As it happens, things have worked out. Jenny's family are going to have him stay in Keswick. I can get a weekend off and nip over there.'

'Everything still rosy on the romantic front then, eh?'

In spite of the light chuckle, John wondered if he could detect an edge of genuine uncertainty in his uncle's enquiry. 'Oh yes,' he replied, and continued to wonder whether his own confused emotion would show through the confidence of his answer. 'It's not ideal, of course. Up to the Easter hols we'd only seen each other twice since Christmas. But it'll be worth it in the end, I suppose. We should be able to get quite a sum put away. Ready to put down on a house. Perhaps after the summer we can get things sorted.'

'Don't leave it too long,' Dan laughed, his joviality too close to what John really felt for his comfort. 'A pretty girl like that. Can't leave her on the shelf too long, you know.' John was glad that Dan quickly changed the subject. 'Speaking of houses, how's Marian getting on?'

Although the girl had been typically reticent about her views, May had cajoled her into going ahead with the planned move to the new house at Chow Dene, on the edge of Gateshead. The new semi had been ready for occupation since before the end of last year. 'It'll be in your name,' May told her daughter-in-law. The girl had looked tearfully embarrassed, but she had not put up half as spirited a resistance as May's own solicitor, whose firm had served the Wright family for years.

'It's rather unusual, Mrs Wright. I mean – shouldn't we stick to what we arranged? In your son's name. His wife of course would be the beneficiary of—'

'I want the deeds to be in Marian's name,' May insisted, the gleam of contest clear in her brown eyes. 'Teddy at present shows absolutely no regard for either what's morally right or his responsibilities. Now, is there any legal difficulty in having the property in my daughter-in-law's name? The terms of the mortgage will be met. I'm guaranteeing it. Payments to the Rock building society. First of every month.' She was determined to have her way, and she succeeded.

She could see how nervous Marian was. She had emerged, it seemed almost sleepily, from her utter absorption with her baby in the first few weeks of Edwina Helen's life, to gaze with childish apprehension at the outside world facing her so threateningly. 'It's a long way away,' she offered diffidently.

'Nonsense!' May countered firmly. 'It's much nearer for your mam.' Perhaps that wasn't such a useful argument, she acknowledged privately, and hurried on. 'Iris and I can pop through in the car in no time. You'll see more than enough of us, I can tell you.'

She had set her mind on infant and mother starting out as soon as possible in their own home, as they had originally planned before Teddy's desertion. It wasn't as though she found Marian a burden any more, May assured herself, and Iris. She had got used to the girl's silence, her too readily submissive manner. And the baby was captivating. May had spent almost as much time with her granddaughter as Marian had. No, she didn't want to be rid of them, far from it. But she felt a deep-seated conviction that Marian must begin to find some measure of independence, for her own sake and her infant's. She began to suspect that it was partly, if not largely, the girl's enduring passivity, her pliability, that had led her into her present tragic situation.

'You'll feel better once you're standing on your own two feet,' she urged the timid figure, who gazed at her dumbly with those great, sad blue eyes, until May wanted to hug her and shake her all at once.

April was well advanced before the move was effected. The three-bedroomed house was spick and span, with its brand new furnishings, though beyond the three steps of the porch the garden was a churned up heap of clay and rubble, and the road-way was still an unpaved, muddy track, with large puddles the colour of milky tea everywhere. At the end of the road, corn-fields still stood, and the new green shoots grew on the steep slope below, beyond the skeletal roofs of the uncompleted build-ings opposite. The greenery of Silver Hill billowed to the horizon, beyond the wooded bottom of the valley with its small beck.

'You're right out in the country here,' May commented enthu-siastically. 'It'll be lovely once the estate's finished. So nice for Edwina. No soot or smoke at all.'

'Yes. Teddie loves it, don't you, pet lamb?' Marian cuddled the baby in to her ample breast, and May stifled her instinctive quiver of protest at the use of the diminutive. Unchar-acteristically stubborn, Marian had insisted on using the name Teddie, however unsuitable it sounded for a girl. May suffered in silence, for she could understand that it was the poor girl's perhaps simplistic way of clinging on to a link with her missing husband.

It hurt May deeply to be reminded of the countless, desperate ways she had done the same herself after Jack's death. Papers, books – clothing even. She could not bear to let anything go through those first nightmare months. His shirts, neatly folded in the drawer. She would run her hands over them, tortured, recalling everything of their love. . . .

An unexpected ally in helping Marian to settle at Low Fell turned out to be none other than May's sister, Julia, and her family. Perhaps Julia felt sympathy for a girl from Marian's background, for her feeling of being somewhat out of her depth, mixed up so inextricably with the Wrights and their privileged world which Julia seemed to think May had somehow disloyally aspired to. Whatever the reason, she was on hand from the very day of the move. She lived not more than two miles down the road, in the rows of pit cottages surrounding the Lady Mary pit, on the northern edge of Birtley.

In particular, her eldest girl, Dora, fourteen years old and longing only to leave school and begin growing up, became an almost daily visitor. She made herself very useful about the house, and as a companion for Marian, who enjoyed having a confidante, someone to whom she could chat with no trace of inferiority.

'Teddy's such an ass,' John confided to his uncle, sitting in the smoky intimacy of the Angel. He sighed regretfully. 'Marian still dotes on him. That brand new little house. Brand new baby girl.' He could hardly believe his brother's rejection of such an idyll.

'Complicated business, love, eh?' Dan mused, staring unseeingly ahead as he groped for another cigarette.

Chapter Thirteen

'I'm sorry, John.' May managed to sound both resentful and apologetic at the same time. 'I know you think I'm being unreasonable. This is still your home, and I've always made any friends of yours welcome, but honestly, I just couldn't face this lad, Horst,' she even found his name unpleasant to pronounce, 'without, well, showing my feelings. It wouldn't be fair. To you or to him.'

It was late on Friday evening. John had driven over to Hexham to spend the night at home, and planned to set off for the Lakes from the cottage at first light. 'It's all right, Mam. I understand. I don't agree. I don't think it's fair as you put it to hold Horst responsible for international events that happened over twenty years ago. But I can understand. There are plenty more who feel the same way.'

'Has it occurred to you that there are German bombers over in Spain? Trying to put an end to the life of your own brother?' Only a few weeks ago, the papers had screamed apocalyptically of the terrible damage caused by the air attack on the small town of Guernica.

'For that matter, there are British who are doing that,' he answered curtly. 'It's not just the Republicanists who've recruited foreigners. They're fighting on General Franco's side, too.'

'Mind you,' May resumed bitterly, 'here's me talking about making your friends welcome, and your own fiancée doesn't even come over to visit. It must be nearly a year since she last came to see us.'

John fought down the powerful urge to answer roughly, it's precisely because she *doesn't* feel welcome that she stays away! He didn't say it, in spite of his hurt, because he didn't want to hit back, and, partly, because he felt that blame was far from one-sided; that Jenny was deliberately thin-skinned in her attitude towards his mother. With effort, he strove to change the subject. 'How's Marian and the baby?' He knew that his mother and Aunt I had driven over there as usual earlier in the day.

'Fine. Young Dora was there. It's a wonder our Julia hasn't got the school board man after her. That lass is never at school. Mind you, she helps Marian no end about the house, and with the bairn. She dotes on her. Julia's down there herself every other day, apparently. It's funny how she gets on with Marian.' She pulled a face, gave a disparaging laugh. 'Maybe not, though. No wonder my ears are burning so much!'

'Oh, come on, Mam. Marian thinks the world of you, you know she does.'

May grunted again, perhaps in acknowledgement. 'It's hard to know what that lass thinks. She won't say boo to a goose, that one. But she keeps the place nipping clean, I'll give her that. She's had another letter from Teddy.' Her lips thinned. John saw and heard plainly the disapproval in her voice. 'That's two she's had. Not a word to me. It's a fine thing when a mother has to learn if her son's alive or dead at second hand, eh?'

'She *is* his wife,' John protested again. 'And you were mad with him before for not writing to her.'

'All right, all right,' May conceded, 'not that he said much. She let me read it. Not exactly lovey-dovey. Not like a newly wed to his bride. Wasn't more than a page. Asking after Edwina, telling them he was all right. Didn't say where he was, or what he was doing.'

'Probably not allowed to. Perhaps they've got some kind of censorship going. After all, our letters go through Central GPO, don't they?'

May nodded. 'I just wish the daft young beggar would get himself home to them,' she said sombrely. She had recognized like an ancient adversary the clutch of fear lodged permanently at the back of her mind.

The May morning was chilly, and a low mist hung at tree level, when John motored off early next day. But in little more than an hour, on the road between Alston and Appleby, the sun was shining brightly, dissipating the white trails of vapour, and he pulled on to the grass verge to fold down the hood. For a large part of the journey his mind dwelt on Teddy, and on Marian, but, as the sun climbed high, and he began to see the distant crags of the Lakeland mountains, he felt that odd mixture of excitement and tension at the prospect of seeing Jenny once more. It was strange how he felt himself something of an inter-loper, as though he was moving into hostile territory, when he thought of Jenny and her family. Even more disturbing was the realization that, instinctively, he was coming to range her with them, as part of the opposing force.

This trip was complicated by the fact of Horst Zettel's pres-ence. The German had been staying with the Alsops for more than a week already. As well as the awkwardness of not being able to offer Horst hospitality himself, John was plagued by the ambiguity of his own feelings towards the reunion. He recalled vividly the magnetic friendliness of the slight blond figure, his knack of establishing so quickly a kind of intimacy which normally came only after long acquaintance with somebody. Jenny had felt it, too, he remembered. He had pretended to feel-ing quite jealous of her enthusiasm for their new friend, to their mutual amusement.

But now there was a real stumbling block, for, although John could never condone his mother's prejudice, his own views had become far less sympathetic towards what Germany stood for. He knew that Horst was an ardent supporter of many of the German Chancellor's policies. And there was no doubt that the dynamic leader had achieved much for his country. But, like the majority of his fellow countrymen, John was uneasy with the belligerent air of new nationalism, the blatant flouting of the rearmament controls, however harsh they may have been. Any day now, it was rumoured, Hitler was going to move against Austria, just as he had occupied the demilitarized zone of the Rhineland last year. There was a growing number of people in Britain, not just politicians, who were beginning to talk as though war against Germany would be inevitable, given this mood of aggression. 'They don't forget easily,' Uncle Dan had said one evening, over his whisky. 'Last time the army felt let down. They would have fought on, believe me. They'd welcome another go.'

Horst Zettel's eager cry, his rushing down the steps of the Alsops' villa with arms outstretched, his almost too classically handsome nordic features lit by pure joy as he hugged his friend, scattered John's reservations as the sun had dispersed the morning mists. The German had even beaten Jenny to embrace him. She stood by laughing before it was her turn to hug John, which she did with far more restraint, settling for a quick brush of lips on her blushing cheek.

To John's deep discomfort, that restraint remained painfully in the foreground. Of course, Horst occupied a great deal of the short time of the weekend, so that John could explain their friend's presence as the reason for it. But then, after the family attendance at matins on Sunday, Horst made his loud and pointed comments on the necessity of 'the lovebirds' having some precious time to themselves, almost pushing John and Jenny towards John's motor car, with the blessing of the Alsop elders' tolerant laughter. The couple were waved off, and John found himself driving in a silence from his pretty companion more jarring than the throaty roar of the engine as the little car tackled the familiar, steeply winding road up to the western side of Derwent Water.

He had chosen his route deliberately, without reference to Jenny, and soon he was pulling off the narrow road at one of their favourite spots high above the lake, which gleamed silver and then dark, almost charcoal, as the sun danced behind the high, summery clouds. When John stretched his arm over her shoulders, he sensed at once the unnatural stiffness, the unyield-ingness of her posture. 'Have I done something wrong?' he asked rawly.

She didn't meet his look. 'No, of course not. I'm just a bit – tired, that's all. It's been – having to entertain Horst, keep him amused. As well as working each day. I felt I had to make the effort. Get out with him in the evenings and so on. A bit wear-ing, that's all.'

John was struck with contrition. 'I know. I'm sorry, Jenny. I wish I could have helped. If he'd come over earlier – at Easter. But it's difficult. The way Mam feels. I tried again to talk to her—'

'Oh, I'm sure you wouldn't want to upset your mother!' she cut in so waspishly that John was taken aback. He coloured deeply.

'I'm not defending her. But I can appreciate her feeling. I should've thought you would, too,' he couldn't help adding, reproachfully.

'No, I can't, frankly. If everyone took her attitude, there'd be no progress made at all, would there? Or is Christian forgiveness just a nice little myth we keep for sermons on Sunday mornings? I'm sure there are thousands of German wives, and mothers, who grieve still for their lost ones.'

He pulled his arm from her shoulder, yanked at the starter,

roaring the engine back to life. 'We'll drive on a bit. No point in staying here.' He had no need to explain how closely he associated it with happier, more tender memories.

Her mouth pulled together, she stared ahead. 'I'm sorry, John. I didn't mean to upset you. It's something you'll have to put up with, I'm afraid. That sometimes there are people who have opinions that don't always agree with your mother's.'

He drove badly, almost blindly. He could feel his trembling anger, and his confusion, for he could not properly understand why he felt so deeply disturbed. Why he felt himself torn so vitally. When eventually he glanced across at Jenny, he saw that her head was bent, her chin on her chest, and that the tears were flowing silently, her mascara running on to her cheek.

He slowed so suddenly that it was lucky there was no Sunday driver close behind. He pulled into the steep bank of spiky grass in front of a drystone wall, and let the engine die. He groped for his handkerchief and passed it on to her lap, then he put his arm once again around her shoulders. He swallowed hard, 'Don't let's quarrel,' he said miserably. She didn't answer, but her dark blonde hair shook almost angrily, then her chin dropped again, and she clutched the handkerchief to her, her shoulders heaved, and she sobbed noisily. He twisted awkwardly, tried to take her in his arms, to pull her head down to him. She half resisted. Distracted, his gaze fell on her knees, where her rayon stockings sparkled in the sunshine. He murmured huskily, 'I miss you so much, Jen. It's awful being away from you for so long. I love you.'

This time her head bobbed in acknowledgement, but sadly, still. She gave a convulsive heave, snuffled chokingly, then blew into the handkerchief, and dabbed at her eyes. Her make-up had run, her face looked blotched, smeared with her grief, her nose pinkly shining. She was far from the glamorous poise she aimed for, and his heart constricted with his love for her.

'Why don't we just go ahead? We love each other. Let's not go through all this any longer. Marry me, Jen?' He sounded desperate, pleading. He didn't care. That was how he felt. Suddenly, he felt an enormous threat to their love and happiness surrounding them.

To his dismay, the fit of weeping which she was having some success at controlling seized her again and her breast heaved once more; her frame shook with the violence of her desolation. Dumb now, and afraid, he held her as closely as he could in that awkward little space. Long minutes slipped by, before, once more, she blew and sniffled and dabbed vigorously, and finally let her tears subside.

Gently, she eased herself from his grasp, and rummaged in her handbag to begin repairing the ravages to her features. 'You haven't answered my question,' he said, his heart thudding.

'I can't,' she said wearily.

'Can't what? Answer or marry?' His smile was crooked, part of their overwhelming sadness. All at once the significance of the 'I' struck him. Not 'we'. No qualifications, about practicalities, about waiting. The flat finality of her response alarmed him. Yet somehow, compassionately, he sensed that he should not pursue it now.

As though in tune with him, she said softly, 'It's not a good time for me. Not just now. A girl thing. Please be patient.'

Oh, God. A girl thing! Her monthly period? he wondered, feeling the beginnings of a blush stirring. She ought to say something, come out with it. They were going to spend their lives together. Make love. There should be nothing they couldn't say. Or should he know anyway? Was it something a fellow – a fiancé – should be able to recognize? He leaned in to her, kissed her damp temple tenderly, without passion, to make up for his hopeless, helpless ignorance. Patted her silk knee, then snatched his hand away again. He started up the engine once more.

When they got back the others were sitting down to Sunday lunch. 'I'm not hungry. I'll get something later,' Jenny said, hurrying upstairs before anyone should note her red eyes, and John joined the family, struggling over his inner turmoil to be outgoing and lively, uncertain whether he was making a good job of it or not.

Jenny was palely withdrawn when she joined them later. He had no more opportunity to be alone with her before it was time for him to start on the long drive homewards. They hugged and kissed in the afternoon sun, bodies briefly clamped while the others studiously chatted and ignored them. 'Write me a long letter,' he pleaded into her sweet-blonde hair and she nodded. But he felt her vulnerable eyes flinching from his, and again that disturbing sense of alarm and loss swept over him. 'I love you.' She nodded, put her hands on his upper arms, gently released his hold.

Horst had said he would ride a little way with him, and enjoy the walk back. As they drove through the quiet Sunday streets of the market town, John told him, 'I don't like leaving Jenny like this. We don't see enough of each other. I wish we could get married right away.'

'Of course. She is a beautiful. girl. You are a lucky man.' He put his hand on John's leg, pressed his fingers into the flesh above the knee. He kept it there, and John felt deeply uncomfortable, had to make a conscious effort not to jerk his leg away. We don't do that here, he wanted to say. We don't touch like that. But then he recalled the way Horst hugged him, clasping him to his breast, pressing his face into his shoulder. He had done so when they had said goodbye that first time, in Germany. 'You British!' Horst had laughed, as though he knew exactly what was going through John's mind. And that pomade, or cologne, that he wore. He could smell it now. Pleasant, of course, not offensive. John was ashamed of the word 'pansy' which nudged its way unpleasantly into his mind, and he pushed it angrily away. What nonsense! He had given ample proof of how interested in females he was. They were just different over there, that was all.

'You will come in summer to stay? You and your Jenny? You promise! I can fix up nice apartment for you. You do not need to stay in my house with my parents.' He laughed. The fingers dug tightly into John's flesh again. 'You will have chance to be alone together. Good, yes? To make love so much.'

John smiled, moved his leg, the hand left him. His mind rioted with the hazy vision of sexual desire – and gratification. He did not tell Horst that they were both virgins still. 'I hope we can make it.' He smiled. 'I'm looking forward to it very much.'

Jenny lay back in the scented water, watched the little islands of bubbles breaking up, dissolving around her. The warmth hugged her caressingly, she felt the ache deep in her belly eased. Very lightly, she touched her breasts, teased the nipples, which tingled and peaked, and she shivered at their sensitivity. A corresponding spasm tightened the muscles of her thighs, and she caressed herself between her legs, even more gently, with her flannel, clenched her buttocks at the fierce thrill she gave herself.

Her face felt hot. The tears squeezed perilously close to the surface of her eyes once more. She banished them. She would not cry any more. Her head throbbed, she had wept so much today, especially after John's departure, when she had immediately retreated to her room. She lifted one foot out of the water, held it aloft, wiggling her toes, observing the shape of her calf, the drip of the water. Another sexual spasm caught her, and she moved, her belly lifted slightly, she studied the dark cap of her hair against its paleness.

It was always like this when her period was due. She both hated and thrilled to the arousal she could feel coursing through her, her awareness of the nerve centres of her sexuality. Now, more than ever, she wished she could make love with John. Of course with John! The heat rose, enflaming her, the tears prickled once more.

She relived vividly the touch of Horst's hands, on her neck, her shoulders, as he massaged her. Such thin, delicate hands, like his features. Too good-looking almost for a man. Too softly unblemished, too smoothly beautiful. And his manner, too. So strange, so knowing. As though he could see right into her, into her secrets, the way John never could, or would want to.

That was what had undermined her, why she had not been able to resist, to behave properly, as she had always managed to do with John. There was something almost sinister, hypnotic, about the way Horst had got so close to her, to those disturbing inner feelings, sensations she had kept so secret all her life. It was – she blushed fiercely at the thought – as though his intuition was feminine, that he knew her as well as she knew herself.

Even his voice could be like a caress. It was deep, sensual, yet almost androgynous in a way, like his touches had been. 'You are so tense, my dear. So rigid, with your inhibitions. Just relax. Look. Feel. The tension, in your body and your mind.'

He had laughed, with supreme confidence, as though he did not even contemplate her refusal, her rejection of his impropriety. His hands, long fingers, at the base of her neck, pressing down on her, hard, under the collar of her blouse, into her skin, the hollows, the bunching of her muscles. Then on, widening, over her shoulders, while she bent her head forward, and he swept the hair off the nape of her neck, so that she thought of Mary Queen of Scots, Lady Jane Grey, being prepared for execution. His laughter, slow and strong, made even the idea of her objection seem prissy and foolishly prudish.

Then his hands were at her neck again, his fingers tracing the line of her jaw, and she was shaking. Now she did make a stumbling protest, but without the strength to accompany it as he pulled her back, so that her head lay folded in his lap, and she looked up at the fair, golden beauty of his face, his white teeth, smiling, his fingers stroking her hair, and her face, on which tears now shone wetly. When he moved again, capturing her face between his hands, holding her as he swivelled round, soared darkly above her, she did not resist, held her mouth still while his descended, covered her lips. Slowly, helplessly, those lips opened, and he was kissing her passionately, lingeringly, drawing out of her such depths of sensation she thought she must faint.

He brushed aside her tearful outrage, her shame, as if it were totally meaningless. To him it was. He talked shockingly. 'You are still a virgin? At how old? Twenty? With John – you have never made love? How is this possible?'

He told her of the new sexual mores in Germany. She had seen enough of it on her trip to believe he was telling the truth. 'It is not healthy to be like you British. To be so full of repression, yes? You are ashamed of your body. You do not wish me to see you naked. You should be proud. If you love someone. Sex is a natural thing. Not to do it, when you want so much to do, is what is unnatural.'

He showed her photographs, proudly, with no shame at all, of naked or almost naked girls, in the most public of circumstances. There was some kind of pageant, depicting scenes of Germanic history, or legend. The naked females rode on horseback, displayed their bodies for the crowds of onlookers to stare at. She was shocked, yet fascinated. When he kissed her a second time, and held her, he put his hand on her leg, moved it under her skirt, moved even higher until, belatedly, she twisted free, clutched at herself, held him off, ashamed not of what he had done but of what she had felt, the damp excitement and hunger she had experienced.

He touched her whenever he had the opportunity. With his knowing laugh, an oddly innocent glee, like a worldly school-boy. It seemed to negate all her inbred standards of decency, to render them useless. She was dreading John's visit at the week-end. By the time he came, she felt as guilty as if she had already been unfaithful to him. In fact, in essence she had, by her complicity in Horst Zettel's wicked behaviour. In not stopping it, branding it as intolerable, she had condoned it. She *was* guilty. It confirmed the doubts she had been having, long before Horst's visit, about her relationship with John.

'I don't know if I love him,' she had confessed to Horst, near the end of their week together.

'You are ignorant. Untutored,' the German told her, in his carelessly forthright manner. 'You know nothing of yourself, or of men. Let me teach you.'

She knew what he was saying, what he was asking, and she made a show of her shock and outrage. 'You are evil!' she squeaked, 'utterly terrible! You want to corrupt me.' He laughed in that deep way, and she found herself afraid, and more excited than she had any right to feel. There was a feeling that she had not answered his request at all, that it was still hanging over them.

Tonight, when her parents had said that after evensong they were going to the Maddisons for supper, Jenny felt the tension between her and Horst enclosing them like the oppression of a thunderstorm. Her brother, Paul, and sister, Joan, were going with their mother and father. Jenny had already made excuses for their guest and for herself. 'We'll be back about ten,' her mother said. 'You'll get something for Horst and you, won't you?'

'Yes, Mummy. I'll probably have a bath and an early night. Work in the morning, and I feel a bit queasy.' She put a hand on her tummy, exchanged one of those looks of telepathic feminality with her mother, who nodded sympathetically.

When she heard his steps on the stairs, her heart raced fearfully. He made no attempt to disguise his approach. When he put his head round the door she was already crouching forward, the warm cloth spread over her chest, her arms folded, hugging it to her, hiding herself – Her knees were slightly hunched, and pressed very tightly together. She gasped, her voice soft, shaky. 'Please don't. Get out.' She sat there, her back curved, her chin down, not turning to look at him.

'You did not lock the door,' he said. She could hear the deep note of mockery and laughter in his tone.

'You shouldn't – you knew – we've been taught never lock the bathroom door.' She was breathless, had to force the words out. She felt she was about to cry again. 'Leave me, please. Don't look at me. I've never been – naked – with anyone.' The tears came, but quietly. She sniffled like a little girl.

He came forward easily, and now she was giddy, trembling violently. Her dark head bowed lower, her protest was a feeble whisper. He perched on the edge of the tub, beside her arm, and she felt his hand on her cold, wet shoulder. 'No more games, Jenny.' There was no laughter in his voice now, only a hint of patient inexorability. 'Now you are – you say – grown up, yes? You are young woman. It is time for honesty now.'

She shivered, looked up imploringly, the tears trickling down her flushed face as he leaned over her. Gently, he took her wrists, and drew them away from her shoulders, held on to them, keeping them away from her body. The flannel clung for a second, then fell into her lap.

Chapter Fourteen

Teddy stared at Rosie in dismay. He still could not take in the import of her words, nor her casual way of telling him that she was leaving. That they might never see each other again. She even looked different, in the ugly, stiff new uniform. The belted jacket with its pouched pockets hung on her, looked far too big, the cheap material stiff as canvas. The ugly, wide skirt, still creased from the way it had been folded, was no better. It came down almost to the top of her dusty leather boots, allowing a glimpse of just a few inches of her black-stockinged shins. She looked like a schoolgirl, or some slip of a peasant girl, in spite of the supposed military styling. The loose beret came low over her forehead, hid her cropped black hair entirely.

He had loved the way she normally looked: bareheaded, the ragged jacket, the voluminous man's shirt, the trousers, their ample waist bunched round her, gathered with the plaited belt. Her flashing smile, the dark, gypsy looks, laughing eyes. They had been lovers for only two months, yet he seemed to have known her slim, hard little body a lifetime. A body so slight it could seem as yet unformed, yet the happy ferocity of its uncomplicated loving drove him wild.

He had expected something to happen, for them to be reprimanded, for Leonid to interfere in some way. Yet all that only added to the excitement, the need for her which he felt constantly. Even the guilt when he thought of Marian and the baby could not detract from his fascination with her. Now, it seemed incredible that they had lasted this long, but he was stunned, nevertheless, by the suddenness of its ending, and by Rosie's bald acceptance of it. Worst of all, it seemed that she had initiated it.

'I'm going back on the truck tonight,' she said. 'That's why I'm done up like a dog's dinner.' She gestured at the crackling uniform, and gave a brave imitation of her usual face-splitting grin.

'Is this that bastard Leonid's doing?' He glared at her wildly. 'Let me have a word with him.'

'No, Teddy, please. You know it was bound to come anyway. They were going to transfer me out. They don't want us here – the women, I mean.' She scowled fiercely, shook her head. 'And I've played right into their hands.' He stared at her, at a loss, and she gave a little grimace, hunching her shoulders, with a sheepish smile which made her appear even more youthful. She glanced about them, as though she wanted to seek a more private place than this busy thoroughfare that ran through their temporary camp of long wooden huts.

'Listen,' she resumed, with a reluctance he could clearly sense. 'I have to go. I can't stay on. It's medical. I've to go to San Sebastian. There's a place there. A clinic.' He was still staring uncomprehendingly. She gave an impatient, irritable toss of her head, as though he ought to have caught her meaning. 'For God's sake, Teddy! I'm going to have an abortion.'

He gaped at her. Somewhere inside his head, he could hear a savage scream of laughter. You've done it again, my boy! Got her up the spout! His mouth opened, he fought for words. 'But you can't – I mean, I thought you were, you know, taking precautions.' A string of obscenities raced through his boiling brain. He even sounded like the last time! He had an appalling sense of helplessness, of hopeless ignorance, and foolishness.

Rosie smiled, but tautly, not in her typical, carefree manner. 'Come off it, my man! You knew there was nothing like that when we shagged.'

He winced, coloured hotly, still hating her to use foul terms like that to refer to their loving. 'But surely . . .' he let out his breath in a great sigh of hopeless frustration. 'You can't – let them do it. You'll have to have it. The baby.'

There was a split second of hesitation, then she gazed straight at him, her face lifting in that challenging way she had. 'Don't worry. It's not yours,' she said matter-of-factly. 'I've worked it out. It can't be.'

He gazed helplessly. He felt like a fighter hanging on the ropes, the blows thudding into his unprotected body, one after the other. 'What are you on about? Don't be mad. It must be—'

'What do ye want? To populate the whole planet? You've got a kid at home, don't forget. And a wife!' Her voice went back to its flat tone. 'I missed my monthly just before we started doing it. There was a feller when we were up in the forest, above Laguardia. We got a bit pissed. Stayed out all night. He's your man all right. Why'd you think I never bothered – about frenchies and all that? I had a feeling.' She shrugged, gave another brave smile. 'Ah, I'll be all right, don't fret. That's one thing about the doctors in this mob, they don't care about that sort of thing, thank God! Not like those sanctimonious buggers back home. They'd have me roasting in the fires of Hell for all time.'

'I'll come and see you,' he promised desperately. He made to grab her, and she held up her arms, fending him off.

'Let's not make a song and dance of it, eh? You'd best be on your way, before someone comes looking for you. It's been a great gas, Teddy, hasn't it? You're a good man, and no mistake. But it's the end of the road for us. And best way, too.' She darted forward, clumsily stabbed a kiss at him and withdrew again. 'If ye want my advice – which I'm sure you don't – you'll get yourself back to that wife and child of yours before you get your arse shot off here. They're making a right old balls-up of it all round, I'd say. Take care. So long, comrade! I've got masses to do.' She turned and ran from him. He stood, watched her go, the ridiculous skirt flapping stiffly. She didn't turn round again, and he never moved until she was out of sight.

Everything seemed unreal for hours afterwards. His friends showed sympathy, and tact, too. They left him largely alone, no one made jokes at his expense, or tried to draw him out, and he was deeply grateful to them. He felt closer to them than ever. After the early evening meal, Leonid came and sought him out, walked with him to the hill of coarse, tussocky grass and low brushwood which they used as a makeshift firing range. 'Are you all right?' the commander asked gravely.

Teddy nodded. 'I still can't take it in. You know . . . believe it. I had no idea.' He glanced enquiringly at Leonid. 'She said it wasn't mine.'

Leonid shrugged. 'It is the problem. Times like these, in war. Not good. It is better she go.'

All at once, Teddy felt too weary and dispirited to argue. I loved her! he wanted to cry out, thought again of Rosie's flat, disinterested voice as she made her announcement. His eyes stung, his throat clogged with his hurt. It was from that moment that his disillusionment grew. Her words stayed with him, nagging away inside: 'Get yourself back to that wife and child of yours'. He realized that any enthusiasm or belief he had in the cause of the forces he was fighting for had withered. He kept thinking about those terrified young prisoners, soiling themselves in their final fear. The pop-eyed priest, the mumbling indignity of his ending. The butchered corpses after that first air attack, the stench. Since then he'd seen women and children reduced to carcasses like that, or weeping and damaged, scarred physically and mentally, and, like him, uncomprehending the savage madness released all around them.

The Fascists had carved a great wedge through the country, splitting it in two. Not long after Rosie had left for the northern coast, their unit was part of a great push south-east, to try to break through the enemy barrier cutting them off from the Republican forces in the south. In the blazing heat of June and July, he witnessed more air attacks, saw their advance halt, turn into a retreat. They passed through the ruins of villages where the inhabitants had cheered them on their way only weeks before. Now the villages were deserted, or small groups would appear, watch them in sullen silence. Once, when they bivouacked for the night, a figure dressed all in black appeared, and began cursing them, her cracked voice growing shriller and shriller. She spat at them, until, eventually, one of the sentries drove her away, pushing her until she stumbled and fell, hitting her across her bent shoulders with his rifle butt. No one protested, glad only when her sobbing imprecations faded to nothingness. Teddy felt sick with self-disgust.

People were beginning to disappear. Men just slipped away, their names were recorded, nobody said much. At the beginning of August Teddy sought out Leonid.

'I want to leave.'

'What do you think?' the Russian shouted. 'You can just walk from us? I can have you shot! I have the power!' His eyes were veined, bloodshot, his beard unkempt, the black curls sprouting in all directions.

'I don't want to just sneak away, like a dog,' Teddy explained, 'but I've had enough. I need to go home. I have a child I've never seen.'

'I tell you – you are soldier. You cannot leave. You have duty.'

'I have a duty to my family,' Teddy said, aware of the savage irony of his words. The mocking laughter screamed forth inside his head.

'You must make request!' Leonid yelled, the spittle clinging to his lip. 'Things must be done military. By procedure.'

Teddy drew himself to attention, clicked his heels. 'Sir! I request permission to leave!'

'Get out,' Leonid said, his voice scarcely more than a whisper.

Next morning, the company commander sent for him. He handed him a whole sheaf of documents, and a considerable wad of money. 'Here are your orders. You will proceed on leave today. You have done well, comrade. Thank you.'

The anticlimax of his leaving this group of men with whom he had shared so many dangers over the past months was part of the dreamlike quality which had settled over him. He felt numb, cut off from what was happening around him. The following day he arrived in Bilbao, and reported to the group headquarters there, a scene of apparently insolvable chaos. He moved from office to office, from harassed clerk to clerk, handing over the documents Leonid had given him, clutching them tightly when they were returned and he was moved on elsewhere. Finally, someone gave him a large, flimsy sheet with several impressive stamps on it. He was told to take it to the dock, where arrangements would be made to ship him out. When he got there he was told to report again the next day, that he would be transported across the Bay of Biscay to the French port of Nantes, in a small coal-burner sailing the following evening.

He scrounged a meal with the men working at the dockside, and was told he could doss down in a shed for the night. Faced with hours of idleness, he had a sudden powerful urge to head off along the coast, to try to find Rosie. She might have been lying about the baby, telling him it wasn't his, to make the parting easier for them. But that wasn't Rosie, he acknowledged. She was too straight, too devastatingly honest to use that as a subterfuge, even to be kind. On the other hand, she might simply be wrong in thinking that it was this other nameless one who had made her pregnant. He knew little about such things, except that he recalled it had taken Marian some time before she was sure. She had kept it from him, she said, because she wasn't certain for a while. In any case, whoever had implanted his seed in Rosie, its killing would have been done long ago now. She could be anywhere, perhaps no longer in Spain at all. And she no longer wanted him. If she did, she would have found him again.

He walked away from the busy area of the dock, found a pile of old timbers on which he sprawled in the enervating sun, hiding his eyes from the glare of the water. He lay back, closed his eyes, let the heat soak into his body, let the tense muscles relax. Did he love Rosie? Certainly she excited him. Even now he felt his body react to the memory of their lovemaking. She was so vital, so alive, she fascinated him. But there had always been that sense of temporariness about their relationship. The last thing he associated her with was a settled, stable life; with children; with one man. She had given him fair warning. 'Bird of passage, that's me,' she grinned. He hadn't minded. It was part of the attraction, that heady impermanence. After all, they were living literally with death, for most of the time.

Now, as always, came the comparisons. Marian's fair, voluptuous body, surrendered to him. It had excited him, too, as had her ready acceptance to yield to him, her placid deferral to him, in everything. But it was not, could never be, as it was with Rosie. That tingling knife edge of vitality, the electricity of their loving, both physical and mental. Marian's passivity had come to feel smothering, until he was truly scared of that feeling of being trapped, sucked down into a sugary nothingness. He couldn't stand it. He had fled – like Rosie, a bird of passage. Could he stand it now?

He stayed, drowsed away the evening, and the fitful night, the long following day, until, the sun beginning to tinge with blood pink over his shoulder, he squatted on the crowded rusty deck of the little steamer as she rolled out her clouds of black smoke and shuddered over the placid water, taking him away from the land he had been prepared to give his life for, whose bloody fight he had never really felt part of, but during which he had, in some ways, grown to manhood.

It took him a further two and a half days of travel, north through France, sitting in the uncomfortable third-class rail carriages on the wooden seats, shared with peasants and their offspring, and their animals and wicker crates of smelly poultry. He spent a wet night in Cherbourg, again sleeping rough in a public shelter close to the sea-front. He had enough money left to purchase a modestly priced bed somewhere, but he wanted to take as much home with him as he could. The inconveniences of insufficient food and no lodgings were penances he considered well deserved.

The nearer he got to home the more anxious and sickened he felt. Like a boy who has run away and now has to return to face the exacting music. The day he landed in England, after almost a year, was his mother's birthday – 10 August. He worked out her age. Forty-three. He wondered if she would be having a cele-bration. Aunt I and Uncle Dan, of course. Would Grandma Wright be there? He doubted it. She hardly ever left the house these days. John and Jenny. They must be on holiday now. John had started at some boarding-school in Corbridge, had been there since the beginning of the year. Why had he and Jenny delayed their marriage? Perhaps they've been made wary by my fine example he thought, with grim humour. He pictured their faces when this unshaven, tramplike figure turned up out of the blue.

Then he pulled himself up short in startled dismay. All at once he realized he had been thinking of his return to Hexham. The prodigal son. Never once had he thought about Marian – and his baby. Of course he must go to them. He knew where they were living well enough. He remembered Mam picking out the site of the house, their ride out on the tram to the terminus at Low Fell, and their walk out to the very edge of town, where the estate lay, pegged out among the fields.

'We must call in on your grandma,' May told them. 'She'd never forgive us, this close.' The Wrights' house was less than a mile from the new Chow Dene building site. He had been nervous about seeing his grandmother. There was no doubt that she would heartily disapprove of the marriage, and the circumstances that had made it necessary. She could be a fearful snob, as he well remembered. Though his mother always loyally defended her, and reminded the boys constantly of how much she owed to their father's mother for her support after his death, Teddy knew that there had been tensions, that, at the beginning she had not thought his mam good enough for his dad. Like mother like son, he thought, and felt pity for Marian's pale, tense face, for the way the silent girl was shaking with her own fear.

Marian had enthused about the new house, then he had caught her glancing warily at him, curbing her own delight in case it should annoy him. It was that about her which drove him to distraction, made him sick at himself for his sudden urges to hurt her, which was so cruelly easy to do.

Yes, he must go straight to his wife and child, assume the responsibility he had shirked. He tried to push away his reluctance to face Marian, his spontaneous wish that he could see his family first. Mam. Tell her how sorry he was. And John. He was looking forward so much to seeing his brother again, and the pretty girl he was going to marry. He hoped they would be happy together. Not like me. The thought came as a stab of pain, and he vowed solemnly he would make Marian happy, never let her see or know the secrets of his heart.

'You have been very foolish, Herr Wright. Or perhaps you are in fact very clever.' The affable looking individual stared at John. His plump, jovial features, and his expression of tolerant amusement were at odds with the serious threat he represented. 'Please. Don't talk about your rights as a citizen of Great Britain. You have abused our hospitality, broken our laws. Laws your government expects you to respect and to obey when you visit. We have enough evidence to accuse you of spying. We can have you detained.'

'I was just trying to help someone. A family friend. That's all. Fräulein Arad is just a schoolgirl. Her family want to give her the opportunity to study – train abroad.'

The official waved aside John's explanation. 'The papers; the travel documents you brought for her; the money. We have a very strict code of conduct here, as I'm sure you were aware when you embarked on this affair. Clearly you sympathize with those elements who are subverting the state here. But whatever your views, however divergent, you cannot ride roughshod over the law here, Herr Wright. As I have said, it is a serious matter.'

John felt his head spinning. The tight nausea of his fear gripped him again. Distractedly, his mind raced over the sequence of events which had led to this unreal moment in state police headquarters in the German capital.

He had been looking forward to escaping – that was how he saw his coming trip to Germany as the term drew to its busy close in July. The letter from Jenny had floored him, even though, in some hidden compartment of his mind, he found he had been expecting something like it for a while: 'For some time now I've felt full of doubts. For both our sakes, I think we should no longer feel committed by any former promises, and so I'm taking the step I feel I have to. I hope you can understand how painful that is for me. I've wept, a lot, had to force myself to go through with this. But I still feel I have to do it. It's not that there's anybody else. Please believe me. I'm still very fond of you – still love you, if you can understand that. But like I said, it's a feeling I can't ignore any longer, that I need some time, more time, without any obligations.

'You're still my closest friend. Can you believe that? And can you forgive me? I want you to stay my friend, always. Perhaps all I need is this time on my own to get things straight in my mind. Then who knows? But, for the moment, like I said, it's something that I just have to do. Let's just be friends for now.

'I can't come to Germany with you, with things like this. It will be better if we don't see each other for a while. Let's leave it until after the summer at least. I'm going down to Devon, with Rosemary and Gerald.'

The ring was there, neatly hidden in the folded sheets. He had phoned as soon as he received the letter. Mrs Alsop had answered, her tone sad and compassionate. 'She's really too upset to talk now, John. Do try to understand. Please leave things a while.'

Devastated, close to tears himself, he had whispered his goodbyes, while part of him screamed with fury at her sympathy. It was what she wanted, what they all wanted, damned smug, middle class snobs! He calmed down, his misery blotting out his anger, and his honesty forcing him to face the fact that it was Jenny alone who had done this, For whatever reason. And she was deeply unhappy too, he knew it. But that could not ease his pain. He loved her, and there was nothing in the world to keep them apart, except her own compulsion to do so.

He had to dig deep into his character, to find a strength he didn't know he possessed, to carry on. He daren't let his guard down. His mother understood something of what he was going through, and he came dangerously near to being unmanned by her compassion for him. He fled from it.

When his Uncle David – David Golding, his Aunt Cissy's husband – wrote to him and asked if he could arrange to see him, he was intrigued, and more than happy to have a little mystery to distract him from his gloom, if only for a short while.

He had never had a great deal to do with his Aunt Cissy, especially since her marriage just over ten years ago. She was already thirty-two when she suddenly returned to the north, leaving her job in London, with David Golding in tow. John remembered her chiefly as an exciting, exotic figure, a 'glamour puss', as Aunt I and his mother labelled her. Quite the opposite of the serious-looking individual, already well up the ladder of commercial success, to whom she became engaged, then married within three months.

For most of their ten years together, she and her husband had lived either in the south or abroad on the continent. John still vividly remembered the occasion of the opening of the New Tyne Bridge, the ceremony performed by King George himself. He and Teddy and May had got special seats in a stand with local dignitaries because of Uncle David's influence. His company was part of the steel industry and had connections with the north-eastern firm Dorman Long, which had built the bridge.

The marriage had not produced any children. There was even a whiff of scandal at one time, when John and Teddy had been in their mid-teens. Discreet whispers of Cissy's dangerous behaviour, a liaison with some other man. Uncle Dan, Aunt I and his mother used to discuss it, and clam up, with compressed lips and knowing looks when the boys appeared. He and Teddy were intrigued, vicariously thrilled at the idea of such a wicked aunt. However, the marriage had endured. For the last four years they had lived in the north-east once more, in a fashionable Victorian property in Gosforth. Part of the 'smart city set', as Dan mockingly dubbed them.

John was puzzled by the air of secrecy hinted at by David when he made arrangements to pick John up from the school and take him somewhere for a meal. He was a distinguished-looking man, more of an ascetic intellectual than ruthless tycoon, John thought, studying him with new interest. He wore thick-framed, dark spectacles. His hair, and severely neat moustache, cut in vertical lines at the ends of his upper lip, in the style of the German leader, were already grey. He looked considerably older than his still good-looking wife, though there was an age difference of no more than three years between them.

He had always given John the impression of being a very private individual, not shy, but distant, lacking in easy, effusive charm. Now was no exception. 'I'd rather you didn't mention our meeting to your Aunt Cissy, John. Really, I'd prefer it not to be mentioned to anyone in the family. It's a matter of some delicacy.'

Deliberately, he waited until they were settled at a table in the country hotel he had chosen, and had ordered their meal, before he broached the reason for their rendezvous. 'I hear you're going over to Germany. To spend some time with that friend of yours. There's something I'd like you to do for me. I'll understand perfectly if you say you can't. We'll say no more about it, no hard feelings either way, I hope.'

John felt the brown eyes fixed on him. There was a slight pause, as though his uncle were deciding on the wisdom of proceeding. All at once John realized that behind the contained, urbane manner, there was a real hesitancy, an uncertainty.

'I expect you're aware – even though Cissy and I have never made anything of it – that I have Jewish connections. My family – I'm not a practising Jew, neither was my father. But our roots are Jewish.'

John nodded, wondered what he should say, found there was nothing he *could* say. That's quite all right, it doesn't bother me. How could he say anything as patronizing as that? He waited for David to continue.

'I hope you won't find what I'm about to say offensive, in view of your friendship with young Germans, but you must know the way things are going over there – with regard to Jewish people. These Nuremberg Laws that they passed a couple of years ago – they've taken away citizenship from so many. Forbidden Jews to marry with Germans of other faiths. And that's just the beginning many people feel. It's a campaign that has been going on for a long time now. And it could get much worse.

'A cousin of my father's has been in touch. Asked for help. He needs travel documents for his daughter. They want her to come over here to study. But all the normal channels are being blocked. I have some papers that will help to get her out.'

John agreed readily enough to carry the documents, in their special folder, which David had brought with him. He insisted on showing them to John, explaining each one to him, though John did not pay much attention. His uncle gave him the address of a legal firm in Berlin, and also a telephone number. 'Louis Schevitz is a cousin of the Arad family. He will see that the papers are safely delivered to them.'

He paused significantly, and reached out to put his hand over John's forearm. The gesture, from such a reserved and private man, was not lost on John, who was embarrassed. 'I'm very grateful to you, my boy. It will mean so much to them.' His brow furrowed, he gave a small, sombre shake of his head. 'I think families like the Arads should look for ways of emigrating. I mean all of them. There's no future for them under the National Socialists.'

He insisted John take fifty pounds to add to his holiday fund. 'You must let me show my gratitude. On behalf of Sara's family,' he said, when John protested. 'And listen: be careful, won't you? Don't take any risks. Make sure you hand over the folder to this man Schevitz. Nobody else. I'm not being melodramatic, but as I said, things are not good over there just now.' He made a visible effort to lighten the atmosphere, flashed John a smile all the warmer for its rarity. 'But have a splendid holiday. It's a wonderful place in many ways. I've had lots of good times there. In happier days.'

John had felt rather dashing, his romanticism spiced by the idea of secrecy, and the Pimpernel flavour of the adventure. Rescuing a young maiden from the clutches of a blatantly racist regime certainly smacked of derring-do. But there seemed little of such high-flown excitement about the mundane task once he arrived in Germany. He had the good sense not to confide the true nature of his undertaking to Horst, putting him off with some vague reference to seeing someone in Berlin on his uncle's behalf. 'Some family matter or other, I'm not sure what it's about. I just promised to see someone for him, drop some papers off.'

Horst was attached to one of the government ministries, working on some research studies which followed on from his university course. He was on vacation during John's visit. 'Of course, I must make certain I am free for my dear friend,' he told him, with that engaging grin.

His handsome face clouded with sympathy when Jenny's name was mentioned, as it was within minutes of their meeting. 'I am so sorry for you, my friend. But I am sure it is not final.' John had already written briefly, explaining that Jenny would not be with him, and that the engagement was 'in suspension'. 'Jenny is good girl. She loves you so much. That I know. She told me when I stay with her. All will be well.' John could not help responding to his sympathy, and his warmth.

They stayed with his parents, in a village near Magdeburg. When John mentioned the task he had promised to carry out for his uncle, Horst was enthusiastic. 'That is good. We will take trip to Berlin. We spend some days there. I know it very well now. I spend much of my work-time there. I know room where we stay. Not at all expensive. For me and my friend.'

The room, which they shared, was in the south-eastern suburb of Kopenick. The landlady clearly knew Horst, and made them welcome.

'Listen. Let me get this business out of the way, then we can enjoy ourselves,' John said. 'I just need to telephone this firm. Make an appointment. It shouldn't take long.'

'What is the company name? I find the number for you.'

'It's fine. I have the number. I'll just nip out and find a phone-box. I won't be long.'

'There is no need. Frau Kupe will allow you to use the telephone. I ask her for you.'

John made the call from Frau Kupe's own rather overpowering sitting-room. A portrait of Adolf Hitler frowned sternly down during his brief conversation, a fact which John found privately amusing. Louis Schevitz came quickly to the phone, and John gave his explanation. The voice answered in carefully precise English. 'I will meet you at two p.m. It is possible? Good. I will be at the Zoo Station. At the entrance. I find you there.'

Horst offered to go with him. 'No, it's fine, honestly. I'll find it. I can always take a cab. Where shall we meet afterwards?'

'Perhaps it is better you return here. You may be long time. Perhaps you have many things to discuss.'

'No, no. It shouldn't take long at all,' John assured him. 'But that sounds like a good idea. I'll see you back here then.'

As soon as John had left the lodging house, Horst made a phone call himself, spoke briefly, then turned to Frau Kupe, who was standing just outside the door, hands clasped over her apron. 'I'm afraid I have to go out, too, Mrs Kupe. If Mr Wright comes back before me, tell him I won't be long.'

She gave a little nod of the head. 'Yes, Mr Zettel.' She watched him go, thinking how youthful he looked. No more than a schoolboy, you'd think, with that pretty face of his, and that dimpled smile. A proper little darling. But she knew better. She had a number of guests of similar mettle. Always best to treat them with caution. You couldn't be too careful with these young party officials. High fliers, the lot of them. Shop their own mothers as soon as look at you.

Chapter Fifteen

Dora gaped at the darkly tanned, travel-weary figure standing on the top step. He had an untidy beard, just beginning to curl, and his once good suit was crumpled and bore the marks of recent hard wear. He was supporting a canvas rucksack by one shoulder strap.

'Hello, Dora. Don't you recognize me? Is Marian in?'

'Teddy!' Dora gave a shriek, whirled about, and left him standing there while she fled inside, this time screaming out Marian's name. Teddy smiled, stepped into the dim coolness of the hall, gratefully eased the rucksack from his shoulder and lowered it to the wooden floor. To his right a staircase led off, turning at right angles after three steps to continue upwards. The dark wood of the banister rails was highly polished. To his left he caught sight of his own face, with something of a shock at its gypsylike appearance, in the central mirror of a large coat and hat rack, also of dark wood. Several doors, in pristine white contrast, led off from this small square vestibule, from one of which came his wife, at a run.

Her yellow hair was tied in a scarf, emerging in tousled strands from the upper edges of the brightly dotted cloth. The youthful face, pink with exertion, was redder still, and its expression told her utter astonishment and confusion. She was wearing a sleeveless, summery blouse with its top buttons undone, showing the cleavage of her full breasts, the paler skin contrasting with her face and the light tan of her bare arms.

'I was working in the back,' she stammered, standing in front of him like a guilty schoolgirl, the simile reinforced by the grey ankle-socks and sturdy, dirty shoes. Her husky voice was soft, full of contrition. 'I didn't know – I had no idea. . . .'

Teddy felt his throat close, his eyes sting with tears. 'Come here!' he said gruffly, holding out his arms, and, with a wounded cry, she flung herself at him, buried her face in his neck and shoulder, and burst into a fit of weeping the effect of which he could feel through her entire frame as he held her tightly to him, his face tickled by her hair. He could smell the aroma of her fresh sweat and sweet femininity.

'Oh, God!' she sobbed. 'Thank God you're safe, Teddy. I thought I mightn't see you again, ever!'

'Shush.' He held her, savoured the cool, sweet smoothness of her upper arms, stroked the back of her head. 'Come on, lass! A bad penny like me. You know I always turn up in the end.' His vision was blurred, the tears were closer than ever. 'I'm sorry for everything,' he whispered into her ear.

Over her shoulder, he saw the grinning Dora. 'By, you've grown and all, haven't you? I hardly recognized you. Put the kettle on, there's a good lass, eh? I'm gasping for a decent cup of tea.' He held the still weeping figure a little away from him. 'And where's this bonny bairn of ours, then? I think it's high time I met me own daughter, don't you?'

'She's out the back. Having her afternoon sleep. I always try to make sure she gets plenty of fresh air. That's what's so nice having a garden.'

She led him through a small, modern kitchen, and a narrow, glass-roofed outhouse attached to the main house, which in turn led to the rear garden. The mark of taming civilization had already been laid on it in the few months of occupation. There was a postage-stamp-sized lawn of fresh green grass, the indi-

vidual blades showing, evidence of careful twice-daily water-
ings against the heat of summer. Its outer boundaries were still
pegged out, marked with string on which the tiny shreds of rags
still fluttered against marauding birds. It was clear no one was
allowed to set foot on it. The lawn was surrounded by neatly
levelled, weed-free flower-beds, with uniform clumps of herba-
cious border plants in whites and blues, and slender young rose
bushes supporting surprisingly fulsome blooms. At the further
end of the grass patch, away from the house, was a line of young
fruit trees, no taller than Teddy and bound to tall stakes. From
here on to the low, wooden boundary fences the ground was
uneven, with brown clay showing and tufts of hummocky grass,
to remind them of the undeveloped site it had been a short time
ago. On either side Teddy could see, between the rows of fences,
similar proud efforts of cultivation and the imposition of order.

There was a narrow path of concrete running along the rear
wall of the house. Other even narrower paths of crazy paving –
broken slabs begged or filched from the builders still working
across the untarmaced road – ran past the lawn and through the
flower-beds to the no man's land of miniature hillocks beyond
the fruit trees.

But Teddy's eyes were drawn to the high, black perambulator,
with its elegant, sprung-carriage shape, its huge, white-tyred
wheels, the gleaming, silvery swan-curve of its handles. Above
the folded hood rested a fine, white silk canopy, fringed with long
tassels, in the shade of which lay Edwina Helen, bundled and
swathed, in spite of the August warmth, her brown curls poking
out beneath the summer bonnet and resting on her creamy brow.
Her lips, slightly parted, were twin bows of pink perfection, the
curled lashes of silky brown rested on exquisitely dimpled cheeks.

Teddy was caught off-guard, in spite of his preparation, at the
surge of emotion. Unable to prevent himself, he turned automatically towards Marian again, compelled to whisper, 'Sorry.
I'm really sorry, Marian.'

She blushed and glanced typically down, away from the naked intensity of his look. 'It's all right,' she murmured, embarrassed. 'I think the world of her. I wouldn't be without her.'

He turned again, bent low, his head under the canopy, smelt the new, fragrant, unique baby smell of his daughter. 'Hello, Edwina. Your daddy's back now.'

'I call her Teddie,' Marian said, on a note of confession. She pulled a wry face. 'Your mam hates it. So does mine.'

She had already written and told him this. And why. 'It's fine by me,' he answered, straightening up. He gazed down at his child. 'Teddie it is then!'

There was a phone-box on the main Durham Road, at the top of the hill, where the first houses of the estate had been built. He and Marian wheeled the pram up there, after she had washed and changed into her best summer frock, insisting on putting on tan silk stockings and heeled shoes, in spite of the still warm day. He pushed, and she clung tightly to his arm. He fancied he could almost hear her heart beat with her joy and pride. She clung to him as though she could not believe in her happiness, as if it were all too good to be true, and that he might disappear again at any second.

He was glad that it was Ruby who answered his call, though after her first incredulous shriek, his mother's voice was in his ear, trembling, then unable to choke back the tears. 'You bad boy!' she wept, in heartfelt relief and happiness. 'Can I come over? We'll be over right away. Just let me get Iris, I can't believe it. Thank God you're all right!'

He pulled a comic, rueful face when he emerged from the telephone-box. 'They're coming over. Her and Aunt I. I couldn't stop them.'

'She's been worried sick. We all have.' Teddy knew Marian's simple words were not meant to chide, but he nodded soberly.

Marian flew about in a mini panic, dashing round tidying, worrying over what she could give them to eat, rattling the best wedding china as she set it out on the table under the window which looked out on to the back garden. There was no dining-room, so that the living-room had windows at each end, and was thus constantly light and airy.

'Don't fuss,' Teddy chided affectionately. 'It's only Mam and Aunt I.'

Marian gave him a reproachful look. 'She's been so good. They both have.' She glanced round her. 'They've helped so much. With all this. If it hadn't been for them – I'd never have managed. . . .' She stopped, blushed visibly, and Teddy knew she was ashamed that he might take her words as criticism of his conduct. 'I like things to be nice for her. Let her see that I appre-ciate it,' she ended softly.

His reunion with his mother was as emotional as his first home-coming. He felt the fragile slimness as she clutched him to her, felt the tremors as she fought to hold in her tears, the over-whelming relief of having him safely back. She made a good job of it, and swiftly dashed the trace of tears from her cheeks, though they shone in her dark eyes as she surrendered him to the equally engulfing embrace of Iris's more substantial frame.

'You young blackguard!' Iris huffed, thumping him on the back as she pressed him to her pillowy bosom. 'Your Uncle Dan's away, at one of his dreary meetings,' she told him dismis-sively. 'I couldn't get hold of him. He'll be back tomorrow. He'll be delighted to get the news.'

It wasn't until later, as the daylight faded, the sky a beautiful mixture of bruise-dark cloud, faint salmon and deepening pink over Silver Hill, that May managed to speak seriously to Teddy. She and Iris were making ready to leave. Marian was nursing the baby, and he walked them down the front path to the car. May put her hand on his arm, holding him back. Her eyes gazed steadily at him, and he braced himself, having some idea of what was coming.

'It was a wicked thing you did,' she said quietly, the level tone adding to the weight of her words. 'Cruel and unbelievably self-ish. I wouldn't have believed either of my boys capable of an act like that.' Her head, in the light felt cloche hat, jerked back towards the lighted windows behind them. 'That poor girl. No more than a child herself, to be left to face something like that.'

May shook her head. 'I still don't understand how you could bring yourself to be so cruel.' She gave a kind of shudder of distaste, drew herself up as though she were thrusting it away from her. 'Never mind. She dotes on you, you know that, don't you? Absolutely worships you.' It seemed to Teddy that the note of accusation was still there. 'And she's coped so well. I thought she'd go to pieces. But she's made a real home here. For the baby – and you. You're back now, thank God! Don't let them down again. You've got an awful lot to make up for.'

He saw them safely away, watched the headlights dancing as the car bumped over the uneven ground and vanished at the corner of the avenue. The windows were lit, the interior hidden behind the drawn curtains. The bars of light fell on the dim patch of garden, insects flickered around him as he climbed the steps and went inside.

Marian was sitting in an armchair. He saw the white spill of her breast, the large nipple and its rosy surround, the shining, parted lips of the baby as she slept on the soft fecundity of the swelling round. Marian blushed, made an instinctive movement to turn her shoulder, half shielding herself. 'Sorry. She still – I feed her myself. As well as her baby food. It's good – the doctor said.' Awkwardly, she shifted the baby, hastily covering her breast with the gaping dress. She stood, held the shawled infant over her shoulder, rubbed at the curved back. 'It's late. I'll go up. She should settle down now. She usually goes right through without waking.' There was a pause. A suddenly pregnant silence. Marian looked at him, a kind of defencelessness on her face. 'Where – do you want to sleep in – our room?'

Her pathos smote at him like a blow. He cleared his throat. 'Of course I do,' he said strongly. 'You go on. I'll, be up in a jiffy.'

He shivered suddenly, in spite of the warm night. All at once, the euphoria of his home-coming drained away. His mother's words echoed in his brain. Like a judge passing sentence. A lot to make up for. His mind spun off to his brother. They had told him about the broken-off engagement, and John's trip to Germany. He was shocked at how an insidious envy of John's solitariness lodged like a splinter in his thoughts. Resolutely, he turned off the lights and climbed the stairs.

The light drilled painfully through John's closed eyelids into his aching skull, and he slitted them open against the stabbing morning brightness. He felt the great, swamping thrill of fear which made his body jerk violently, then the huge surge of relief at his escape. Drifting to full consciousness, he was again shocked by the feel of the naked limbs draped heavily over his, the warm contact of the body next to him. He turned, saw the girl's face close to him on the pillow, at the same time smelt the staleness of their combined sweat and the cloying sweetness of her perfume.

The relaxed face was heavily made up, the lipstick smeared on her parted lips, through which she blew lightly, but the cosmetic only emphasized the extreme youthfulness, as did the tiny imperfections of incipient pink spots around the curled sides of her nostrils. She looked no older than some of his young cousins. He felt a shamed disgust at the recall of his aching excitement, the frightening lust for her he had experienced a few hours ago.

His mind reeled. So much had happened in the last eventful forty-eight hours, it all seemed like some unreal screen epic. First, the day and night of being shut away in the police cell, the terror of being entirely cut off from the world, utterly helpless. He had told them everything. Afterwards, he felt sickly ashamed, though he reasoned with himself that they knew everything anyway. They just wanted him to confirm it. He wasn't betraying the Arads, or his uncle. Or the unfortunate Louis Schevitz, whom they had surely by now questioned. No doubt they had all the documents in the folder he had handed over.

The long evening dragged on, and they left him alone, the distant clangings and voices in the corridor adding to his unease. He tried to work out how they could possibly have known about him, how the innocent ordinariness of his mission could have become this convoluted plot of intrigue, of criminal behaviour. A few papers for a 17-year-old girl to go and study in Britain. It was ludicrous; would have been as laughable as his own romantic fantasy of the Scarlet Pimpernel, except that the reality of this fetid cell and its locked door was all too fearfully real.

He almost fell into Horst's arms, unable to hold back his weakness, the torrent of his relief, while Horst held him close and patted his shoulders. 'It is fine now, everything,' the German murmured, his mouth close to John's ear. 'We can go.'

John was swaying with exhaustion, scarcely taking in anything, obediently signing the papers they pushed at him, letting the forbidding tone of the plump official wash over him, nodding like a naughty, repentant child.

'You have been very foolish, Herr Wright. You do not understand what has been going on in our country. The network of evil that has been woven into our society, which we must root out. I hope you are a little wiser now.'

He was surprised at Horst's good-natured teasing. He had expected his friend to be at least furious, perhaps even scared at what he had done. 'So! You try to steal a litle Jewess for yourself, my friend? I do not know you have friends among the Jews. Even in your family?'

'No. Not really. My uncle – he married my father's sister. But he's not Jewish. Not since his grandfather's time.'

Horst shrugged, laughed easily. 'It is in the blood. Like disease. But do not worry. Your little Jewess will be allowed to go. We do not want them. We wish they would all go.'

John's breath caught in a huge, shivering sigh. Outside, he

breathed deeply of the night air. 'I was really frightened,' he confessed. He reached for Horst's hand, gripped it powerfully. 'Thanks. It was very good of you. I'll never forget it. Getting me out of there.'

Horst laughed, put his hand on his shoulder, digging in his fingers. 'I am your friend, yes? I must do for my friend. I talk much. Very fast. They listen to me.'

The sky was paling as they let themselves quietly into the lodging house. Horst came into the room when John was in bed. He was wearing a robe. When he sat on the covers beside John, the gown parted its upper folds, and John could see the smooth brownness of his naked chest, also the lean brown thigh where the gown's lower edges parted. He leaned forward. The rather overpowering scent of cologne wafted over John. The handsome face came closer. His breath was flavoured with a minted toothpaste.

John was suddenly deeply aware of his proximity, and his nakedness, the encapsuled intimacy of the bed, the startling atmosphere of sensuality that cloaked them. Horst's brow was almost touching his, that too good-looking face almost simpering, the long lashes lowering, flickering, like a girl. The smile, too, was alluring, provocative.

A thin hand came up, its slim softness rested on John's own chest, in the gap of his pyjama jacket. His heart beat under its cupping embrace. 'You are good now, yes? No more worry. Everything is good.'

John was rigid, almost holding his breath. He nodded, unable to move to break the contact. The whiteness of Horst's teeth showed in another dimpling smile. 'Tomorrow I find you nice girl. You do not look for little Jewess, my friend. You must have good German girl. For love, is the best.'

He was as good as his word. They went out on the town. John tried not to let Horst see how shocked he was at the degeneracy of the club-life his host showed him. He felt that Horst was watching him closely, waiting for just such a reaction, so that he could mock the primness of the British. He supposed there were places like this in London, if you knew where to seek them out. He had no idea. The patrons seemed a cross-section of almost every level of society. Rich, silk-scarved, evening-suited plutocrats, with stunning female partners on their arms; strutting, jack-booted army types; flashily cheap tarts; down-at-heel drunks; and young couples who looked the acme of suburban respectability, all rubbed shoulders in the packed nightclubs, watched the sex shows on the tiny, brilliantly lit stages with guffawing enthusiasm.

Along with his still euphoric sense of relief at his emergence from his fearful ordeal, John felt again a tiny *frisson* of that fear as he took in the scene about him. There was something frightening, alien and hard, about the people pressing round him, about their wild gaiety. He could feel it, strongly, like a low-humming generator: that atmosphere of danger, of violence lurking somewhere not too distant.

He strove to shake off his mood. After all, he owed his liberty to his German friend, who had risked a great deal coming forward like that, speaking out for him. He could so easily have deserted him, proclaimed his outraged innocence and condemnation. Besides, the girls *were* beautiful. He could not deny the excitement they aroused. He had never seen naked girls in the flesh. Now his vision was filled with a dizzying succession of them. He began to mock his prudery, to see himself through Horst's eyes. And, as he got drunker, his senses took over more and more, and he pushed his moral niceness to the background.

They found the girls in a *bierkeller* frequented by students. Horst had laughed at John's ogling of the attractive whores who approached them in the clubs. 'You do not touch the professional, my friend. I tell you – I find nice girl for you. Clean, good girl.'

Inge was one of a crowd, many of whom hailed Horst with friendly recognition. Horst brought her to John, laughing paternally, put them together. 'Tonight I am maestro,' he declared, his arms around them, pulling them into him.

For such a momentous occasion as the loss of his bodily innocence, John's recollections as he surfaced to painful awareness beside Inge's sleeping form were hazy. He had no idea whose apartment they were in, or whose bed. He remembered fumbling out of his clothes, his clumsy haste, his fear as Inge's warm body finally enveloped him and he thrust blindly at her, enormously relieved when she competently took charge, guided him aright. Only the brief but vivid sensation of coupling remained. And the bursting satiety of the climax. After that, oblivion, until this confusing awakening.

The first clear emotion was shame. Revulsion almost, at the smells and touches surrounding him, smothering him in sexuality. He lay still, enduring the damp heat of the girl's limbs, her slack body against his. Then reason locked in, and he argued with himself, at war now with his own instinct. Why should he condemn what he had done? What his body had urged and compelled him to do? What was wrong with that?

He glanced about him. The room was shabby, that much he could see, and cluttered with ancient furniture. A typical student den, he guessed. Inge's? He wondered how many men had slept in this bed. In these sheets. He felt his skin crawl, and automatically he stirred, sought to withdraw his leg from under hers. She stirred, grunted, obligingly rolled away to the far side of the mattress, presenting the pronounced curve of her back. He followed the knobs of her spine, down to the darker shading where the divide of her buttocks peeped from the displaced sheet. Carefully, he eased himself out, covered her again.

He shivered violently, feeling vulnerable at his own nudity. Thankfully, he found his underpants and trousers on the floor, hauled them on, tiptoed barefoot across the floor to the door. He found a high, draughty bathroom with a toilet down the corridor, and used it thankfully. When he got back to the bedroom, he found his place had been taken by Horst, who was lounging, his bare upper torso showing above the sheet. Inge, her face still creased with sleep, was nestling into his chest, and he had an arm draped loosely over her shoulders.

'Aha! The master spy returns! You enjoy?' He squeezed Inge significantly as he spoke, and she giggled and slapped at his arm. He said something in German, and she laughed even more as she answered. 'That is the British. Always in hurry.' John blushed, looked for somewhere to sit, and for the rest of his clothes. A tall girl, with hair as fair as Horst's, came to the doorway. She was wearing a black robe, carelessly tied at her waist, and was clearly naked beneath it. She showed neither surprise nor displeasure at the sight of Horst in bed with Inge.

'You like eggs?' John realized she was addressing him, and he nodded, blushing.

'Good girl, Käthe!' Horst called out. She pulled a face at him and went out again. 'We must replenish the body after our hard work, yes?' He patted the bed. 'Come and join us. Inge can be the meat. We make sandwich.'

John tried to make light of it. 'No thanks,' he said. 'We have a saying in English. Two's company, three's a crowd.'

'Nonsense! Poor Inge. She want you, I know. Don't you, Inge?' As he spoke, he flicked back the sheet, exposing her, and she gave a little scream, her legs lifting as she grabbed and tugged at the cloth, hauling it to her breasts. She pouted and let fly a torrent of German, but she was not perturbed, John could tell. Unlike him.

He stood, searched for and found his shirt, and socks and shoes. 'I'll just go and wash. And see if your friend needs help in the kitchen.' Horst's taunting laugh followed him out.

He was glad when, much later, they made their escape. He was hot with embarrassment all the while, through the leisurely breakfast and the chatting afterwards. All he could think of was that he had slept with Inge. Had sex with her. The first girl he had ever had sex with, and here they were, sitting and talking, politely, perfect strangers. Again, the unreality of it all gripped him.

On their way back to Frau Kupe's in the taxi, Horst put his hand on John's knee, kept it there. 'That was your first time. To do sex, yes?'

John's face flamed. He nodded. 'Yes,' he confessed. He moved his knee, plainly letting Horst see that he did not like such tactile familiarity.

'It is not to be ashamed,' Horst said, in that tone that was half-mocking, half-tender. 'You Englishmen, you are too – how you say? – too bashful. With sex. We are flesh and blood. We should not be shame of our bodies.' He leaned close again, confiding, but did not try to touch him. 'That is problem. With Jenny. She is flesh and blood. Not abstract. You must love her, Johnny. Make love to her. She want it. The girls do. Like we. You will have no problem, I tell you.'

John felt a surge of anger. It blazed up inside and he fought to stifle it. 'That's rubbish!' he answered, his teeth clenched. His head jerked back in the direction they had come from. 'She's – Jenny's not – like that.'

Horst's chuckle was infuriating. 'You are wrong, Johnny. I tell you this. I know, my friend.'

John's mind reeled. What on earth did he mean? He felt himself shaking, and all at once a murderous desire to strike the smiling figure beside him made him clench his fists. The fit passed, and he leaned back weakly, wearily. He was overwhelmed by his wish to be far away from Germany; to be back home; to be back with Jenny, whose face he could see so clearly now, and of whom he was so totally unworthy, whose very love he had sullied, forever. She had been right after all to have her doubts. He didn't deserve her. He closed his eyes against the sudden sting of tears, and against his own torturous awareness of his baseness.

Chapter Sixteen

The truth about John's escapade in Germany did not come out until several months after his return. He had met with his Uncle David soon after he got back, and gave him a full account. His uncle was very apologetic, and blamed himself for putting John at risk. He had heard from the Arad family. Contrary to Horst Zettel's flippant words of reassurance, there was no sign that the German authorities were prepared to let Sara Arad out of the country, while the unfortunate Louis Schevitz had been taken by the police. So far nothing more had been heard of him. 'I guess he will be sent to a work camp,' David Golding surmised bitterly.

John was wretched. 'I mucked things up. But I still don't understand how they could have known. They were ready. Picked me up as soon as I'd left Mr Schevitz.'

'Did you say anything to your friend? Did he know anything about it?'

'No. He's a party member. I made a point of keeping quiet. I knew he wouldn't approve.'

John was ashamed of the suspicion half-formed in his mind, which had been lodged there almost from the day after the incident. Horst couldn't have known. Unless he had somehow been through John's bags, discovered the folder. But it was through Horst's intervention that the police had eventually let him go.

None of it made any sense. Ashamedly, John wondered if his suspicions of the German stemmed from his behaviour after John's release, That strange intimacy which Horst had adopted towards him, with its undertone of homosexuality. John couldn't forget it.

And then, Horst had been responsible for John's sexual initiation with Inge. Had been eager for it, had arranged everything, putting them in bed together. His whole manner had changed, become openly decadent, corruptive. It had soured the rest of the holiday, which John had cut short. Worst of all had been Horst's strange and offensive manner towards Jenny. Suggesting that she was as libidinous as John had proved to be. That she would welcome a sexual approach from John. Could he not see how insulting it was to Jenny to talk of her like that? He had tried to tell him, without quarrelling, and Horst had made it worse by that sneering, superior attitude. 'I know, my friend.' As if the assumption was beyond doubt.

All in all, John's trip had been a severe learning experience, both at a personal and more general level. Germany was dangerous. Of that he was now convinced. He confided as much to his uncle, who once more apologized for having behaved, as he put it, naïvely, in asking John to carry out his quest.

Then, out of the blue, or rather grey, for it was early in the new year of 1938, Sara Arad turned up. John met her when she came up to Gosforth on a brief visit to his aunt and uncle's. He smiled wryly to himself at his fanciful Pimpernel scenario, for Sara was plump, bordering on fat, her skin was a sallow brown, her black hair cut in an unbecoming fringe, and she wore thick spectacles.

He was ashamed of his pettiness, though, when she told, in her heavily accented English, of the troubles facing her people in Germany. Her family had been interrogated, her father's business had virtually been taken from him because he had been forced to take on a German partner. 'I am so worried for them. I wish they could come to England too.'

During her short stay up north, she let slip something about John's trouble with the German police. It was seized on by his Aunt Cissy, and all at once there was another family crisis, it seemed, with everyone talking and rowing. John first learned of it when his mother came in one evening, her face white and closed in an expression that he knew of old meant trouble.

'So! You didn't see fit to tell me, eh? That you'd been arrested and locked up by the Nazis while you were staying with your *friend* in the summer!'

He tried to calm her, but his reasoned tones only served to anger her further. 'What is it with you lads? Are you determined to worry me into an early grave? First your brother runs off, deserts his pregnant wife and goes to fight in Spain. Then you go and nearly get yourself imprisoned or worse in that Godless place! And never a word!'

'Look, it worked out all right. It's precisely because I didn't want to worry you that I kept quiet—'

'Worry? Worry? Hah!' Her voice soared to shrill vehemence. 'I'm just your mother. Why on earth should I be worried? Just because you've got yourself mixed up with Nazi friends and all sorts.'

'Not any more, Mam,' he answered hotly. 'I saw what's going on over there. I told you. I just wish I could do more to help folk like Sara Arad and her family.' He paused, flushed, as he added painfully, 'There's some poor fellow suffering God-knows-what because of me. The chap I met and gave the papers for Sara to. He's in a camp somewhere. . . .'

'Yes, well, I'll give David Golding a piece of my mind when I next meet up with him. He had no right at all to drag you into it. It's not as if he's Jewish himself. Cissy's livid.'

John let her rant on, knowing she would soon calm down and realize that it was all in the past. The danger, if any, had been over in a couple of days, six months ago. Next week the new term at Beaconsfield would begin. Tomorrow, he would go up to school, see what he could do in the way of preparation. One thing was sure. He would find the head already hard at work, John realized just how eager he was to get back to work again after the month's break. Especially now, with this awful feeling of instability on the international scene, the threat of Armageddon hanging over everyone, whether they acknowledged it or not. It was something worthwhile to cling on to. More than ever when he was alone like this.

He had refrained from getting in touch with Jenny when he came back to England. Partly through his abiding sense of guilt at his downfall. He lashed himself endlessly. He even condemned his own weak excuse in setting up Horst Zettel as some kind of devil's agent engineering the corruption of his soul. No way! he savaged himself. It's you! All he did was show you what you're really like.

Eventually, well into the Autumn term, he had weakened, wrote a long, soulful letter to her, expressing powerfully and poignantly, he thought, his desolation at losing her. The curtness of her reply cut him deeply. 'Please don't go on about how lonely you are. You're not the only one who's suffered, don't forget. And besides, I find it rather hard to take when I hear of how you managed to enjoy yourself with your Nazi chum. Not the kind of behaviour I'd have expected from someone who claims to think something of me. But just what I *would* expect from fellows of Horst's persuasion. He had the gall to write and tell me all about your diversions.'

At first John felt sick with disgust and apprehension. But then, surely Horst would not have told her the truth about their debauchery? He couldn't have written of that to Jenny of all people. No, he must have bragged on, like an undergraduate, of drinking sprees, nights out on the town, that kind of thing. Damaging enough, though, it would seem, from Jenny's cruel tone. Still, at least now she had had her eyes opened about the young German. He recalled his own pique at the way she seemed to have fallen for Horst's admittedly magnetic personality during his stay in England. Now, she, too, had seen the truth behind the façade.

Only a few days after the start of the new term at Beaconsfield, John read in the papers of the arrival in Britain of the Austrian psychoanalyst, Sigmund Freud. John was annoyed by a caustic remark from one of his colleagues from the depths of a staff-room armchair: 'Huh! He's lucky he's got us as a bolt-hole to run to. We let any nutcase in. He can spout his weird ideas as much as he likes here. Probably make a fortune doing it, too!'

Like most people, himself included, John guessed that his fellow teacher had probably only read reviews of Freud's theories and writings. The work he had produced in conjunction with Jung five years ago on religion had not gone down well with the more traditional elements of British society. John was well aware that, although largely unexpressed, there was a considerable amount of anti-semitic feeling in Britain, as elsewhere. Formerly, his sentiments had been fuzzily liberal. But not since his trip to Germany. When Mosley was laid out by a brick in Liverpool last October, John had felt almost savagely delighted. Now, he could not stop himself from replying sharply to his colleague's remark. 'You're right. He *is* lucky. There's thousands of poor blighters of his religion who can't find anywhere to run to.'

At the beginning of February, a letter came from Horst. John was embarrassed at its intimately friendly tone, in particular at the references to the night they had spent with the two girls, Käthe and Inge.

'I hope by now that you have put what you have learnt into practice with your beautiful Jenny. If so, you will know by now that what I told you is true. If you have not, you will find it too late, my friend. Someone else will teach to her about love and you will lose her for ever. Please heed my advice to you.'

When he read those words, John felt again that murderous surge of fury, so that the paper trembled in his hand. The fact that the offending paragraph was followed by the news that Horst was planning to return to England in the summer, and looking forward eagerly to their meeting again, maybe even staying for some days with 'your beautiful Jenny and her family' was salt in the wound.

That night, John sat up late in a deserted staff-room and penned a short but pointed answer. Even though he felt his anger and distaste were justified, he did not find it easy to let Horst know his true feelings, but it did not deter him.

He wrote, 'I feel I have to be honest, and tell you that too much stands in the way of our continuing friendship. Normally, political differences would not matter, but I have to tell you that the policies of your country, which I know you endorse, are too extreme for me to ignore. I cannot sympathize with or accept any of them, and they stand in the way of my continuing on a friendly footing with anyone who supports them.

'On a personal level, I also have to say that your remarks about Jenny and our relationship upset me a great deal. I suppose they stem from your notions of free love, which I can't subscribe to either, nor, I am quite sure, could Jenny. About what happened that night with Inge, I can only say that I feel an abiding shame. I let myself, and, worse, Jenny, down badly.'

With compressed lips, he quickly wrote a few closing lines, terminal in more ways than one, and sealed the envelope. He felt he had sullied her by writing her very name in such a letter. He was glad he was done with the strange figure. Somehow the shade of Horst Zettel seemed irrevocably bound with the disaster which had befallen his relationship with the girl he truly loved.

'So! Running away again, are we?' May's face was set in a mask of bitterness, behind which lay a great press of anguish and helplessness. The pain she was experiencing was increased by Teddy's lowered, hangdog expression, the stubborn, surly set of his features which reminded her so powerfully of earlier childhood obstinacy. She had come a long way since those days, learned to master and hide her emotions, especially where her sons were concerned. It was as well, she reflected grimly, for in the past year or two they had caused her more than her fair share of grief. Immediately she was assailed by a feeling of guilt at this thought.

Poor John had done nothing to hurt her. Except to fall in love with a girl who didn't want him, and through no fault of his own, as far as she could see. In fact, she was proud of the way he had borne what was clearly a serious blow to his happiness, the way he had flung himself into his work, though out of the way Beaconsfield was not the kind of place she would have chosen for him to start his professional life. Not that it was up to her. She had interfered little in her sons' choices, had seen, with help for which she would always be grateful, that they had both got the best start she could give them, morally and academically.

But in a way it was John's very containment of his grief which hurt her so much. She had ached to comfort him, to let him see that their bedrock relationship would never fail him. And he had shut her out. Not cruelly, perhaps not even consciously, but that did not lessen the pain of it. There was a distance between them, and one she felt was growing wider each day. They were drifting slowly further and further apart, and there seemed to be nothing she could do about it. Even though the school was less than ten miles down the road, he hardly came home at all during term time. She was lucky if she saw him more than once a month.

As for her younger son, he was nothing but heartache to her. It was odd. In some ways she felt even closer to him, could feel and recognize his moods and thinking, for he was so much closer to her family traits than Jack's. She had felt it particularly ever since he had gone to work at Swan's, and moved in with his grandparents. He had more of a look of her own father – inches shorter than his brother, with that strutting, cocksure manner. The same impulsive way, plunging into things. Like now.

She knew Marian had been weeping half the night. Her eyes were red, puffed up, her nose blotched. As always, May felt the irritation flow like bile in her at the girl's passivity. Her dumb, masochistic acceptance of the wickedness with which Teddy treated her. She knew how desolate the girl must be at the bombshell he had dropped, and yet she sat there, silent, suffering, ready as always to let him kill her with his selfishness.

Marian looked at her tragically. The pale eyes filled yet again. She made a helpless little gesture, and May thought vindictively, Perhaps if you made some effort, smartened yourself up a bit, lost some of that weight, demanded more from him, he might start taking some notice. She gave up, turned back to her son. 'You haven't been back five minutes! You've never even tried to settle down.' She waved her hand around. 'You've got a lovely little home. A beautiful bairn, a wife that thinks the sun shines out of you! What more do you want? What more *is* there to want?' She gave a kind of gasp of frustration, gazed appealingly at him.

Teddy returned her look, with the same kind of helplessness she herself was feeling. He gave a small shake of the head, as though acknowledging his incapability of answering her question. The 'five minutes' his mother referred to had been almost a year. How could he tell her how swiftly each day had turned into an eternity of smothering depression, and of growing desperation to escape?

In spite of all his best promises, to himself and to others, he had not been able to live up to the vow he had made to himself. He hadn't the cruelty in him to tell Marian the truth – a truth that would be worse than the most savage beating. Her love, her blind adoration, stifled him, made him groan, and, in his blackest moments howl inside himself with his pain. The happiness which had shone like a light from her during the first weeks when he had been back had comforted him only briefly. Then it became a secret scourge to his own emotion, making his despair far worse as he endured day after day.

It emanated from her, an aura of pure contentment, in having him near, walking beside her with the pram each Saturday as they headed along to the Fell for their shopping. The cups of tea she brought to him as he dug the garden, put fresh coats of paint on things that did not need painting. Even, saddest of all, her doting on 'Baby Teddie' became part of the claustrophobic atmosphere in which he was drowning. It was like some sick parody of all the women's magazines and Hollywood epics they sat through at the Capitol on a Saturday night when Dora or some other willing accomplice baby-sat for them.

There was no escape. Least of all in physical love. The soft, pillowy receptiveness of her pale body – that too added to the drowning sensation. Sometimes, after his first cautious efforts at sex, he had felt a shameful desire to brutalize, to shock her into seeing just what lay beneath the surface of his tumbled emotion. Haunted by the spectre of another, leaner, darker body, to which he had cleaved with such fiercely simple joy, he had begun to be rougher, more demanding, even to suggest sexual techniques and practices which he thought would shock and dismay. But she had proved there was nothing she would not do for him, and he had desisted, more ashamed and sickened than before. His insistence on precautions to ensure she would not get pregnant again must, he was certain, have hurt her deeply, yet she accepted, as always, and went through the ritual of preparation for sex with the painstaking thoroughness he demanded.

At last, this suffocating sweetness had tainted even the real joy he found in his infant daughter. Part of Marian's stereotype of family-hearth-home happiness was the ideal that child-rear-ing was part of the matriarchal duties. The babe was an object to be cosseted by Daddy at certain prescribed moments when, bathed and fed and fragranced, the infant was presented for paternal approval. Dirty nappies, milky sick, disturbance in the night – such things were not for father's sight or hearing. He often felt that the women in the family were in a conspiracy to make sure he had little time to attend to his daughter's needs at all.

'Ye'll be gannin' back tae Swan's, eh?' his Granda Rayner asked, soon after the first euphoria of his return. Teddy was shocked at how old his grandfather had become. Stooped shoulders, shuffling gait, broken-veined cheeks and the strawberry, boozer's nose. Jimmy and Kathy and their family were still living at the house in Sidney Terrace, looking after him.

'I've tried time and again to get him to move out with me,' May told Teddy resignedly, 'but he won't leave that blessed club of his. He spends all day and half the night there. He won't last much longer. He can't. He can hardly get his breath on a morning. He's sixty-eight now.'

He was secretly ashamed at the relief he felt when McAlister, now chief draughtsman of the drawing office at the Wallsend yard, refused to countenance his return. 'You could have had a job here for life,' Mr McAlister reprimanded him. 'You should've thought of that when you chucked it in to go gallivanting off like that.'

'Never worry, lad,' his grandfather told him. 'Gan ower to the naval yard. The've got stacks of orders, now that we're all gettin' in a panshite wi' the Jerries at last.'

'It's different, working on naval vessels, Grandad,' Teddy said uncomfortably. 'I don't know anything about it.'

'The' still bloody ships, aren't they?' George retorted fiercely.

He had been taken on, as a junior. He was not happy with the work, but, in his spirit of contrition he had conquered his reluctance, promising himself that he would look for something different, as soon as he had settled in and earned something to make up for his neglect of his new family. He owed it not least to his mother who, though she had not said anything about it to him, had virtually carried them financially throughout his desertion of them.

His idea had begun as a tiny grain of irritation in his mind, a particle that would not go, that gathered bulk as it lodged within him, and as the fateful year advanced, and the atmosphere of unrest and instability all around him grew to match his own. Treaties were being broken, all the European powers were rushing belatedly to rearm, as the threat of war loomed ever closer.

When he told Marian of his still half-formed plan, she was as devastated as he had feared. 'Wait,' he said, already on edge, as she was making the usual preparations for bed. 'Don't go up just yet.' She had got into the habit of going up before him. He used the excuse that he wanted to stay and listen to the wireless. She seemed capable of shutting out any unpalatable facts that did not affect her own domestic world directly. 'I want to talk for a minute. It's important.' The look of wide-eyed fear which came over her, that expression of vulnerability, added to the tension he was already experiencing.

'I've been thinking. I'm not really getting anywhere at the naval yard. There's no prospect of me getting promoted. There's lads two years behind me passing me in the office. I'm going to pack in.' He drew a deep breath. Her face looked sickly in the lamplight. She was staring at him with a terror-stricken look. 'I've been looking into the army. I think there could be a good career in there for me. With all this expansion. And the way things are going, chances are I could be called up soon anyway. All young men could. You know there's talk of making us register. They'll have to conscript, to build up the forces. If I get in now, I could do really well.'

'You want to leave me.' Her voice was a whisper. Even her lips looked white. She was sitting on the edge of the chair, hunched forward. She began to whimper softly, and to shake, hugging her breasts. 'It's me, isn't it? You're sick of me.'

'No, honest, Marian. It isn't that. Believe me. I'm doing it for you – and Teddie.' He hated himself, the urgent effort at sincerity in his tone. 'If I join up now, maybe I'll stand a better chance of not being posted abroad – when the time comes. It's—'

'Please! Don't go! Don't leave me! Just tell me – what it is – what you want. I'll do whatever . . .' With a wail of despair she slumped on to her knees on the carpet, then fell forward like a little child on to her face. Great, ugly sobs from deep within shook her frame, her stockinged feet began to drum softly on the carpet, her fingers clawed at it.

He stared, appalled. 'For God's sake, Marian! Stop it!' He knelt, took her by her shoulders, gently at first, then gripping her tightly, shaking her, trying to turn her over. He was both repulsed and torn with compassionate guilt. She moved, came round, and flung her arms round his neck like a drowning person, almost pulling him on top of her. Her face was red now, and smeared with tears and mucus. Her mouth gaped.

'Don't leave me!' she moaned, and he sat, folded her into his lap, held her and rocked her gently back and forth, shushing and soothing her, for an ageless time, while the storm of her grief swept through her.

He had already been to the recruiting office in Newcastle, and taken the first steps towards enlistment when he told his mother of his plans. Now, in his own living-room, he faced May, and his Aunt I and Uncle Dan. And Marian, choking back her tears, supported him by her loyal silence as he faced their combined amazement and wrath. She could not trust herself to speak.

May finally turned away in helpless defeat. She had conquered, thrust aside her own grief for later, more private moments, of which there would be many. Her dark eyes glittered, and she waved her hand, with the two rings of engagement and marriage on her finger, at Dan. 'For God's sake, tell him! Tell him what it's like. What it's really like, Dan. He has no idea at all! He thinks it's Beau Geste and all that nonsense. Talk some sense into him, will you?' Automatically, she moved close to Iris's sturdy frame, and her arm came out, slipped just as unconsciously about the slim waist.

'I think,' Dan said carefully, 'it might be an idea if we all cooled off a little. Time for us menfolk to slip out for a pint while our ears burn at the home truths you ladies are lining up.'

'Hah! The all-wise one's answer to all life's problems!' Iris commented caustically. 'Why didn't Mr Chamberlain think of that? "Come on, Herr Hitler. Let's just pop out for a pint and we can solve all this rearmament nonsense!" '

Dan smiled easily. 'Mightn't be a bad idea at that. Couldn't be any worse than the mess they're making of things right now.' He turned to his nephew, who had stood with alacrity. 'Where's the nearest? The George, I suppose? You don't mind driving, do you? We won't be long, my love.'

'No. Only till closing time, eh?' Iris fired back sarcastically. But it was a relief in a way to see them go. As the car drove away, Marian could at last permit herself the luxury of the tears which she felt had been so easily and so frequently spilt over the past few days, and to savour at least the understanding and sympathy of her two companions in sharing her sadness.

Dan and Teddy sought out the mid-week solitude of the best room, with its round, iron tables and polished linoleum. When the barmaid had brought their drinks, Dan sipped philosophically, and said, 'You never fail to surprise us, Teddy. I thought Spain had got it all out of your system.'

Teddy shook his head. 'It's no good trying to tell them,' he began. Dan waited but there was a lengthy pause. 'I just can't seem to settle,' he attempted finally. Another shake of the head, as he gave up. 'Anyway, there's going to be a war. Isn't there?' he added almost belligerently. 'It's bound to come. Even John reckons so now. Hitler's hell bent on taking over Europe, and we've got to stop him.'

'You're probably right,' Dan conceded. 'But that doesn't mean you have to rush out and meet it before it gets here.'

Teddy gave him a wounded, indignant look in return. 'You did!' he said accusingly. 'I mean – you went straight off and volunteered. As soon as war was declared.'

'Come on! That was different. It was mass hysteria. Just a lark. Everybody did.'

'Dad didn't, did he?' Teddy said quietly.

Dan made no answer, stared at his glass for so long that Teddy blushed, feeling that he had gone too far. His uncle had never really talked about the war, except to joke about it. It was a subject which the boys had always felt was more or less taboo in their household. Then Dan cleared his throat, and spoke, just as softly. 'No,' he said. 'He didn't. He waited until it came to him. He had something far more important to care about. And precious. Your Ma. And Johnny. And you.'

Dan's heart ached at the tortured look on his nephew's face. He regretted his impulsive speech, true though it was. He knew that, at the bottom of it, it was a purely personal restlessness, unhappiness, which was driving Teddy. In marrying Marian, he had tried to take the right course, do the right thing. It made his subsequent running away all the more ignominious. And now, for a second time, he was deserting his post, fleeing from a responsibility he couldn't take.

All at once, he remembered Jack's mate, Arty, that irrepressible character at Jack and May's wedding, who had scored such a success with Marian's mum, and who had perished before a British firing squad. Jack had been lucky not to be cashiered for his refusal to be one of the execution party. Lucky? Dan grimaced. A few weeks later Jack himself was wiped carelessly out of existence.

Duty. Jack should have stuck to his own ideals, his first duty, of loving and protecting his wife and children. And what of Dan's own marriage? Born out of a night's lustful madness right in the midst of the nightmare of war. Coming to sickly fruit years after the event, because of a hopeless need for companionship and comfort. He certainly was not the one to upbraid Teddy for failure to carry out his duty towards his marriage partner.

He thought of Iris's clenched distaste, finally her undisguised abhorrence of the sterile physical side of their union. And of Madge Wheeler's splendidly abandoned, hot and eager body, the simple, sensual joy of their coupling, which he would return to as long as he was able, No casting stones on his part, that was for sure.

He smiled, tapped Teddy's arm, 'Drink up, old son. Time for one more before we face the second half!'

Chapter Seventeen

The official who had questioned John stared with a mild reproach which did nothing to ease the wary discomfort Horst Zettel felt. 'I thought you said you were extremely close to Wright?'

Horst's edginess heightened. The stir of disapproval from the other two officers in the increasingly important *Schutzstaffel*, or SS, was obvious. His flash of resentment was no less intense because of his careful effort to keep it hidden. Damned hypocrites! Their élitist superiority infuriated him. He gave the three older men a disarming smile, and another shrug of false modesty. 'I think maybe he's since found out just how friendly I got with his girlfriend during my last trip to England. His ex-girlfriend now. I'm still in touch with her. She'll be a better source than him, anyway. I'm sure she'll be happy to see me. Put me up for a while.'

One of the SS duo frowned with distaste, picked up the documents in front of him. 'I thought the idea was that you would make contacts through the student movement. With people sympathetic to our cause. Establish links with the British Fascist movement?'

'Of course, sir,' Horst answered, 'but it is useful to make some personal contact. To find places where I can stay. Form friendships, shall we say?' He smiled again, suggestively, but his humorous innuendo encountered only that expression of lofty disdain.

That night in his room at Mrs Kupe's, Horst sat late into the night, with pad and pen, and dictionary, struggling to further his nefariously patriotic scheme.

'My dearest Jenny – you are that to me, you know. Very dear, more than any young lady I have known before. I take this trouble to write to you because I fear that John is no longer my friend. I think maybe he knows, or suspects, about the way I am feeling for you, my dear, although I do not tell him anything of what happens between us. I am sad, for he is a dear boy to me. I want him to be happy, and you also. You especially, and now I think I can tell you this for you and he are no longer affianced.

'I do not forget how you are beautiful. Many times, especially in the night, I remember. I think perhaps you forget, but I never. My great fear when John writes that he is no longer my friend is that I can not see you again. Please allow me, Jenny, to visit with you and your wonderful family once more. I must see you again. Please do not be like John, to blame me for the politics of my country which I do not help. Such things can not spoil a true friendship which I feel for you, my dear. And stronger than friendship.

'Please do write to permit that I may come and visit you. I hope to come to England in August. I wait impatiently for that time to see you. Understand I am truly your loving friend, Horst.'

He sighed with weary satisfaction as he sealed the letter in its envelope. He felt he had struck just the right note, without making his desire too blatant. And the prim little English girl, for all her blushes and tearful modesty, would be wet with eagerness for him. He felt the excitement flare up in him, despite his tiredness, and he smiled in real anticipation.

But the politics he had so easily discounted in his letter to Jenny forestalled his intentions. By the summer he had been diverted to duties concerning the planned dismemberment of Czechoslovakia, where the fermentation of unrest was an urgently necessary prelude to Germany's move in that direction. He had little time to reflect on the fact that his love letter to the English girl had gone unanswered during the build up that led to the crisis of Munich, and Neville Chamberlain's triumphant return with the paper fluttering in the September breeze. Four days later, German troops marched into the Sudetenland.

The policy of appeasement was soon revealed as useless, its only dubious value the fact that it had bought Britain a little more much-needed time. By December, a national register for war service was opened, and money was being allocated to the building of air-raid shelters. In April of the following year, conscription for twenty and twenty-one year old men was introduced, a month later the government was urging farmers to plough up pasture to grow more food, and the fateful Anglo–Polish treaty was signed in London.

Teddy was home on leave in July, when the British Prime Minister issued yet another warning to Hitler that this time Britain would not stand by if he moved against Poland. There was almost an air of resignation in most people's minds. 'I'll be off to France as soon as the balloon goes up,' Teddy confided to his brother. 'You should try and get in our mob when the call-up comes. It's not bad at all. Not too much spit and polish once your basic training's over. And the job's interesting enough, once you get used to army ways.'

He had been transferred to the REME, where his skills at technical drawing had been put to some use. He was in a unit which was working on plans for prefabricated huts, and for a new type of pontoon bridge. He was already a corporal, and hoped in the not too distant future to be promoted to sergeant. Because of the emergency, he was wearing khaki, and people treated the uniform with new respect and admiration.

Though his conscience still troubled him in more reflective

231

moments, he was glad that the uproar he had caused at his enlist-ment last year had died down. He had managed to get home for fairly regular leave, even from the distant depot near Salisbury, once the basic training had been completed, and Marian had accepted his absence uncomplainingly, as he knew she would. Though the misery in her eyes when the goodbyes came made him wish she would let loose a stream of vituperation against him. She seemed to think that it didn't affect him, leaving Teddie and her and the neat little house behind. It did. But, shamefully, that feeling of nostalgic sadness faded once he was back on the train and heading south, with uniformed figures all about him, and his heart lifted with boyish lightness at the camaraderie of service life in which he was once more happily immersed.

The one person who had not, he felt, accepted his decision to join up was his mother, though she had said nothing directly critical of him since her bitter tirades before his enlistment. At least this time she had no financial burden to bear as far as his family were concerned. His pay as a regular was better than he had been getting at the naval yard, and his allotment to Marian was as generous as he could afford. He kept little back for himself and lived a fairly abstemious life in barracks. He knew his mother still spent on Teddie, and bought frequent 'treats' for his wife, like a new pair of rayon stockings, or cosmetics, or underwear, or things for the house. But they were not necessi-ties. He understood the pleasure his mother got from doing such things. He was pleased that she had taken Marian under her wing, and showed such motherly affection towards her. He knew, too, how highly Marian valued it.

John had finished another academic year at Beaconsfield, and drove over to Low Fell to spend the night with them a few days before Teddy was due to return to his unit. After supper, the brothers walked up through the pleasant summer evening to the George IV, the pub which stood at the tram terminus. They settled with their pints in a corner of the best room, at the very table where Teddy had sat with Uncle Dan on the occasion when he had first faced his mother after his announcement that he was signing on in the forces.

'P'raps you won't get called up,' Teddy observed. 'Teaching might be made a reserved occupation, eh? There's loads of jobs we can't do without when you think about it.'

'Like draughtsmen, for instance,' John answered wryly, and Teddy grimaced humorously.

'Don't rub it in. You sound just like Mam.'

'I don't really know how I feel about it any more. I wouldn't mind joining up. I thought about it seriously after you'd gone last year. And now it's just about inevitable. Some time sooner or later, we're going to have to fight the blighters.' He took a long pull at his beer, and wiped his lips with the back of his hand. 'James has already made plans to take in a host of new kids. Evacuees from the city. I must admit, I'd feel a bit bad about deserting him if I did go.'

'No. You wait till they send for you, kiddo.' Teddy glanced rather sheepishly at him. 'Listen. Don't say too much at home about what's going to happen. Marian gets a bit upset about it. Naturally.'

John nodded, made noises of understanding. Teddy gave another speculative glance. 'How's your love life these days? Have you heard anything from Jenny recently?'

John stared ahead, didn't meet his gaze. His tone was falsely casual. 'No. Nothing since that letter at Christmas formally ending our relationship. Not that that was anything new. Just dotting i's and crossing t's. It was over a long time ago. I've written it off. Pastures new and all that.'

'And are there? Pastures new, I mean?' Teddy matched his lightness of tone.

'Naw! Chance 'ud be a fine thing! Stuck in a prep school in the back of beyond? I tell you! I'm beginning to have erotic dreams about matron, and you've seen *her*, haven't you?'

'Have you not seen Jenny at all then? Not been in touch?' Teddy pursued cautiously.

John shook his head. 'No point, really. Made it quite clear she wasn't interested. I rang a few times but it was the big brush-off. I suppose it's – Oh, more than two years now. Ancient history. Not since that Nazi swine came over on his visit.' He murmured his name softly. 'Almost worth going to war just to put a bullet up that bastard's backside!' He tipped his glass, let the remaining foam slide towards his mouth. 'Just as well I'm not involved with anybody, really. Not exactly the time to think too far ahead, is it? Better off on my tod with things the way they are.' He paused, carried on a little awkwardly. 'It's different when you're already hitched. A family and all that.'

'You're probably right. Got enough on your plate looking after number one, I reckon.' He gave his wide, comfortingly familiar grin of old. 'Eat drink and be merry, that's the ticket!' He nodded at the bell wired into the wall. 'Give that a push, old son, and we'll get on with the real business of the day!'

The Sunday morning announcement of the outbreak of war, broadcast on the new BBC Home Service, in the Prime Minister's solemnly apologetic tones, should not have come as a shock, yet to many it did. John was called in from the garden, where he had been helping the workman, whom May had engaged to erect the Anderson shelter, bail out the two feet of muddy water the colour of milky tea with which the new, sunken edifice had filled during the previous night. As he listened, he, too, experienced that clutch of disbelief that it had finally happened. 'This country is now at war with Germany.'

Teddy had already telephoned May two nights before. 'We're on stand-by to move. I can't get out of camp. There won't be any leave.' He paused. His voice sounded gruff, hoarse with emotion, and embarrassment. 'Tell Marian – give her my love. And Teddie.'

234

May closed her eyes, a lump closing her throat, a sob shaking her chest. She saw yet again another young, khaki-clad figure, standing before her, his eyes eloquent with tragedy. She bit her lip, bit back the tears. 'I will. Take care, Teddy. God bless – I love you!'

The next day had come the expected news that military service was to be made compulsory for all men aged between eighteen and forty-one, and now this long-awaited, and dreaded, declaration of war. May could no longer hold back her tears. She moved to embrace her eldest son, unmindful of the workman standing awkwardly in the doorway. John could feel her trembling, though she quickly conquered her weeping. 'You won't have to go,' she said, trying to disguise her sense of desperation. 'They'll need teachers. Just like the pitmen.'

John was kept busy enough in the next few days. Evacuation plans were already being put into action, and he worked from dawn until well after dusk with his colleagues, meeting train and coach loads of Tyneside children, checking off lists, marshalling them into some semblance of order, getting them installed in the school, where camp-beds had been squeezed into every available corner and corridor.

'Hey, mistah. Me ma sez tae tell ye wor Franky's a bed-wetter.'

Little Franky stood forlornly, snotty-nosed, his grey jersey little more than a series of holes held together by strands of wool. He was scratching at his head in a suspicious manner. He had a few threadbare items in a brown-paper carrier-bag. They did not include any change of underwear, or pyjamas. On closer inspection, despite Franky's bawling protests, John found he wasn't wearing any, either, and that, under the ragged shirt and shorts below his knees, his body was almost uniformly black. 'Come on, lads. Bathroom, now!' The tears at this frighteningly alien world increased, as John tried vainly to reassure him that no harm would befall from such comprehensive contact with soap and water. As he knelt, soaking himself, and rubbing at the skinny, grimy little body, he wondered with grim humour what the regular, privileged inhabitants of Beaconsfield would make of their new chums, when they themselves returned in two weeks' time.

A lot was to happen before then. Teddy actually left for France as part of the BEF vanguard a week after the declaration of hostilities, by which time the war at sea had already begun with the sinking of the liner, *Athenia*. And the first air raids, both British and German, had been carried out. Yet the much feared blitz had not brought its apocalyptic rain of terror down from the skies, and, as autumn moved into the intense chill of a severe winter, people began to relax just a little. Only at sea was the conflict sadly real. Five hundred men had been lost when HMS *Courageous* sank in the Atlantic, followed only a month later and disturbingly nearer home by the sinking of HMS *Royal Oak* while at anchor at Scapa Flow, with the death of over 800.

It was tragedy of another kind which hit the family, just after the first wartime Christmas and the entrance into the first year of a new decade. The weather was exceptionally bitter. A harsh frost brought icicles and frozen pipes, and folks hoped for a snowfall to make the cold ease a little. May had brought Marian and little Teddie, who was tottering uncertainly from one article of furniture to another, to Hexham for the holiday. John had braved the icy roads in his car to keep checking on the house at Low Fell, setting up heaters and climbing into the loft, where his breath rose in clouds about him as he bound sacks round the water pipes as lagging.

The evacuees had long since departed, back to their city homes, once it was seen that the menace of wholescale bombing was not forthcoming, so that his Christmas holiday was virtually uninterrupted. Indeed, he felt quite guilty, for his mother had joined the Women's Voluntary Service, and had got caught up in a veritable whirlwind of activity, from knitting socks and bala-clavas to learning how to deal with incendiary bombs. His tender conscience was pricked further by Marian's presence, whose blue eyes tended to fill with water at any mention of the military situation, which, in the circumstances, it was not easy to avoid. However, she was nowhere near so shy with him now, nor with Iris and Dan, who joined them for Christmas. They did their best to make it as festive as possible, with goose, and Christmas pud, and party hats and expensive crackers.

They gathered again on New Year's Eve. Everything went well, until John, shivering in the starry night, waiting for the midnight chimes, was let as 'firstfoot' into the black-out-curtained cottage, with his coal and salt, and received due homage, including a swift kiss on the cheek from the blushful Marian. But, at the toast to the new year, and to absent friends, Marian gave a kind of snort, her blonde head went down, and she ran from the room, her wails trailing like a flowing veil behind her.

The others looked at one another in consternation. May said quietly, 'Why don't *you* go up to her, John?' An automatic protest began to form, then he nodded and left the cosy sitting-room. He moved tentatively up the stairs, hesitated on the dark landing outside the bedroom, from which came the muffled but poignant noise of her grief. He tapped softly and peeped round the door.

Teddie was snuffling in her sleep from the cot in the corner. Marian was slumped face-down across the bed, but she wriggled round, and sat forward at his entry. She smoothed the skirt of her best woollen dress down over her knees. 'I'm sorry,' she whispered pathetically, her inadequate, lacy handkerchief clutched to her face.

'It's all right. Don't worry. That's how we all feel, really. Just making the best of it, I suppose.'

'Oh, John!' Somehow, he was holding her, she had flung herself into his arms, and he sat there, hugging her, while her body heaved and shook in the violence of her crying. The perfumed smell of her, the wisps of fine golden hair tickling his cheek, the soft femininity of her, stirred him deeply. She was plump now, far more than was considered fashionable, but her fragrant softness was powerfully desirable, and he pushed away his physical pleasure in her contact as he held and comforted her.

Soon, she sniffled and gulped, and brought her weeping under control. She leaned her brow gratefully into his neck, savoured the grip of his arms around her. 'I miss him so much, John. I can't tell you – it's – I'm that worried for him. I pray – every night. I just wish he was back safe.'

He felt the quiver pass through her, felt her great effort not to break down again, and he hugged her even tighter to him. One hand stroked at the hair at her temple. 'I know, Marian. He's a lucky man. And he knows it. I'm certain of that.' She turned with a small cry, of longing and of gratitude, and her mouth moved over his, searched for his lips, held them in a kiss that was both rousing yet oddly innocent. Then, characteristically, she blushed, and lowered her gaze in confusion. At that second, he thought how beautiful she looked. 'Dry your eyes and powder your nose and come down again.' She nodded, like an obedient child, and he smiled and left her sitting there.

He volunteered to run her home again after the holiday, and stayed for the afternoon, getting the fire going and the house warmed through, sharing the lunch she set out from the things May had insisted she bring back with her. Teddie played happily, and John enjoyed his role of surrogate man-of-the-house, sitting before the warm fire, enjoying the sight of Marian bustling about in the bright home she had created. He felt a rekindling of that old feeling of impatience with his brother for his apparent disregard of all the warmth of love and caring he could feel here, then a sudden, much deeper pang of loneliness and loss when he thought of Jenny.

The afternoon was closing in, with a thick and chilling fog, which grew thicker still, yellow and abrasive, as he approached the town and crept down to the river and the High Level Bridge.

The new regulations of the black-out and the slitted hoods which had to be fitted over car headlamps, made the hazards of the journey far worse. He was thankful that there was very little traffic about. It felt more like the hours of deep night than early evening, and it was a great relief when he approached the outer limits of Newcastle, and the air became a little purer and the fog less dense.

The look on his mother's face when she met him in the open doorway warned him of disaster. At once he thought of the pretty girl and the warmth of the domestic scene he had left. Not Teddy! he prayed. 'It's your grandad. He's in hospital. It's not good, I'm afraid.'

George Rayner had been out as usual the previous evening, despite the cruel cold. In the night, Jimmy and Kathy had woken to hear his retching and coughing. They found him slumped on the floor, his face purple, and blood among the viscous fluid he was vomiting up. He was scarcely conscious, and his chest rattled like a bag of broken bones, as Jimmy put it later.

John turned the car round, and began another journey through the murk, in the direction he had just come from. He was reminded unavoidably of the time of his grandmother's death. It was the same month, the same time of night almost, the bitter weather only slightly less atrocious. The feeling grew, inevitably. The same hospital, the same helpless waiting.

There were differences. George lingered for almost a week, the drowning sounds of his breathing searing to the nerves of those who kept vigil at his bedside in the public ward. May wanted to move him, once she learned that the doctors held out little hope. 'I could bring him home with me. Make him comfortable. There'd be a nurse—'

'And will ye make him better?' Julia rounded on her with all the old enmity. 'Can ye save him, eh?' She shook her head. 'He's got no time left. He's where Mam went here. Leave him be, for God's sake!'

May faced her, white-lipped. Jimmy intervened diplomatically. 'He'll not last much longer, May.' He put his calloused hand on her wrist placatingly. 'Ah reckon our Julia's right. Movin' him now won't do any good.'

He drifted in and out of consciousness, sometimes acknowledging them with a weary smile, and a flick of his gnarled, twisted hand on the white sheet. Other times, his eyes, rheumy and unfocused, drifted restlessly by them without recognition, and he muttered unintelligibly. Once, he called his wife's name, clearly, in a high, querulous voice, as though he could not find her: 'Bobbie?'

On the sixth morning of his illness, May got up, wrapped in her thickest dressing-gown, bed-socked and slippered, and stood in the chill, still dark hall, telephoning the hospital as she habitually did. She would have to go briefly into the Tea Cosy first this morning, before she took a taxi across to the hospital. John would come as soon as he could get away from school in the afternoon, and stay with her until they drove back together.

'Oh, Mrs Wright. I'm so sorry. We were about to telephone you. Your father passed away earlier this morning. Not more than an hour ago. Very peacefully, I'm able to tell you.'

'Thank you. Yes, I'll be in touch later.' She hung up the receiver, padded back upstairs, tapped on John's door. 'John? Your grandad. He's gone. Just a little while ago, apparently.'

He came sleepily to her, warm from the bed, and they held each other close. It was odd, she thought, but she felt quite calm. There were no tears inside her at all. Had she cried when Mam died? She couldn't remember. Of course she had tears later, at the funeral. All quite decorous, though, tastefully sniffling into her hankie.

She shivered, smitten by the memory of her great, tearing, gut-wrenching grief at Jack's death, the hours of solitary, hot-eyed weeping as she desperately tried to deny its awful finality. The almost sweet relief of her tears after her dream, when he had

240

come back to her, to help her face the inescapable truth. Perhaps, she thought tiredly as she turned to go downstairs again, she had shed enough tears then for all their lifetimes.

Chapter Eighteen

The 'phoney war' ended with appalling swiftness after the real onset of spring. One minute the tone in the press and on the wireless was cautiously optimistic, even when the German forces made their first advances into Luxemburg and The Netherlands. The British army crossed into Belgium to meet them. Then, suddenly, Chamberlain was resigning, and a new national government under Winston Churchill was set up. He talked of blood, toil, sweat and tears, and days later the BEF was in what seemed to be disorganized rout, being swept back towards the coast of northern France.

May and Iris drove over to Low Fell, to find Marian moving around in a daze of grief. Her distraction was affecting Teddie, who trailed round clutching at her mammy's skirts in uncomprehending dismay at the transformation. 'I've no idea where he is,' Marian told them, the tears welling up again at their appearance. 'You know the last letter I got? Over a week ago. He said he'd been on the move.' She shrugged hopelessly, brushed at her glistening cheek with the back of a hand. She gathered Teddie to her, lifted her and squeezed her convulsively. The brown curls shook as Teddie struggled, began to whimper.

The heaviness in May's breast, that cold leadenness, was all too fearfully familiar. The intervening twenty-three years seemed to have folded like a telescope. She reached for her daughter-in-law and took her into her arms, while Teddie wriggled free and sat sniffling on the carpet at their feet. Marian's body shook with the strength of her weeping, while May held her, her own, quieter tears trickling in compassion.

Iris blinked against the stinging in her own eyes, cleared her throat. She said almost aggressively, 'He'll be all right. You'll see. He's not PBI – infantry. He's technical support. They'll get them out. Things are bound to be chaotic. You'll hear soon enough.'

The miracle week began during the last few days of May, though people were slow to recognize it. By 4 June, over 300,000 men had been lifted off the beaches surrounding Dunkirk. Once safely back over the Channel, the exhausted troops were dispatched on leave as soon as possible. Marian waited every day, her nerves twisted almost to breaking point. May came over daily, and young Dora, who was working at the Co-op stores in Birtley, longing to be eighteen so that she could join up, stayed over every night.

One afternoon, May found her sister, Julia, there, with her youngest daughter, Rose, who was nine now. 'Listen,' May said to Marian, whose youthful face was etched with the lines of her weary tension, 'why don't you come and stop over at our place for a while? It'll do you good. There might be news—'

'I'd have thought they'd inform the wife first!' Julia said, with her accustomed acerbity. 'She *is* the next of kin, I suppose.'

May glowered at her. 'I know that! It's just that we are on the telephone, and—'

Julia gave a loudly expressive sniff. 'Oh, aye. Of course. But they do manage to get news to common folk and all, ye know. We can get telegrams.'

The crackling atmosphere between the sisters, as of old, penetrated Marian's anxiety, and she reached for May's arm appeasingly. 'I'd better stay here, I reckon. They will let me know as soon . . .' she smiled pitifully. 'Or if Teddy phones you, you'll let me know, won't you?'

Dora came straight from her work, and Julia grudgingly allowed herself to be persuaded to accept a lift back to her cottage home beside the pit, a couple of miles down the road. Alf was back below ground again, with all the overtime he could want, and more. 'It's all right,' Julia had said caustically, 'we can get a bus, ye know. We're quite used to it.' May felt the familiar tingle in her palm, indicative of her desire to slap her sister's aggravating face.

'Our Julia's no sweeter, is she?' she observed to Iris, who was at the wheel as they drove away from the row of identical terraced dwellings. 'You'd think she'd be a bit less bitchy now that Alf's back in regular work again.' She sighed, her thoughts dragged back to her deep worry over Teddy. 'I wish we'd hear something.'

Iris glanced across at her. 'Too early yet. Just imagine what a mess it must be. All those boats, men pouring back every hour of the day and night.'

May nodded. She looked about her at the still sunny late afternoon, the gentle roll of the green fields falling away to their left, the rise towards the high fell on their right. 'You're not in a great rush, are you? Let's drive over Silver Hill. Run back through Sunnyside, all right?' She was moved oddly to savour the links this countryside provided with her past, with the sweetness, and the pain of it, as though, by doing so, she might somehow fend off any threat to Teddy which might be hovering over them.

They dropped down the steep hill, and drove along the narrow road at the bottom of the valley, past the old pub, the Ravensworth, and Lamesley Church. At the crossroads they turned left, began the long, slow climb, up towards the Iron Well. 'Remember the day we had the picnic?' May said. She saw Iris give a kind of flinch, saw the redness at her cheek. 'Slow down. Let's see if we can find it. The gateway into the field. It was on the right somewhere, wasn't it? We got the dog cart along there, I remember.'

They went on more slowly, May leaning up, staring out past Iris, 'There! Was it? No, go on a bit. It was here somewhere. Stop a minute. Let's look.'

There were traces of an entrance into the field. The shallow ditch was filled in at the spot, but there was no break in the hedge. May scrambled up among the twisted branches, staring through the gaps. 'I'm sure this was it. But – there were trees further along. That's where . . .' Her throat closed. She wanted to cry, and yet it was a warm, sweet remembrance, of walking with Jack's arm about her, of their utter happiness in the complete-ness of their love for each other.

'I don't know,' Iris said doubtfully. 'It doesn't look the same. It's hard to tell.' She was thinking of the picnic to which May had referred, of the quarrel that had flared up between them, which had led to May's racing off, sobbing. Iris had been sounding off, in her high-toned, moralistic way, about patriotic duty, and the need for all the menfolk to rush off and offer themselves for King and country. For cannon fodder, she acknowledged now, bitterly, and writhed inwardly with self-disgust for her high-blown, drum-banging fervour, as she had so often over the past twenty years.

May's Jack had been one of the few sensible ones. He had recognized the higher claim, of love. Real love, not some trum-pet-blaring abstraction of nationalistic pride. Not that it had done him much good. He had perished, along with the thou-sands of others, and blighted permanently the life of this dear girl standing beside her now.

June came, fresh, dancing green; pure blue and high rolling white cloud, and still no word of Teddy from among the thou-sands who had been saved. May and John telephoned whoever and wherever they could, with no success. In the grip of their own tragic anxiety, they were impervious to the state of national tension and uncertainty, scarcely registering Churchill's defiant growl about fighting on the beaches.

The first official communication told them that Teddy's unit had linked up with an armoured infantry battalion at the Belgian border, which had then begun the pull back towards the coast. Examination of the lists of survivors landed at various points in the British Isles had failed to reveal his name, and he was, therefore, categorized as missing in action.

Marian collapsed, took inconsolably to her bed. Though May strove her hardest to hold in her pain, John and Iris and Dan could see how much she was suffering. She remembered all too vividly the days after the news of Jack had come through. He had been classified as missing presumed killed. She had clung pathetically to the uncertainty of that phrase, for weeks convincing herself with deranged fervour that she would have known, felt it, if he had been dead. And all that time, long before she had been made aware of the possibility even, his undiscoverable remains had lain, his life snuffed out in less than an instant.

This time she felt nothing, except that heavy, cold despair, deep in the pit of her, like a dead embryo. Only Iris, with urgently tearful eyes, begged and bullied them all. 'We don't know yet. Don't give up yet, for God's sake!' Sometimes May felt like screaming back at her, telling her to shut up, yet part of her, a tiny part, clung to the desperate hope she offered.

On the first Sunday in July, Iris drove May over to Low Fell again. When they pulled up in the road, Marian appeared at the front door. Her yellow hair, unbound by any headscarf, hung over her face in lank rats' tails. Her cheeks shone with tears, her eyes were slits in her puffed countenance. She was holding a crumpled piece of paper aloft, and Iris recalled incongruously the late Prime Minister on the steps of the plane: 'Peace in our time.'

'Oh, God!' May whispered, clutching at the green wooden gate.

Iris turned, held on to her. 'Buck up.' She hurried forward, reached up and snatched the telegram from Marian's fingers.

She gave a gasp, turned to May, whose brown eyes held hers pleadingly. 'Oh, May! He's alive. It's from the Red Cross. He's a prisoner of war. It's all right. He's unhurt!'

Dan carefully drew the heavy black-out curtains together, making sure there was no chink through which light might escape as he closed them, before switching on the standard lamp and then pulling the inner curtains across. He heard the soft rustle of clothing, saw Madge's still trim figure bend supply as she stepped out of her dark skirt, laid it neatly over the wooden back of the chair on top of the discarded blouse. He was touched by the sight of her dainty, lace-trimmed slip, the gleam of silk stockings. She always dressed in her finest underwear, to please him.

He glanced round at the intimate cosiness of the room in the subdued light. It was much more homely than the hotel rooms they used to meet in. He had been renting it on a regular basis for nearly a year now, from Mrs McAlpine. She had other lodgers in the large, old three-storeyed house, as well as a number of passing 'B&B' guests, but she let this room to him permanently, even though she was well aware that he used it quite infrequently. He guessed she knew why, but she showed remarkably little curiosity for a landlady, a trait both he and Madge appreciated deeply. They had their own key, and very often they saw no one as they passed through the dim hallway, and up the flights of stairs to the second floor.

Madge was sitting on the chair now, unclipping her stockings, sliding them carefully down her legs. She looked good. Dan felt his heart quicken at the sight. He realized it was almost four weeks since they had been to bed together, though he had met her last week in the coffee bar of the News Theatre for half an hour.

There seemed to be something different about her tonight. Quieter. Something on her mind. Though who hadn't in these turbulent days? 'We've had a letter from Teddy,' he said, undoing his tie, watching and enjoying her removal of the last of her underthings before she climbed into the bed, making little noises of protest at the chill of the sheets. An early September wind rattled the window frames, to remind them that summer was on the wane.

'At least Marian has. From some camp in France. Though he reckons they'll be moved on soon. Probably back to Germany, I should think. Seem to be treating them decently enough, though. Not that he'd be able to tell us if they weren't, I suppose. At least they're letting them write.'

'Must be awful for her, with the bairn and everything. How's his mam taking it?'

'Oh, May's had her fair share of trials in the past. It's hard for her, though. This lot must have brought back all the business with Jack. It looks as though John will have to go, too. He's had to register, had his medical. His papers should come through any day. It's a mess.' He shook his head, gave a short, angry laugh. 'One thing. You needn't worry about me, my pet. Nobody's going to come and drag me off. They don't even want me for this LDV carry-on. You know, these Home Guards, as they're calling them. I'm too much of a crock even to be in on the last stand!'

'You've done more than your share for king and country,' Madge declared feelingly. 'And you've had more than your share of luck. Otherwise, you wouldn't be here now. With me,' she added, with that tempting, rogue's smile. She sat up, let the sheets fall away, and held out her arms. Letting him see her full, ripe breasts, 'Come to bed, soldier.'

He struggled out of his clothing, sat himself on the edge of the bed and clumsily swung his legs round, while she held back the bedclothes for him. Their bodies were warm as he turned awkwardly and she lithely moved round, half on top of him, to embrace. They kissed slowly, with familiar love and passion. But then he eased back on the pillows, with an apologetic smile. 'How long can you stay tonight? Till ten?' She nodded, her eyes on him. 'Good. Let's just cuddle for a bit, eh?' He gave his wry grin. 'I must be getting old, lass. You look more gorgeous than ever. But I'm not really randy yet. You'll have to push me in my bathchair next.'

'That's all right.' She leaned back at his side, their shoulder and arms touching. Her hair brushed against him as she bent her head lovingly towards him. 'I want to talk anyway. I've got some fairly shattering news to tell you myself, as it happens.'

He tensed at once, though he strove to keep his voice light, as hers was. 'Oh, aye? What's that then? Don't tell me your Peter's coming after me with a loaded shotgun.'

She gave a low laugh, but, underneath, he could sense her trembling emotion, and again he felt a clutch of unease. 'No. Though you might think it's just as bad when you hear it.' She paused, and he waited, not trusting himself to speak. 'You can't be *that* old, Mr Wright,' she smiled, her voice just a little breathy, unsteady. 'I'm going to have your baby!'

'What?' He was totally stunned. Floored. 'Are you sure?'

'Oh, yes. Absolutely certain. I waited to make sure. I'm not exactly little miss innocent, remember?'

'No. I mean – you're sure it's mine?' As the words came out, Dan realized too late their cruelty.

Madge tried not to flinch, not to show the wound his words made. She almost succeeded. She forced a brighter smile, swallowed back her pain. 'Afraid so. I can tell you the mechanics of it, if you really want. It's not Peter's. And I haven't slept with any other men, however much of a trollop you think I am.'

'Oh, Madge!' he cried brokenly, grabbed at her, buried his face in her shoulder, in shame and dawning, humble delight. 'That is wonderful! God, Madge. I mean it. I love you, sweet!'

Now she began to cry, softly, in a controlled way, loving the feeling of his arms holding her, his body against hers. 'I wasn't going to tell you. I swear I wasn't. But I couldn't keep it from you. Not when it's your child I'm carrying.'

'Will you marry me?' He drew his head back, stared into her eyes. 'I mean it, Madge. I do!' he said vehemently. As though he were trying to convince himself.

She smiled tenderly, cupped her palm around his jawline. She shook her head slightly. 'I'm a wicked, wicked woman. But I'm so happy, Dan, to have your baby in me. I can't leave Peter. Or Mark and Laura. You know that. And I'll make sure he never knows it isn't his. It would destroy him. I can't wreck three people's lives.' She hesitated only briefly before going bravely on. 'Or maybe more. There's Iris, too. And us. We're not that selfish, are we?'

'But Madge . . .' he began a tortured protest, and she put her fingers on his lips.

'No, love. We can't, you know it. But we'll know ourselves. I'll know it's yours. I'll love it. And so will you. I swear it'll be part of your life, Dan. I promise. Solemnly. Somehow you'll share in it. Now. Please – just hold me, next to you, as close as ever we can be. I love you.'

They lay together, touching along every inch. He felt the slow rise of his physical passion, but they lay, doing nothing about it, entirely happy in their closeness.

The still novel rise and fall of the siren penetrated only slowly through their drifting contentment. They heard distant doors banging, voices calling out. 'It's early tonight,' Dan said. They knew that most of these old city houses used their cellars as air-raid shelters, though there was a communal concrete bunker only a block away. 'The warning's gone practically every night this past week,' he murmured, nuzzling at her warm breast. 'It'll be some snooper over the coast, I expect. It's dark now, they'll not see a thing. Let's stay where we are. The all-clear will go in an hour or two, I bet.'

He felt her leg lift, hook over him, and she thrust her belly at him provocatively. 'They wouldn't dare bomb us now. Not in the state we're in,' she giggled, and put her lips to his trustingly.

It was a stray from the squadron of Heinkel 111's which caused the civilian casualties, among the first in the north-east. The bombers had been looking for the Vickers–Armstrong works up river. Several planes, startled and dismayed at the batteries of anti-aircraft guns ranged against them, the wired barrage balloons and the searchlights, dropped their bombs only approximately in the vicinity of the Tyne, and thus demolished several of the houses in the Jesmond area.

Iris was not worried the following morning when she called in at The Tea Cosy, even though everyone was talking of the raid. 'Did you hear the guns?' May asked. 'It was a dreadful racket. I was with the Johnsons in the garden. We could see the flashes and everything. The whole sky was lit up.'

'Oh, May! You shouldn't!' Iris chided. 'Shrapnel could come down; anything! You really ought to stay in the shelter.' She gave a dismissive grunt. 'I was on my own. I was petrified. Dan didn't come home last night. Sleeping it off after that silly club of his. You'd think he'd at least have rung, or come back early this morning, just to see if I was all right. Even he must have heard the racket, however drunk he was.' Or was he too occupied somewhere else? she added meanly, to herself. With someone else? Some cheap, gin-swilling floosie! Her lips tightened, she drove the speculation from her mind.

It was a call from his younger brother, Joe, just before lunch, which started the first stirrings of unease. 'Where the devil is he?' Joe asked May querulously. 'He had a meeting at ten-thirty. He knew damned well how important it was. Not a word from him all morning. Tell him to get himself into the office. He's hardly ever in the place these days!'

'Dan's gone missing,' May told Iris when she put the phone down.

Iris's face soured in disgust. 'He's always going missing!'

But when no trace of him had been found by evening, both she and May were growing increasingly anxious. 'The raid ... do you think. ... ?' May did not finish her sentence. Her face etched in lines of worry, Iris began to make telephone calls.

May got in touch with the school, and John came home and sat with them. For the first time in over a week, the air-raid warnings did not sound soon after dark. They were seriously alarmed now. Stomachs cramped, they sat, and paced, and drank cups of tea, Iris puffing with incessant nervousness at cigarettes, until, at almost eleven o'clock, they heard the sound of a car. The police.

All three went to the police station, where, after some minutes, an exhausted-looking inspector came and led them to his office. The women's faces were the colour of paper as they waited, with almost identical looks of fright, for him to speak. His reluctance to do so was a clear enough indication that the news was of the worst kind.

'We believe we've found your husband, Mrs Wright. We think we've identified him, from some papers, and personal effects.' He unwrapped what looked like a piece of oilskin. Iris gave a small whimper of distress. The wallet was badly charred, but it was Dan's. So was the battered, twisted, blackened wrist-watch. The inspector coughed. Iris said nothing. She was still staring at him intently.

'He was found in a house in Leasdon Terrace. A bedsit. He rented it from a Mrs McAlpine. She's all right. Shaken up a bit. She was in the cellar, they all got out all right. Mr Wright hadn't gone down there.' Again that tortuous pause.

'Who was he with?' Iris's voice was laboured, quivering with her effort not to let go.

The inspector sounded almost relieved. 'A Mrs Wheeler. They met there quite regularly, apparently.'

'A married woman?' Iris said bitterly, and the policeman

nodded. Diplomatically, he refrained from adding more detail. The fact that they had both clearly been in bed, naked. That the dead woman had been with child.

May was crying, Iris wasn't, when the three of them left the inspector's office. They didn't notice the slumped figure in a mackintosh sitting a little way down the corridor, nor he them. The stranger looked utterly bemused, as though he had just woken in a strange place. His eyes were red and sore with weeping. 'Mr Peter Wheeler?' the inspector said. 'Come in, will you, sir?'

John's call-up papers came through a week after his uncle's funeral. He was glad. More than anything he wanted to get away, escape from the misery and the silences of the past days. Somehow, little appeared in the press about the scandal, thanks probably to Iris's father's influence. But to John, it seemed that the air was full of behind-the-hand sniggers, even among his colleagues, and almost everyone he came into contact with. 'Heard about that bloke, Dan Wright? Found in bed with a married tart after the air raid! Blown to bits on the job! What a way to go, eh?' He could practically hear Dan's own quiet chuckle at the music-hall flavour of it.

Except that, for the bereaved Iris, and his mother, there was no funny side to the situation. Only the cruel twist to the tragedy. Iris had made only one abrupt, embarrassing comment, when the shock had eased a little, and funeral arrangements made. 'I never could be how he wanted – make him happy – on the physical side, I mean.'

James Challoner held on to John's hand, and put a hand on his shoulder, in an openly emotional display. 'I'm very sorry to lose you. You're an exceptional teacher. There'll be a place here for you as long as I'm head.'

He had a few days to tidy up things at home before he had to report to Fenham Barracks. He ached to see the brave face his mother was struggling to put on for him. 'Once things get settled, your Aunt I will move back in here with me,' she told him, and he knew she said it chiefly to ease his mind about her after he had gone.

'They'll no doubt give me some sort of pen pusher's job,' he grimaced. It was his turn to comfort her, even though he had already vowed to himself that he would not let them do that to him. Then, suddenly, in the last two days he seemed to have done all he needed to, and time was hanging heavily on him. More than ever he wanted for it to be time; this was torment for both May and himself. 'I'll be all right, Mam!' he blurted one morning, saddened by the deep anxiety he could see stamped on her face. 'I promise. And so will our Teddy. You'll see.'

May's vision was filled with Jack, the burning love in his eyes, in his voice as he had made the promise. 'May, I swear. I'll come back to you, and the boys.' She nodded, smiled, in spite of the tears stinging at her eyes.

'Listen,' she said. 'Why don't you give Jenny a call?'

She had been on his mind almost the whole time recently, no matter how hard he tried to drive her out. 'She won't want to hear from me,' he answered softly. 'She might be away herself now.' He tried to sound jovial. 'She might be married by now.'

But that afternoon, he packed a bag, and told May, 'I'm going to have one last look around. I'll put up somewhere tonight. I'll be back tomorrow. Give the jalopy its last run out.' She nodded, knowing full well where he was heading, and glad of it.

His stomach churned during the long drive. Several times he tried to argue himself out of his foolishness. He had left it far too long, allowed her to slip out of his life. He was just reopening a wound which had all but healed. But he kept going, steadily westward, until he saw again the mountains, their tops hidden in autumnal mists.

Mrs Alsop's face would, in any other circumstances, have struck him as comical, so shocked was she to see him at her front door. But, when she recovered, her pleasure spurred him on, his clenched muscles relaxed just a little. There was, at least, no disaster to floor him at the outset, such as some favoured replacement. 'You should have warned us. Jenny's at school, of course. No, no. Same place.' She hesitated only fractionally. 'She'll be delighted. Why not wait here for her?'

But he couldn't bear his uncertainty any longer, he rushed to meet his fate. He waited across the road, saw her come through the gate in the stone wall, chatting to a middle-aged man, carrying a bag full of books. As she made to cross the road, she glanced over, saw the car, and stood stock still. He scrambled out from under the canvas hood, came over. His heart was racing. 'Carry your books, Miss?'

She fell into his embrace, collapsed in a wash of tears, the sobs buffeting her, choking her, and he clung to her in dismay, swallowing at the threat of his own tears. 'Guh – get me out of here!' she gasped, and he half carried her to the car, wedged her in with a flash of her stockinged limbs, pushing in her skirt and fastening the door on her. She hunched, sobbing, lost in her grief, for long minutes, until she blew and sniffed, and controlled her outburst. 'Where are we?' She glanced around, answering her own question, seeing the dark and light over the grey surface of the lake far below.

He pulled in to the grassy side of the road. 'Don't say it's going to rain again – like it did last time!'

They clung together, twisted in the narrow seats, knees jammed, mouths pressed desperately together, until her tears flowed again. 'It's too late,' she wept, hiding in the comfort of his breast, shivering in his embrace. 'I could never tell you. That's why – I'm not worth it – not worthy. . . .'

His stomach felt empty, as though the world itself were falling away from him. 'I let you down!' The sobs came again, and she fought them in anguish, forcing out her words. 'With Horst. I let him – it wasn't love. It was – I don't know. Wickedness!'

She collapsed again, her arms still round his neck, trembling violently. 'I'm so sorry, John. I've been so miserable. I've hated myself for so long! You mustn't think of me any more.'

His brain was spinning. He wondered dazedly why he should feel so shocked, when, somehow, part of him had known all along. There was a sadness, too, a great sense of regret, but then his urgent feeling took over. 'I love you. Always. I let you down too. It's too late – to change that. But I love you. I never stopped loving you. That's the truth. That's what matters. All that matters. I'm going into the army the day after tomorrow. I have to say it. Marry me, Jenny?'

'But—'

He grabbed her, kissed her, hard. Now his fingers dug painfully into her upper arms. He was almost shaking her. 'Do you love me?'

The tears streamed down her reddened face. She nodded.

'That's it then!' he said fiercely. She felt him grabbing at her hand, fiddling with her fingers, felt the drag of the ring forced back on to her finger. She closed her eyes, leaned against him, weak with weary relief, and nodded once more.